People of the Storm 2

People of the Storm 2

HRB Collotzi

People of the Storm
Text copyright © 2023 HRB Collotzi
All rights reserved.

Published April 2023
Cover designed by Getcovers
Copyright © 2023 HRB Collotzi
All rights reserved.

ISBN: 978-1-962628-04-4
Library of Congress Control Number: 2019909507
Published by HRB Collotzi
Rosemount, Minnesota

www.peopleofthestorm.com

For My Kids

Thank you for inspiring me, encouraging me and never
giving up on me!

People of the Storm

HRB Collotzi

Chapter One

I knocked on the door and waited, sparing a glance for Ella on my right. We had done this a few times together and were getting pretty good at it. Of course, having a girlfriend who could literally read my mind made it pretty easy for her to know what I needed in situations like this.

The girl is upstairs in her room. The parents think we might be someone from the psychiatric hospital in town.

I heard Ella say it in my mind. When we were on the surface, as opposed to hundreds of feet underground at our base, she often spoke in my mind so we didn't possibly compromise our people.

Our people are the People of the Storm, or Storm People as we call ourselves. We've been struck by lightning and gained special powers. Saying things like that out loud could certainly compromise us if the wrong people heard it, so we kept our audible communication to a minimum. Anytime we visited someone recently struck by lightning, we needed to watch every word.

Since she's so young, we'll have to stick with the "theraputic" story. We had been over this before we showed up at this quaint little suburban neighborhood, but I repeated it to make sure we were on the same page.

The way Ella's powers worked could be hard to explain, but to put it simply, she could reach out and connect to someone else's mind – reading thoughts and planting her own words as well. The communication worked, and Ella learned to hover on the surface of my mind so as not to intrude too much. Then, when I chose to share my thoughts, I focused on pushing them through to her. It took some practice, but having been doing it ever since I met her a couple months ago, I didn't have to think about it too much anymore.

When the door opened suddenly, a tall, balding man stood on the threshold. He looked us over briefly then leaned closer to me. With a low voice he asked, "Are you from St. Anthony's?"

"No, sir," I corrected him politely. "My name is William McCurdy. This is my associate, Ella Hemlock." I motioned to Ella next to me. "We're from a teen support group for lightning strike survivors. We'd like to talk to you and your daughter about the effects of her being struck by lightning."

He's still afraid for us to find out. He thinks we'll be just as freaked out. Ella informed me.

"You're a little young to help, aren't you?"

"No, sir," I told him. These conversations were so common, the answers rolled off my tongue. I had heard just about everything. "Both Ella and I have been struck by lightning. We understand the difficulties it can create. We represent a group like ourselves who support each other."

He's warming up.

"I was struck just about a couple months ago," Ella said. "If we could speak with your daughter, we might be able to help. If nothing else, we can let her know she's not alone."

The man, Stan Lancaster, nodded his head then moved away from the door. "Please, come in," he said.

As we followed him inside to a sitting area to the left of the foyer, a woman with strawberry blonde hair in her mid-40's came out of the kitchen. She eyed us as we removed our jackets, then turned to her husband, quietly asking him, "Are they from…."

He quickly cut her off, shaking his head. "They're from a support group. They've been struck by lightning too. They said they might be able to help Heather," he told her quietly.

They acted as if they were at a funeral, speaking in whispers and tiptoeing around the house. I also noticed many of the curtains drawn although it was a beautiful, sunny summer afternoon.

"I'm sorry, this is my wife, Marie Lancaster."

"Nice to meet you. Where is Heather, if I may ask?" I figured we should see her as soon as possible.

"She's up in her room." Marie answered. "She's been refusing to come down." Her eyebrows scrunched together as if in pain. I felt sorry for the woman but also knew it would all work out. "I'll go see what I can do." She crept up the stairs on the other side of the hallway.

"Do you really think you can help? I worry that what's going on in her head is beyond a support group," Stan said.

"Often times," Ella spoke again, "all someone needs is to be understood." She said it gently. I admired how well-spoken she was. Of course, I also knew she could just knock him out with a strike from what she called her "little serpent," the multi-faceted unseen appendage she used to read minds, but she was much more tactful than that.

Mrs. Lancaster came back down the stairs alone with the pained look still on her face. "I'm sorry," she told us, "she doesn't want to come down."

"Maybe we could go talk to her?" Ella asked. "If you're comfortable with that."

They're willing to do just about anything. It's like they're afraid of her. She told me.

"Sure," Stan nodded.

He started to follow us up, but Ella stopped him. "Maybe it would be best for us to speak with her alone first. She might be willing to open up a little more without interference."

Stan agreed and the parents huddled at the bottom of the steps as Ella and I went up. Of course, Ella knew exactly which room it was even though there were five bedrooms upstairs to accommodate the family of six. I followed as Ella knocked on an unadorned door down the long hallway. No answer, but Ella opened the door anyway.

I'll let you take the lead on this. I can hardly relate to a teenage girl, I told her.

I don't know about that. You and Tony can gossip like teenage girls sometimes. She retorted.

As I started to protest, she shushed me and entered the room.

Heather sat on her bed facing the window, even though the blinds were drawn tightly shut. She had long blonde hair tumbling down her back in tight ringlets. Only the left side of her face was visible, and her expression was blank, not even reacting to our intrusion.

I expected a frilly pink room, but she had everything decorated in deep red and blue. She had posters of popular rock bands on the wall, but also charts of star constellations and the periodic table. The most prominent display was the samurai sword hanging from the ceiling by fishing line over her bed. If it had been me, I would've been terrified it would fall and kill me in my sleep.

"Hello, Heather," Ella said gently. I could tell from the shushing I had received that Ella was looking into Heather's mind to see how best to approach the situation. Ella couldn't communicate with me while in Heather's mind or Heather would hear it. I would have to wait to ask her what she needed me to do, but I knew I wouldn't wait long.

"I know why you're here." Heather said sternly. I glanced at Ella and she just shook her head slightly. "You want to lock me away somewhere. I knew I never should have said anything to my parents." She said it with no emotion, like it didn't matter to her at all. Heather must have already known her parents' plan. She seemed like a pretty smart girl.

"Actually," Ella answered her, "we're not the people from the hospital. Besides," she added very seriously, "we know it wouldn't do any good anyway."

Heather turned to stare at us with a blank face. She looked both of us over carefully, although she came back to me twice. I saw part of her hair cut away from the right side of her head. She had a large gauze square covering her scar. Her hair hung as if trying to conceal it.

Introduce yourself. She thinks you're hot. Ella told me in my mind.

I cracked a small smile. I hated it when she told me stuff like that. Putting my hand on my chest, I said, "I'm William McCurdy, but you can call me Liam." I gestured to Ella briefly again. "Ella and I have both been struck by lightning. We know a little of what you might be going through."

Her eyebrows scrunched together suspiciously. She looked uncannily like her mother when she did it. "You do?"

"Yes," Ella said, pointing to the fern-shaped scar on her forehead. The scar was a mark of the Storm People. My scar was under my hair, which our doctor, Gretchen, had helped grow over it, so I couldn't show it to Heather, but Ella was proud of her scar and kept it uncovered for anyone to see. It often helped with people like Heather. "Unbeknownst to the rest of the world, the same things happening to you, happen to many people struck by lightning."

Heather seemed to breathe again. Her face lifted as she began to stand up, then she seemed to think better of it. She sat back down. "Prove it." She crossed her arms and fixed us with a determined stare.

Ella and I looked at each other. I was used to this. The others I met, after they had been struck, always wanted proof that I wasn't just leading them on. That was why I was most often sent to meet with new members of our people. Heather, like so many others before her, wanted proof we weren't just humoring her, telling her what she wanted to hear in order to distract her enough to slap a white jacket on her. Like I said, she was smart.

Ella nodded for me to take over. I said to Heather, "Promise not to scream?"

"No," came the defiant response.

I looked at Ella, who said, "Well, it was a stupid question."

I just rolled my eyes and reached my hand out to the samurai sword. The stretchy membrane around my mind acted like a net I could throw over whatever I wanted to make invisible. With a thought, I threw the net out from my scar, down my arm and over the sword. Instantly it disappeared.

With a small yelp, Heather disappeared too. My eyes popped open, but Ella remained poised. She knew Heather's powers, but she had left me in the dark. I pulled my hand and my net away from the sword. The sword reappeared, but Heather didn't. "I didn't do that," I insisted, pointing to where Heather had been.

"Sorry." We turned towards her voice to see Heather hiding behind the door to her room. "I wasn't expecting that."

"She's fast." I commented out loud to Ella. I turned to Heather. "Did you run? Or did you actually transport yourself over there?"

"I...uh..." Heather's eyes darted around the room. She probably didn't want to answer because the real answer is what made her parents so scared and confused.

"Transported," Ella answered for her. "And she's not just fast, she's wicked fast," she said looking at me from out of the corners of her eyes. I knew the comment referred to our former friend Wiki.

Cole "Wiki" Wickludi had once been a transporter for the People of the Storm but had turned against us and colluded with our enemies to kill us all. He had always claimed we called him Wiki because he was "wicked fast," but I had given him the nickname because his last name was hard to pronounce. Ella was subtly suggesting Heather might be able to take Wiki's place as our transporter.

Suddenly, Ella stiffened. "Your parents are coming," she told Heather. "They heard you yell." She urgently whispered to her, "Let us tell them whatever they want to hear in order to get you out of here. You can come with us to meet all our people."

"Really?" Heather brightened at the prospect.

"Don't worry," I told her, "We'll be back in the morning for you, and everything will make a lot more sense."

She nodded, and a smile stretched over her face as her parents appeared in the doorway.

"Is everything okay?" Stan asked.

"We heard a yell." Marie added with a curious yet frightened look.

"Everything is fine," Ella reassured them with a warm smile.

"I just got a little excited. That's all." Heather put in. Smart *and* helpful.

"We just told Heather she could come to a special therapy clinic for people struck by lightning." Ella addressed her parents, "She'll be able to meet more people like us and have the support she needs to get through these difficult times."

Oddly enough, both her parents looked relieved. Her father looked ready to have her off his hands. Her mother looked sad but resigned to her daughter's fate. After all, Heather was fifteen years old, and with her being the second child out of four, they were already learning to let her go. It would be easy enough for her to transport back and forth in order to spend the time she needed at the base learning how to control her powers. It would look to her parents like some new friends were picking her up and dropping her off for group therapy.

"We can come back in the morning to pick her up and give her a tour of the facility," I told her parents. "You're all welcome to come along and see the facility for yourselves or check it out on our website, if you like."

"How much will this clinic cost?" Stan's questions were predictable.

"There's actually no cost to you," I said. "The costs are covered by private donations. Usually from others who have lived through a lightning strike as well."

"Oh," He seemed surprised, but not at all hesitant to take us up on the offer. "Well, that's nice."

"How often would she be there?" her mother asked.

"As much or as little as necessary," I said. "She can come in for an assessment tomorrow, and then she can decide what to do from there."

With the heavy rainy season, we'd been recruiting quite a bit. Jancarlo, our defacto leader, felt it necessary to start putting together a cover institute on the surface. Heather's parents and their like were just the reason for it. As much as they loved their child, they didn't have the resources or even know where to start with such a "problem."

At the same time, the culture had changed enough so parents these days were more vigilant in everything related to their kids. Back in the old days, when I met a few of the other People of the Storm, if they were underage, I just had to feed the parents some story of a private school for their kids. These days, parents would look up the information on the internet or even ask about accreditation, and we had to forge documentation. We had a private school run by one of the Storm People that we were using, but too many of the parents had begun asking questions. We thought it would be best to switch to more of a therapeutic approach, teaching the kids in conjunction with their regular schools.

With Heather being past the proper age for some medical decision-making, she could choose for herself how often to be involved. Either way, we desperately needed a transporter, and I couldn't wait to see the extent of her powers. Unfortunately, new powers were difficult to control from the start. That's probably why Heather didn't want to be around anyone. It's most likely why her parents were scared and confused. We needed to get her to the base as soon as possible and help her control her new abilities.

I followed Stan and Marie down the hallway to the stairs. We had to leave quickly to avoid too many more questions, but I left Ella talking to Heather in her room for a minute. She would explain to Heather that what looked like simple psychological counseling to her parents would in truth be individual "counseling," including practicing using her powers and hiding them. I covered the covert conversation by leaving with the parents.

Before we could get back down the stairs, a heavy knock came at the front door. Heather's parents exchanged a glance, and Stan hurried ahead of us to open the door.

Outside stood two men with name tags and matching scrubs.

Chapter TWO

"What did you tell them?" I asked Marie Lancaster as her husband spoke to the men at the door.

Marie Lancaster's face drained of color. "I…I don't know…" she stammered.

"It's very important, Mrs. Lancaster," I pressed.

"We…" she tried again between glances at the men and her husband and me. "We were afraid," she finally whispered.

I didn't need to hear anymore. I ran back up the stairs as the two men came in. Mrs. Lancaster joined her husband, but they stood off to the side as the men looked around the house. I saw them look up the stairs toward me as I turned the corner out of sight.

I burst into Heather's room. "They're coming," I said, addressing Ella. We both knew it was a possibility the local psychological hospital would get involved. Blood pumped in my ears as I waited for her to use her mind-reading powers to see what was going on downstairs.

Heather stood. Her hands shook, but she curled them into fists. "I'm not going to some crazy house." Her face burned.

"It's ok," Ella said. She had a soothing way about her. "You can go with them. We'll just have to get you out of there later."

"I don't want to go," Heather said again. "And they can't make me stay either."

"I can go with her," I offered. I'd done it before. Multiple times. But that was back when the insane asylums were the worst place you could go. Jail was better.

"No," Ella said. "Both of us have to be seen leaving. Heather, we'll meet you at the hospital and get you out. I promise."

The two men walked around the corner as Ella and Heather stared at each other.

It's okay, Heather, Ella said in both of our minds. *We'll follow you. My powers can reach through objects and around the world. I'll stay in your mind the entire time. We'll be with you every step of the way.*

Heather's eyes popped open for a split second, but realization dawned on her quickly. She reluctantly turned to the men.

"Please come with us, Miss Lancaster," one of the men said.

As Heather was led down the stairs, she couldn't look at her parents as she passed. Her mother whimpered softly behind her hand. Her father gently cajoled and tried to comfort his daughter as the men led her outside to a van.

Liam, Ella said to me, *make them no promises. Make it sound like we're just going along with it, and we think it's probably best as well. We can't be seen as confrontational or we'll be suspects if Heather disappears.*

"It was nice to meet you," I said to the parents, as I tried not to grimace while watching Heather be taken away. Speaking with them also served the purpose of covering the fact that Ella stood staring off into space. She was good at following, finding and tracking people with her mind, but she had the tendency to phase out while she did it. "I'm sure we'll see you at the hospital and we can discuss treatment plans for your daughter."

As we walked to the car, I surveyed the suburban neighborhood while contemplating the scandal this poor family had to endure. Some of the neighbors watched our every step without actually staring.

Are the neighbors watching? Ella asked.

I led Ella gently to her side of our car knowing she couldn't focus on it at the moment. She watched through Heather's eyes in order to get directions to the hospital where the younger girl would end up. Being in someone else's head allowed Ella more than just access to thoughts. If she focused, she could see the world through that person's eyes as well. But it came at a cost. Imagine wearing virtual reality goggles while trying to walk up your own staircase.

I'm sure they're wondering what's going on, I answered her, trying to be delicate for Heather's sake since she could hear all our communications. *I've seen this too many times to be affected by it anymore.*

The whole neighborhood seems to think they know what's going on, I heard Heather's bitter tone, *and they're the only ones who know best how to deal with it.*

These days, I agreed with her, *the world may be more civilized to your face, but behind your back, it's even more barbaric.*

I'm glad I'm leaving, Heather answered. *I wouldn't be able to live with these people anymore anyway.*

How are you going to get me out? Heather asked in our minds as we followed the van to the hospital.

Well, I hemmed, *it can either involve lots of paperwork or none.*

I prefer none, Heather said.

No paperwork can bring lots of trouble later, Ella said.

I don't care, Heather bit back. *I'm leaving one way or another. My parents are afraid of me, and these people won't believe anything I tell them, will they?*

I sighed. *No. No, they won't.*

What usually happens in these situations? Heather asked. *What happened with both of you?*

Well, I said. *What happened to me happened a very long time ago.*

How long?

Over one hundred years ago.

Heather remained silent a moment, then asked. *How is that even possible?*

When someone is struck by lightning, if it doesn't kill them, sometimes they gain powers of some kind, Ella explained. *But it also changes many other things in our bodies. We live much longer than normal humans. We can see in the dark a little better. We eat a little less often. Most computers and electronics don't function well around us because of what our doctor calls "residual lightning" in our makeup.*

Is that why my phone stopped working? Heather asked.

Probably, Ella said. *Our bodies and brains function on a higher level, almost like a higher plane of existence.*

Are you telling me we're more evolved? I could hear the skepticism in Heather's voice.

Evolved? Glorified? Mutated? Whatever you want to call it depends on your view of life and our purpose, Ella said. *But whatever it is, it still varies. Your life cycle will slow depending on how strong or complex your powers are. Some of our people have powers that are limited so they age a little faster than others.*

So, does that mean you're super powerful, Liam? Heather asked.

Maybe, I answered. *But I've never really understood why. I can just make things disappear. Sure, I've made some big things disappear. And I've twisted my powers in different ways, but I've spent most of my life as a street magician, with occasional work as a spy or P.I. Nothing really spectacular, though. I've tried to live as low-key as I can. Most of us do.*

Why? Heather said. *With the powers just the three of us have, we could do anything we want.*

Almost, I said. *Almost anything we want.*

And if we did, Ella added, *we would end up just like you are now. There's a reason we're a secret society. No one wants to end up as a science experiment or a weapon of mass destruction.*

I couldn't help but think back to my time in several wars, but I didn't send the women the images of the horrible things I had seen. Being able to disappear made me the only person who could get across enemy lines and into the war room with major leaders. That way I could discover passwords and plans. But it hadn't been pretty. I had been questioned several times on how I got my information and usually had to disappear, literally and figuratively and leave the service.

But they would never catch me, Heather said. *They couldn't.*

You'd be surprised, I told her. *Tranquilizers and technology have come a long way from the time I got my powers.*

Even Kin and Kimi, who can create fire, have been overcome by a simple home fire extinguisher, Ella told her.

I chuckled remembering how during the great blizzard of 1978 in Ohio, Kin and I went house to house helping people keep warm. Someone thought Kin's hand was on fire and sprayed him. The look on his face was priceless. I purposely sent that image to the women to help lighten the mood.

Okay, Heather said. *So, we can't or shouldn't take over the world or anything. Are there others that can do what I do?*

Yes, we have a man named Boris, one of the Storm People from Russia, who is what we call a transporter, which is what you are. We'll explain more later, but when you move with lightning speed, excuse the pun, you can take other people with you, I said. *I have a gem in a strap on my wrist that allows me to contact him.. He's been helping us a lot lately, but I know he's anxious to get home.*

You don't have another transporter here in the states? Heather asked.

No, Ella said. *One of our transporters was killed a couple months ago. Charlotte's loss was hard on all of us.* I cringed hearing the words, still reeling from the memory.

I'm sorry, Heather said. *How did she die?*

Another secret organization existed called the Shadow, Ella said. *The Shadow was made up of men and women who decided to shock themselves with man-made electricity in order to gain the powers that the People of the Storm have. The biggest difference was that the man-made electric shocks didn't produce the same intensity of powers. For example, had you been shocked by man-made electricity you might only be able to transport yourself or go only short distances, etc.*

The man that led the Shadow, Devin Ross, hated all the People of the Storm. He and his father were struck while camping when he was young. They both gained powers then they were struck again and those powers were taken away and his father died, all in a matter of minutes. He realized the lightning that night was caused by one of our people, so he blamed all People of the Storm for the death of his father, the snatching of his powers and the ensuing trauma. He then spent his life attempting to regain his powers so he could gather an army and attack us.

What did you do?

Well, Ella hemmed her answer, but I remembered it all too well. Ella had used her powers to knock out thousands of people at a single thought, all because Kimi had been hurt. Ella worked her way through her grief in that one thought and came out stronger than I've ever known her.

We were able to capture them, I answered for her. I knew she didn't want to be so intimidating to Heather from the start. *Once they were captured, we could heal them, eliminating their powers, and return them to a normal life with normal humans. If they didn't want to lose their powers, we kept them in a prison at our base.*

You have prisoners? Heather asked. She sounded more excited than scared. *And a prison?*

Bear in mind, I said, *these are basically people who tried to kill us, wouldn't give up the weapons they used and would seek more help and power to try to kill us again if they could. What else could we do with them?*

So, did Charlotte die in that battle, conflict, whatever you want to call it?

Yes, she was one of the unfortunate casualties.

What about the other transporter? Heather asked. *You said Charlotte was* one *of the U.S. transporters. What happened with the other one?*

Ella sighed. Heather was bright to have picked up on that subtilty. *He sided with the Shadow.*

It seemed Heather knew better than to ask more.

But it's no matter, Ella continued. *I've seen how friendly the other transporters around the world are with each other. I know they'll all be willing to help you test out your powers and learn how to control them. Just give it some time.*

I could just transport to them now. Heather said. *I don't want to go to this place anyway.*

No, Ella said. *Then you would be a possibly dangerous runaway.*

And we would be implicated too, I added.

In fact, Ella said, *you could stay as a patient in the hospital, and we could just work out a system where you visit us regularly. It would allow you to work with us and get to know everything about the People of the Storm. That way you can be integrated back into a normal life quickly.*

Oh no, Heather said. *I'm not staying in that place on my own. I don't care how you do it, either you get me out or I'll leave on my own.*

Okay, okay, I said. *I promise we'll get you out.*

Today, Heather said. It wasn't a question.

The van took a final turn into the parking lot of the hospital.

Today, I said. *But we might have to take you back to our base and hide you for a while.*

Fine, she said. *Works for me.*

No matter what we do, I said in the others' minds, *Ella and I have to go back to our hotel rooms for the night at least. If we leave at the same time as Heather disappears, we'll have an Amber Alert and a manhunt on our tails.*

Agreed, Ella said. *Heather, we can bring you back with us invisibly, but Liam and I will have to be seen leaving town, just the two of us, and acting totally normal.*

Normal? Heather asked. *What's normal for you two? Are you two together?*

Yes, but two rooms, Ella said. *Right, old man?*

I could hear the two women giggling. I knew I was old-fashioned, and I was fine with it, even if I felt a little defensive. *Ella,* I said, *this is the first time your mother allowed us to go on this mission alone. Do you really think I'm going to risk that freedom by getting a single room? I mean, you're only sixteen and I look almost twenty.*

What? Heather asked. *Doesn't she trust you? Did you do something?*

No! I took a deep breath before continuing. *I don't know why she's so protective of Ella. It's not like Ella can't knock me out whenever she wants.*

You can knock people out? Heather almost shouted.

Oh, um yeah, Ella said, but quickly steered the subject away, *but my mom probably acts that way because she had to fake her own death and leave me behind to be raised by my aunt.*

Now that she's back in my life, I think she's trying to make up for lost time by spending every second of her waking hours with me.

Why did she fake her own death? Heather asked.

The men in scrubs were unloading Heather from the van and asking her questions. We had purposely fallen behind as we followed her, but Heather's thoughts helped us understand what was happening as we spoke.

That's kind of a long story. Ella said. *My mom was struck by lightning when I was very young. People started noticing she wasn't aging as fast as she should. Because of rumors to that effect, the People of the Storm found her and learned her story. It was gut wrenching, but she realized she had to disappear and leave me behind at the same time. So, they helped her fake her death.*

Do you need to answer some of those people's questions? I asked Heather when she sent a picture of several men staring at her.

No, she answered me. *I don't plan on speaking again until I'm out of this awful place. Can I fake my own death?*

No! Ella and I yelled at the same time.

We don't do it often, I said. *In fact, because I'm so old and I don't exist on paper, I've never had to do it. Some Storm People have had to do it, simply to lose their paper trail. With all the technology and records out there it's easier to write someone off as a doppelganger if they've faked their death. But it isn't always necessary. We'll work out a plan for you, don't worry. Go ahead and let them get you settled in. We'll come visit you shortly.*

As clouds descended in the sky, a trickle of rain began to fall. Ella gave me directions and we drove around aimlessly until Heather was through her admission process.

I pulled the car to the side of the road across from the parking lot of the institute and pointed out all the security cameras to Ella. We switched places, and she drove around a little, inspecting the area, while I pulled my net over myself skin-tight. Luckily, she had gotten her driver's license right before she had to disappear from where she lived in Florida. We hoped she wouldn't be discovered as we wandered the suburbs and streets of Ohio so far away. While driving, we made plans and discussed alternative back-up options of how to get in to see Heather.

She parked the car then got out pretending to fumble with something inside so I could crawl out the door past her. With me invisible at her side, we jogged through the rain into the foreboding building. The rain was light enough that I knew no one would see my shape through it.

We only got as far as the front doors before being stopped by another set of solid looking metal doors with wire in the glass. The lobby, if you could call it that, had a couple of rickety chairs and a small table with outdated magazines. It was about eight feet by eight feet to complete the prison motif. Every fiber of my being wanted to run screaming from the place thinking of how many other souls had been dragged through here against their will. Let alone the idea that if I told them what I could do they would tackle me too. One other door hid off to the side, but it looked more like a broom closet than anything.

Our final option, it appeared, was to talk to a burly woman behind a thick, wide piece of bullet-proof glass. The woman had bags under her eyes and disheveled hair. Disdain emanated from her. This couldn't be a very happy place to work. Her name badge read "Patty," and she glared at us rather than offer any help.

I watched invisibly as Ella stepped forward to talk to Patty. "Hello," she said with her usual kind smile, "I'm here to see a patient who was just admitted. Her name is Heather Lancaster."

"Do you have her passcode?" Patty asked without looking at anything. She must be instructed to ask but didn't really care either way.

"Of course," Ella paused. She looked into her purse as if searching for something, but I knew she was searching the woman's mind. Patty looked down at her computer screen, and Ella finally got what she needed. Holding up a scrap of paper while reading Patty's mind, Ella recited, "9-3-7-7."

Patty looked satisfied, if that was at all possible, and pressed a button on the wall to open the solid door to her left. Ella slipped through the door. Luckily the door closed slowly enough for me to ghost in behind her.

From behind another glass window, Patty said, "Down that hall," pointing to our left, "then take a right at the second hallway. Her room is 109 on the left." She turned away to pick up her phone before Ella could thank her. Thanking her anyway, Ella started down the hall with me close in her wake.

The walls were painted a fading tan color and the floor was institutional tile. The first hallway we passed was closed off by a heavy windowless door. A sensor hung on the wall next to it to gain admittance. Further along the hallway was an elevator, but we turned before we reached it.

Heather sat on her bed when we came in. She wore scrubs and hospital socks, and her hair was pulled back into a ponytail exposing the gauze dressing. An I.V. line had been started in her hand, but it wasn't hooked up to any fluids or machines. Turning at the sound of our entry, her eyes widened in delight. "Ella!" she exclaimed while tackling her in a hug. Ella hugged her back but pulled back to look her in the face. Tears welled in Heather's eyes. "I was afraid you wouldn't get in," Heather whispered. "I thought I might have to leave on my own."

Ella motioned for Heather to sit back down on the bed, and she sat next to her. "Are you okay?"

"I guess," Heather shrugged, "They already started me on medications. Before I've even seen a doctor."

Are your powers intact? She asked Heather in her mind, but she included me in the conversation too.

Yes, came the answer, *I was able to transport the pills that they gave me out of my mouth before I swallowed them.*

Good thinking, I told her. Catching her off guard, Heather gasped.

"It's okay," Ella said out loud to keep a simple outside conversation going for anyone watching on cameras. Then in our minds she said, *Liam's here too. I think you're right. We can't leave you in here if they're going to push drugs at you without even an evaluation.*

This place gives me the creeps too, but she'll be a runaway if she leaves now, Ella. I insisted. I didn't want this poor girl to leave everything behind because her parents were stupid enough to trust a place like this.

I want to go. Heather put in. *If you don't take me with you, I'll go anyway.*

I looked back and forth between the two young women.

It's dangerous, I said. *You might not be able to come back.*

I already can't, Heather chided me.

Okay, I finally caved. *I'll stay with you. Ella, they have to see you leave to know you weren't involved.*

"I'll talk to your doctor about getting you out. I'll come back and see you again." Ella stood up to leave but said in our minds, *The bathroom is the only place without a camera. You'll have to transport out from there.* She put a picture in our minds of a spot down the road under a tree, hidden from the road. *Once you're out, meet me there.*

She hugged Heather again, then we watched her walk out the door. I knew Ella would keep us connected in our minds so we wouldn't have to speak out loud.

Heather's eyes wandered the room nervously. I think she was looking for me. I reached out and touched her on the shoulder. *I'm over here,* I told her. *Don't worry. I'm staying here with you.*

Okay, she answered, a little shaky. *They're supposed to come get me to meet with the doctor any minute.*

As she said it, a big beefy guy walked into the room, not bothering to knock. "Time for your assessment." He didn't say it as an invitation. He stood expectantly, waiting for Heather to come with him.

"Okay," was all Heather could muster. She slowly got up from the bed. *Should I ask to go to the bathroom first?*

I'm not out the door yet. Ella informed us.

We have to wait for Ella to be cleared before we can disappear, I answered her. *Go with him for now. Ask to use the bathroom when you get there.*

She shuffled toward the burly man. He let her go out the door first but fell into step next to her as they walked down the hall. They went further into the hospital then up a short flight of stairs to another hallway with me following close behind. Just steps down that hall was a large common room, complete with an outdated television and tables and chairs everywhere. Patients were being gathered from all over to meet in the uncomfortable chairs inside.

I'm on my way to the car! Ella hurriedly told us.

Get to the bathroom, I told Heather.

The man motioned for Heather to go through a door next to the large common room, but she looked up at him obviously intimidated. "Can I use the bathroom first?"

He heaved a sigh and rolled his eyes. "You should've done that sooner."

"Sorry." Poor Heather was scared to death of this guy, but I was impressed with her courage. "It hit me kinda sudden." She fidgeted with her hands and shuffled her feet around for effect.

"Over there," he grunted, pointing to a bathroom past the nurses' station (again behind glass) past the common room.

"I'll just be a minute." Heather promised.

That's one promise you're going to have to break, I said in her mind.

The jerk deserves it. She insisted.

She scurried down the hall with the orderly at her heels. For a moment I thought he would follow her inside, but he stopped just short. "I'll wait out here. Hurry up."

Heather opened the door wide when she went inside as if inspecting the conditions so I could slip in behind her. The bathroom was just a small room with a toilet, sink and garbage can. There was no way anyone could get out of it except through the door. Even the ceiling didn't have any access panels. I knew it wasn't up to fire code, but I had a feeling this place didn't run on medical insurance alone.

Once the door locked behind us, I threw my net out from me to envelope Heather as well. I pulled it tight knowing now I could keep tabs on her no matter where she went, unless she transported without me. As soon as the net was over both of us, she could see me as well. She visibly relaxed, and I told her in her mind, *We're both invisible now. Even if your friend comes back in, he won't see us.* She smiled a little at this thought. It was good to see her spirits lifting. *Now,* I asked her, *have you tried to transport on purpose before?*

I knew Ella listened to our conversation, and she would help if she could. Heather answered me, *Only a few times. There's a place in my mind I can put a picture of where I want to go. I kind of push myself and the picture into a kind of hole there.*

I nodded. While Boris and Charlotte had described their powers as sensing everything and everyone around them for miles and miles and being able to pick a spot and zoom in on it, Wiki had often described his powers as Heather had. Hopefully it would all work the same because I had no way to know either way. *Try a short jump first.* I suggested. *Try to just get us out of the bathroom and into the hallway. No one will see us. I'll hold onto you because that's how it seems to work for other transporters.*

She nodded back, and I put my hand on her shoulder. The familiar sensation of breathlessness overtook me as the walls of the bathroom swirled together in a hazy blur. It subsided quickly as everything around us solidified again. We stood in the middle of the hall outside the bathroom. The orderly that had come with us stood with his hands together and his back to the door. He looked right past us when we appeared.

Heather took a small, sharp breath when she stood almost face to face with the ominous figure. He must have heard it because he narrowed his eyes slightly and glanced down the hall right through us again. He checked warily around then leaned back to knock on the door to the bathroom.

"Almost done in there?" he asked through the door.

Heather's eyes widened, and I knew she was thinking the same thing I was. He would get suspicious if she didn't answer. Before I could say anything, the air sucked out of my lungs. It was a good thing I still had hold of her shoulder. We both transported back into the bathroom.

Once the air returned to my lungs, I heard Heather say, "Just a minute."

She really was fast as she took us back out into the hallway, this time a little further down the hall and well away from the orderly.

Very good, I praised her. She looked pleased with herself. *Now can you take us out of the hospital?*

I think so, she nodded to me. Again, the hallway swished around us and soon we stood outside the front doors of the hospital.

Perfect! I praised her again. She gave me a wide grin as I took my hand off her shoulder. *We should be able to walk to Ella's meeting place from here. It's only a couple blocks away.*

Could I just transport us there? She asked me without moving.

I stopped and turned to face her. *Can you sense the space around you?*

She shook her head, *No,* she said, *I just picture it.*

Well, I faltered, *how it works for the other transporter we know is he can only transport to somewhere he's been or can see ahead of him. We should probably wait to experiment until we get back to the base.*

But I've already tried it, she insisted. This time I stopped and listened. *Once I transported on purpose. I went to a place on a postcard. I'd never been there before. I just took the picture, fixed it in my mind and pushed myself into it.*

I was a little surprised at this information. I had never heard of transporters being able to do that before. This new talent was unusual, but I figured if she had done it before, we could try it again.

Ok, I said a little tentatively, *we can try it if you're confident about it.*

I am. She nodded back at me, appearing already to be a rather confident young woman.

I put my hand back on her shoulder, and a second later we stood under the tree where Ella waited for us. Ella leaned casually against the car with a distant look in her eyes. Glancing in our general direction, she opened the door to the car then paused to inspect the neighborhood, giving us a chance to climb in before she got in and drove away.

Being the old-fashioned guy I am, I let Heather sit in front with Ella. I kept the two of us invisible so no cameras would catch us. "Everything go okay?" Ella asked, making small talk. Of course, she already knew it went fine.

"Okay, I'm guessing the plan is drive around a bit to make sure we're not being followed?" Ella asked.

I hadn't thought that far ahead and was grateful someone had. "Yes, sounds good. By the way, Heather is quite a talented transporter," I said for Heather's benefit. "She could give Wiki a run for his money."

Heather beamed. After a minute, she asked the question I had been waiting for. "Is Wiki the one transporter? The one that turned on you guys?"

Ella and I squirmed uncomfortably, but I eventually answered. "Yes. Wiki was very powerful. It was a hard situation for everyone."

"Oh," was Heather's only response. I knew she must have tons of questions, but Wiki was kind of a conversation killer, so I tried to change the subject.

"But you'll probably get to meet Boris. I'm sure he'd be glad to help you learn more about using your powers." The thought made Heather smile.

Ella added, "He's a great guy, but he wants to go back to Russia. So, we could really use your help." Ella glanced in Heather's direction cautiously. "That is, if you decide you want to stay with us."

Heather's face only fell slightly. She didn't seem too put out as she responded, "Where else am I going to go?" She looked between the two of us. "I need to be with people like me. Maybe someday I'll come back, but I've got to be able to learn about myself first, and I can't do that at home, obviously."

Ella smiled again. Having Heather join us would be good for her and us.

"So where are we going to go, anyway?" Heather asked while watching the countryside fly by.

"We'll head to the People of the Storm's base in the morning," Ella answered. "It's down south in Georgia." Her eyes bounced around the car. "Do you think we're far enough away for me to be able to see you guys yet?" She asked me.

"We can't risk Heather's face being seen with us. She'll have to stay invisible." I answered her.

Ella nodded and asked, "What about you?"

I scanned the surrounding area to make sure no other cars were around then pulled the net off myself. As Ella looked at me in the rearview mirror I winked at her, a habit from since I was a young man. Not that I was old now.

"So, what's your story, Liam?" Heather asked. "If you don't mind sharing anyway."

I grinned. "I don't mind," I said. "I was born back in 1905 and lived in Ireland in a beautiful little town called Kinvarra. Lightning struck me when I was seventeen and married to my wife Sinead."

"You were married at seventeen?" Heather asked.

"Things were very different back then. And we were very much in love. At least, I thought we were. Being struck changed everything for me.

"The whole experience and the resulting powers confused and overwhelmed me. I tried explaining it to Sinead, but since we were both so young and inexperienced as to the things of the world, she couldn't accept that I was telling her the truth. Despite my pleading, she left me, taking our unborn daughter with her. I never knew the baby she named Ciara McCurdy, although I met Ciara's son, Nathaniel Van Maren, when he was struck by lightning about fifty years ago.

"By the time I was forty, I had to leave for America because I still looked eighteen and people were starting to ask uncomfortable questions. I met Jancarlo Mecina, the man who now runs the People of the Storm in America while I was doing a street performance. I had no idea such organizations existed all around the world. I joined Jancarlo and the Storm People under the leadership of Paul at the time. A couple of decades later, we found Wiki. I've been helping to share the burden of lightning strike victims ever since."

"How about you, Ella?" Heather asked.

"Oh," Ella took a deep breath, "I feel like I've belonged with the Storm People forever. But I was only struck a couple of months ago."

"When those Shadow people attacked?" Heather asked.

Ella nodded.

"How did you fight them?" Heather asked. "You said you can knock people out?"

I chuckled. "Yeah, she decided they all needed a time-out."

Ella rolled her eyes. "How my powers work," she said. "I can listen and talk through minds, but I can also retain vast amounts of information, much more than the average brain. If I want to, I can force too much information into someone's mind until it overwhelms their senses."

"What does that mean?" Heather asked.

"It means she can mentally knock people out," I said. "Lots of them. At the same time. In a fraction of a second."

"Whoa." Heather breathed. "Cool."

"Not just that," I continued, "but she also transferred her consciousness into a giant rock monster that the Shadow used to attack us. She used it to…uh…stop Devin Ross."

"Not bad for a little sixteen-year-old from Florida, huh?" Ella said.

"Yeah, about that," Heather said. "Doesn't that mean that you're dating a man that's well over a hundred years old? And has been married before?"

"Yes," I said, "but it's not as bad as it sounds."

"Definitely not," Ella muttered.

I chose to ignore her and explain to Heather. "Sinead broke my heart so thoroughly that I hadn't been willing to put myself out there with anyone for decades. A friend of ours, Kimi, showed some interest, but I couldn't let go of Sinead. After that, I assumed I would simply be alone the rest of my long, long life. I wasn't interested in any of our people and too old for anyone aging at a normal rate. But the Storm People, including Kimi who had since lost interest in me, convinced me to look beyond actual age. Even though our lives are lengthened, our physical development remains equal to our outside appearance. That means, in every way I'm still only about nineteen, maybe twenty tops."

"Does that mean…?" Heather's voice trailed off with the implication of her life to come.

"Yes," Ella said. "Depending on how powerful you are, you'll probably live a very long life."

Once we decided it was safe to return to the hotel, we spent much of the night explaining these things to Heather. Okay, most of them. Heather and Ella shared a room, and I'm sure they discussed other things. We needed to check out of the hotel in the morning, and so we did, early.

After a few minutes in the car in silence the next morning, with Heather still invisible, she asked, "Can I go home and get some clothes?"

I thought about it for a minute but answered, "I think it would be too dangerous. If one of your family members sees you, it could cause problems."

"That's what I said," Ella told me.

"Even if I just went straight to my room?" She persisted. "I've got to get a change of clothes."

I realized she was still in her hospital scrubs from the night before and figured maybe it would be uncomfortable for her.

Ella glanced at me, "She would need you to keep her invisible." I wasn't sure if she said it for an argument or not.

"It would just take a minute," Heather insisted.

I looked at Ella in the rearview mirror again and she reached out to my mind at the same time. *She's right. She'll need a change of clothes,* She said, shrugging..

"Okay," I sighed again. It seemed more and more like these two young women were ganging up on me.

Ella pulled over to the side of the road. We were out of town with only a few small homesteads in sight. No cameras. We all got out of the car to talk.

"I'll go with you," I insisted.

"Okay," Heather said as she came to stand by me.

"I'll stay in your minds to make sure you don't need any help." Ella added.

"Can you reach that far?" Heather asked with awe.

Ella raised an eyebrow. "Further."

Before Heather could start asking more questions, I put my hand on her shoulder. "Let's get this over with," I said. She nodded and the air around us began to swirl together again.

A moment later, we stood exactly where we had met her the day before. I made sure my net was over the two of us as we stopped to listen. I didn't hear anything, so I said in her mind, *Just grab a couple things. We have toiletries at the base.*

I watched as she packed a bag with a few changes of clothes, but I feigned interest in her posters when she opened the underwear drawer. She grabbed a brush off her dresser and a few more things then turned to face me.

Okay, she told me, *ready to go.*

Good, Ella said in our minds. *Your mom is downstairs, and she thinks she heard someone upstairs. She's on her way up.*

Heather's face drooped as her eyes strayed to the door. Tears welled up, and I could tell she was realizing she wouldn't see her mother again for a while. She took a step toward the door as her mother came around the corner.

Marie Lancaster looked as if she had been crying. That didn't help Heather. I put my arm around Heather and said in her mind, *Don't worry. You'll see her again, and things will be much better. I promise.*

As her mother stepped into the room toward us, the air swirled. We reappeared by the car next to Ella, but I could tell Heather's mind was still full of her mother's weeping face.

Chapter THREE

Again, I made sure no other cars were in sight then pulled the net off myself. I gave Ella a knowing look and squeezed Heather's shoulder one last time before I released my grip, but I kept my net over her.

"You know," Ella said gently. "Maybe we could let Heather try to transport us to the base. She already seems really good at this transporting stuff, and we could get there a lot faster." I could tell she was trying to change the subject and cheer Heather up all at the same time. I think she accomplished it.

At this point I wasn't going to argue. The worst that could happen would be ending up in Fiji or something. "Sure," I answered, "if you're up for it, Heather?" I stretched my net out into a bubble so we could all see each other, but no one else would.

Heather just shrugged her shoulders, "I need a picture of the place we're going."

"That's easy," Ella said. As she said it, we both saw in our minds a picture of the lobby at the Storm People base.

"What should we do with the car?" I asked her. After we retrieved Heather, I was supposed to return the car to a hidden spot where the Storm People of the area park them.

"I can probably take it with us," Heather offered.

I looked at her curiously. "Any transporter I've ever known has only been able to transport people and what they're carrying," I explained. I wasn't sure if she understood her own capabilities yet.

"I accidentally took my bed with me once." She said it so matter-of-factly that I couldn't help but laugh. Ella joined in and even Heather grinned.

I threw my hands up in the air then turned to Ella, "We might not want to show up in the lobby with a Buick in tow…plus…"

"Oh yeah," she said, realization dawning of a certain new security measure we had recently put in place. "Okay, okay," she told me. She put another picture in our minds of the rendezvous point above ground for the base. That was where we parked the cars for Georgia, although I still doubted Heather's ability to actually transport the car with us.

Ella and I put our hands on Heather's shoulders and Ella put her hand on the car as well. Almost immediately, we stood in the exact spot Ella had put in Heather's mind. Heather had never been here before, but with a picture in her mind, she had brought us to the exact spot with the car still under Ella's fingertips.

I looked at Heather through new eyes, "That's amazing!" I said to her, and she beamed again. "Very nice job."

We made sure the car was parked with the others, then we approached the single tree that stood nearby. It used to be the spot that Wiki would meet us to give us a ride underground to the SP base, but now it hid in its branches a rock we used as a transportation device to get anyone into the base.

Well, almost anyone.

Since we had had problems with the so-called Shadow organization under the leadership of Devin Ross, we had put more security measures into place. The transport took you into a clearing area. It was a small room with a window facing the front desk. When a person transported into the room, and therefore the base, they were stripped of all powers and illusions they might be using. For example, if I had tried to keep us all invisible while we transported into the room, we would immediately reappear once we solidified in the room. Ella hated it because she was removed from her little serpent and any mental connection she retained.

Anyone to appear in the room usually got cleared by Ella. When she wasn't available, a few others were trained to fill in although not with her specific powers. We rarely had any problems, but it was a good security measure to have, and other high security areas had similar features added.

Evelyn, Ella's mother, sat at the desk, but stood when she noticed our arrival. "You're back early," she said. "Is everything okay?" She eyed me for half a moment. The idea of allowing myself and Ella to go out on an overnight mission had been a massive exercise in trust on her part. Although I relished the idea of having time alone with Ella,

I could see how her mother might be a little more hesitant, but I hoped that I had gained some amount of trust from her at this point. It was a miracle Evelyn allowed the mission to happen at all because my level of trust with her seemed even more tenuous than ever these days.

"Everything is fine," Ella answered, but Evelyn's eyes had already drifted to Heather.

Ella's mother was a nice enough woman who looked to be in her early thirties maybe younger, though I knew she was actually in her late forties. She pushed a brown lock of hair out of her face to stare at us with wide eyes.

I gestured to our young companion. "Heather got us here in record time."

At this, Evelyn perked up. "Oh?" she said, "Is she a transporter?"

"Fastest around," I said. She smiled, knowing the importance of a new transporter.

The three of us approached the desk and Evelyn came around to shake Heather's hand. "Nice to meet you, Heather. I'm Evelyn. Ella's mother."

"Hi," Heather answered timidly. I could tell she wanted to know what Evelyn's powers were, but she was afraid it might be rude to ask.

Ella helped her out, "It's okay to ask, Heather." She nodded to her mom. "Mom's a water mover."

Prompted by Heather's confused look, Evelyn held out one hand. Droplets of water formed in the air above it as she said, "Unlike fire manipulators, I don't have to create water to use it. It's all around us and in us." The droplets formed a ball then morphed into a long river flowing over and around her arm like a snake. It traced its way back to her fingertips and dissipated into a little cloud before disappearing.

"Wow," Heather whispered, "that's so cool."

"Thanks," Evelyn answered.

"Evelyn," I asked, "do you know where Jancarlo and Gretchen are?" I still felt a little odd using her first name, but she continued to point out that I was technically older than she was. I think she did it to remind everyone, especially myself and Ella, that I was much older than Ella—too old, according to Evelyn.

"In their offices, I think," she answered. I thanked her then steered Heather down the hall to the right of the desk.

"See you 'round, Heather," she called after us. Ella stayed behind momentarily to whisper something quickly to her mother, probably a promise to report everything that happened later, then caught up to us quickly.

Heather's wide smile quickly returned as we walked down the hall.

"I think she should see Gretchen first." Ella told me as we walked down the hall.

"I think you're right. Why don't you take her while I get Jancarlo?" I offered.

She nodded and led Heather to a nearby door while I continued down the hall to Jancarlo's office.

On the way there, I saw a familiar woman walking towards me with a very unfamiliar look on her face. Her sleek black hair was pulled up into a high ponytail behind her head. Although small, Kimi was a fierce fire starter, meaning she could start her own fire without the use of a lighter or something similar. Kimi was very pretty and, under the right circumstances, not intimidating at all, but I knew better. She was not a person to be messed with. We had been friends since she and her brother Kin had transferred here from Japan in the 1960's. I mostly had her to thank for helping me realize I couldn't pine over my first wife forever, allowing me to move on with my life. Because of that, Kimi had a very special spot in my heart.

As she walked closer, I tried to make eye contact and smile at her, but she avoided my gaze. That was strange. Kimi was always very friendly with me. "Hi, Kimi," I called to her and waved. She was still at least twenty feet away, but I knew she heard me, yet she still didn't look at me.

When she was finally directly across the hall from me, I blocked her path and grabbed hold of both her arms, forcing her attention to me. When her eyes at last met mine, it seemed like anger flashed in her eyes, but it disappeared as quickly as it came. I figured I must have just imagined it as she gave me a timid smile. "Sorry," she said, "I didn't see you there. I'm a little distracted."

Kimi? Distracted? She was always on alert. The only time she didn't see me walking straight into her was when I was invisible. Maybe she had something important on her mind. "Are you okay?" I released her arms, regarding her curiously.

"I'm fine," she answered, waving me off. "Just got a lot to do."

"Don't we all," I responded. Jancarlo had been keeping us all very busy in preparing to open the clinic on the surface. "But things should get a little easier," I told her. "Ella and I brought back a new transporter."

I figured she would be overjoyed like everyone else, but she just nodded. "That's good."

"You sure you're okay?" She seemed distracted, yes, but she had never been as scatterbrained as this.

"I'm fine," she insisted. She edged around me to start back down the hall. "See you later," she mumbled as she walked away.

I let her pass but watched her through narrowed eyes as she swept around a corner. Normally I would have insisted on finding out the matter, but I didn't have time right now, so I continued to Jancarlo's office. By the time I got there, I had talked myself into believing Kimi's behavior was just a fluke. If there was anything wrong, I'm sure Tony would get it out of her.

Tony was another member of the Storm People and Kimi's boyfriend. Through the last struggle with the Shadow, Kimi and Tony had finally realized their feelings for each other. They were a funny couple, but their characters were a perfect match. Tony was a small giant before he received his powers of super strength. He was rough on the outside, but once you got to know him, you could see he was very kind. Kimi was a tiny little fire starter, and she seemed personable enough at first sight, but when you tried to talk to her she was very brash. But I guess opposites attract.

I put Kimi and Tony out of my mind as I knocked twice then opened the door to Jancarlo's office without waiting for a response. Jancarlo sat at his paper-strewn desk with his old-fashioned phone receiver against his ear.

He waved me to come in, so I sat across from him as he finished his conversation.

"Okay," Jancarlo said into the receiver, "we'll send someone as soon as we can. Thanks, Marcus. Bye." He set the receiver back on the cradle and gazed at me sternly even though I knew it was stress-induced. "We need to start taking in the Shadow."

My eyebrows immediately came together. "You mean people shocked by man-made electricity?" I was skeptical for good reason. People shocked by electricity who survived gained the same kinds of powers the People of the Storm did, but we could never tell if they did it on purpose or not, making them slightly untrustworthy. Ella's powers solved that problem, but after so many of them tried to wipe the Storm People off the face of the earth, I was a little hesitant to approach them with an olive branch.

"Devin Ross is no longer in control of the ones who have done it on purpose, but accidents continue to happen. Luckily, people are a lot more cautious these days, but if we don't help the few who really are accidents, the same way we do with our people, then they'll be put under the microscope. And sooner or later that scope will be turned to us." He sounded like he had rehearsed the lines. I knew it had been weighing heavily on him, but I didn't know which way he inclined until now.

"Have you discussed this with Kin?" I asked. Kin Sitlaki was Kimi's twin brother. They had been struck at the same time and had the same powers. Kin's official role was that of security, but I was among the very few who knew Jancarlo was grooming him to someday take over for him, should the need arise.

Kin was extremely tough, sharp as a tack and could read people well. He was great with security, but needed tutoring in the finer points of diplomacy. He was a very capable person, the only other person I would trust with the leadership of our people. Mostly because if he didn't take over, the mantle would most likely fall to me, due simply to seniority, something I didn't relish in the least.

"Yes," Jancarlo answered firmly, "he feels the same way I do."

I nodded while I gathered my thoughts. I figured they would feel the same way, and I certainly thought it would be a good move to make, but a lot of the Storm People would not be very accepting of anyone from the Shadow.

"Can't we have Gretchen or Sheila meet with them to heal them of their powers?" I suggested. Gretchen was our main healer, and Sheila had the same powers to a lesser degree. We had found that most of the time they could heal the Shadow group easily so they could return to normal lives after being shocked.

"We've discussed that as well," He nodded, "but the problem remains if they don't want to be healed of their powers."

"We could heal them without asking." I started to suggest, but he cut me off.

"You know I won't take that choice away from anyone." He shook his head adamantly.

"I know." We stared at each other for a moment. I realized what was being said. I would now be sent out with others to not only gather people struck by lightning, but also those shocked by enormous waves of electricity. Then an idea hit me. "Why not send Ella and Gretchen together?" Once I said it, Jancarlo brightened. "Ella could find out their motivation either way," I continued. "Then Gretchen could heal them before they find out too much, if that's what they want."

He nodded vigorously back at me. "She would have to be very thorough, but she's up for that. Yes," He almost smiled, "I think that would work nicely."

"The travel time might get a little easier too." I informed him of Heather and her amazing abilities, but I also explained the mess we left behind by bringing her back with us.

Pinching the bridge of his nose, he asked a few more questions. I told him about Heather's ability to transport large objects, but he shrugged at the possibility of getting her to move things for us. He or any rock mover could usually transport things down to the base.

"We'll have to see how powerful she is." He told me with a sigh. I noticed how worn he seemed and decided I had better leave him alone.

We had been bringing in large numbers recently because of weather patterns and a higher than normal rate of survival. Plus, many of the new recruits were extremely powerful. Some of them had to stay underground with us until they had their new powers under control, but many of them had remained on the surface.

The task of maintaining our people became a monumental job. I always admired Jancarlo for being willing to take it on. Now he was also being tasked with building and managing therapy clinics all over the country to help newly empowered people cope with their life-altering experience without being forced to remove them from their normal lives. We all did our part, but I could still see the stress getting to him.

I excused myself after he told me to get Heather a room and see that Boris was brought back to train her. I left him with his left hand rubbing his forehead and his right hand dialing the phone.

I followed the hall to Gretchen's office to meet Ella and Heather. Heather seemed to be in a better mood. She had been checked over by Gretchen and even had some hair growing back over the bald patch on her head.

On our way to take Heather to one of the rooms provided at the base, we passed the main desk again and I asked Evelyn to contact Boris. Right outside Heather's new room, we bumped into Kin.

Although Heather had been almost climbing the walls the past few minutes, the moment Kin approached us she fell silent. She stared at him with wide eyes. I wondered at the abrupt change. She mumbled a "hello" and shook his hand, but I caught Ella stifling a laugh. She hid it well, but I knew her better than anyone.

"Welcome, Heather. I hope you settle in well. If you need anything, ask me. I'll see what I can do." Heather's eyes lit up, but she said nothing. "Hey, Liam, have you seen Tony?"

"Sorry, no," I said.

"Okay. I'll track him down." But before he left, he faced Heather and said, "Good to have you here." He then smiled and swept past us.

We took Heather to room number four. I used the key I had taken from Jancarlo's office to swipe the lock so only Heather's thumbprint could open the door. She pressed her thumb on the pad and the door opened to admit her.

As she peered inside, we told her of the cafeteria/kitchen, the gym and practice arena. "Feel free to make yourself comfortable and explore the place," Ella said.

"I'll let you know when Boris gets here," I promised her. "We'll have plenty for you to do before long if you're up for it."

"Sure," she agreed enthusiastically.

"I'm in number fifteen if you ever want to hang out," Ella told her. "I'm sure we'll see each other around a lot too."

As we took our leave, we heard footfalls racing down the hallway. We turned just in time to see Evelyn running straight at us. She skidded to a halt right next to me. "Liam," she panted, "Nathaniel just came in."

Chapter FOUR

Evelyn stopped to gain her breath. Nathaniel had been struck by lightning when he was in his fifties, and his powers were such that he attracted more lightning. At times he could harness it as a weapon, but often, if he got upset or excited, he would attract even more lightning. People around him could get hurt. He never got struck by the lightning himself, but he had watched others he cared about be killed or changed because of him, so he had withdrawn from society.

After decades of work we had finally figured out a way to render a person unable to use their powers, ironically made possible by our enemy. In our struggle with the Shadow, we discovered they had invented a ring that could be clipped around someone's neck, and the metal would capture their powers. By using it, we had been able to imprison the Shadow easily with little chance for their escape. We had also been able to put one of these rings around Nathaniel so he could live a somewhat normal life along with the rest of us. Today, however, I was aware he had taken a break, out west in the mountains where he used to live away from everyone. He got irritated with the ring around his neck all the time, so he decided the occasional trip to the mountains would be good for him. I very impatiently waited for Evelyn to go on, although I was glad she came for me. I would be interested to hear anything concerning my grandson.

Finally, she stammered out, "A lost hiker wandered to his house. He didn't even know he was there." I nodded with pursed lips. This type of thing had been frequent when we first learned about Nathaniel, but it hadn't happened for years.

"Where is he?" I asked in a rush. I figured if they had gone straight to Gretchen, then the hiker had survived, but if Nathaniel had gone to Jancarlo, then he was getting advice on what to do next.

"Gretchen," Evelyn responded concisely.

I didn't glance at the women as I pushed past Evelyn and bolted back down the hall to Gretchen's office. I knew if Ella had anything to say she would just reach out to my mind. I also knew if the hiker had survived we would need all the help we could get to calm him enough to explain things to him. Mostly, I just hoped that Nathaniel hadn't been hurt by anyone, especially an irate lost hiker.

I opened the door to Gretchen's office in time to see a glass container of cotton balls fly into the wall next to me. I flinched and covered my face but the shards hadn't reached me.

Gretchen ran toward me, intent on the mess, but upon seeing me standing in the doorway she said, "Oh good, do you have Ella with you?"

"Who's Ella?" a deep voice snapped from the other side of the room. "What are you people doing to me? Let go of me!"

"Just calm down," came a more familiar voice from the same direction. I searched out the voices to see Nathaniel, with the ring around his neck, trying to gently restrain the man who was, very obviously, the lost hiker. He was probably in his early twenties and in peak physical condition. He was tall and had stubble on his chin from days of being in the mountains. His wavy auburn hair was messy and singed, giving him a moderate bald spot just to the left of the crown of his head. An ugly jagged wound splayed his hair from the lightning strike, but I knew that with Gretchen's ministrations, he would soon have a silvery, fern-shaped scar instead.

"What's going on?" I asked, but at the moment I said it, Gretchen's desk chair lifted off the floor.

"That's what I'd like to know!" The hiker shouted at me and the room in general.

"If you would just calm down," Nathaniel said again, "we can explain everything."

Gretchen turned back to me with desperation on her face. She kept her voice low, "He can't control himself. He's wrecking everything."

I hadn't pulled this little trick for a while. I hadn't needed to with Ella around. I hoped Ella was right behind me, but figured I could buy some time. I stretched the net in my mind out but not over the hiker. I made it into an inverted bubble and the further I pushed it out, the more things disappeared. That way instead of making the hiker disappear, I made everyone and everything around him disappear to his view. I doubled the bubble over around on itself, and all sound muffled as well. I used to use this trick often to calm Nathaniel down. When all environmental stimulants dissolved, it was much easier to keep people at peace.

The hiker gazed around for a moment then his eyes fell on me. I made sure I was connected to the bubble but not in it so he could hear and see me, but everyone else could as well.

"Everything is fine." I insisted with as soothing a voice as I could muster. "You're safe here. We're going to help you." I spoke every word slowly and clearly.

"What happened to me?" he asked. I could visibly see him calming down, and from peeking out of my peripheral vision, I could see objects simply floating in the air instead of smashing to the ground.

"You were struck by lightning," I said evenly. "All of us here have been struck by lightning, just like you. We're going to help you. You just need to try to remain calm."

He started to protest, but without warning, his eyes rolled back into his head, and he slumped straight into Nathaniel's outstretched yet invisible arms. The desk chair and a few other things crashed to the floor. Everyone heaved a sigh of relief as Nathaniel gently laid the newest member of the Storm People on the vinyl couch behind him. I removed the net bubble from around the hiker and turned to see Ella in the doorway.

"Sorry to interrupt," she said slyly, "but he was getting ready to go on another rant."

"Thank you," Gretchen said to both of us. She swiftly moved over to the couch and flipped a chair off the floor for herself. Placing her hand on the man's forehead she tuned everyone else out. She must have realized it might be her only chance for a while.

I took in the smashed containers in the room, papers and medical paraphernalia on the floor. I bent over to help clean things up, and Nathaniel joined me.

"I wasn't there five minutes," he explained. "Tony took the ring off, and I went to see how Bam Bam fared. This idiot," he motioned to the man on the couch, "stumbles out of my own cabin and gets zapped the moment his foot touches the ground. I made sure he was still alive and brought him straight back." He obviously felt bad for what had happened, but a few years of having it happen constantly made him slightly callous to the outcome. "I have no idea what his story is. As soon as he came to, he went raving mad and began smashing up the place."

We replaced the papers, somewhat unorganized, on Gretchen's desk. "Well, I think it's safe to say he's a lifter," I said. Lifters can move objects from a distance. They could be extremely volatile until they learned to control their powers.

"His name is Jacob." Ella said as she picked up broken glass and cotton balls and tossed them in the garbage. "He's twenty years old. He's been lost from his hiking group for more than three days. He came upon your cabin," she nodded at Nathaniel, "and had been there for a day without incident. He hoped you would be able to help him get back to civilization."

"Not exactly the way he expected." Nathaniel said quietly as he picked up more glass off the floor.

After a few minutes, Gretchen left Jacob's side. She had done everything she could to heal his body, but she would have to wait until he woke up to explain his new powers. With the four of us working, we got the rest of her office cleaned up in short order.

Nathaniel went to get Jancarlo so they could discuss with Gretchen how best to keep Jacob calm long enough to introduce him to his new life. Ella and I decided to take the overflowing garbage bags to the incineration room.

As we stepped out of Gretchen's office, Kathryn Noahson stumbled down the hall into us. Ella saw her behind me first and pointed her out curiously. When I turned to face her, I understood Ella's confusion. I caught Kathryn in my arms as she panted and tried weakly to push herself into standing.

"Sorry," she panted. She sounded like she had just run a marathon which was usually the result of her putting powers into an object. That was part of Kathryn's powers. She could touch someone and duplicate their powers to transfer them to an object. It was an imprecise art and took a lot of energy out of her, but she was very good at what she did as the result of lots of practice. And it was the only way to explain her current situation.

"Kathryn," Ella studied her. "Are you okay? Were you working with Sophia?"

"No," she responded weakly. She tilted her head, leaning back against the wall behind her to catch her breath again. Watching the two of us from the corner of her eyes she said, "I'm not supposed to say anything, but I guess you two would probably be able to find out for yourselves anyway." It was true. Jancarlo usually shared top secret information with me, and Ella could find out whatever she wanted, whenever she wanted. "I'll have to wait to work with Sophia because Kimi had me make a certain undisclosed item. I need to get Gretchen's help to recover."

"Then you better go recover," I said. I opened the door for her to stagger through.

Before I closed the door, I heard Gretchen exclaim, "Now what?!"

I closed the door with a smirk. Gretchen could blow things out of proportion sometimes, but she really was busy these days. I looked up at Ella expecting to see her giggling at Gretchen's predicament as well but stopped short when I saw her brow pinched together in concern.

"That's strange," Ella said seriously as we headed down the hall with the garbage. "Kimi knew Sophia had scheduled Kathryn's time today to make me a translation device. In order for her to have the energy to make it, she isn't supposed to be making anything else."

"Maybe Kimi forgot." I said. "I saw her earlier in the hall. She seemed distracted or somehow off. She has a lot on her plate," I finished. "We all do."

"Busy or not, Kimi has never been as forgetful as all that." Ella insisted as we tossed the bag into the incineration room. The incineration room was where we put all our garbage. It was a simple, large, usually empty, cavern room. The fire movers and starters took it in turns to burn everything. It was good practice and, according to them, lots of fun. The walls were blackened with signs of past ignitions. The only thing that broke up the charred walls was a small opening in the ceiling.

As we inspected the room this time, it was filled to the ceiling with piles of garbage.

Ella and I looked at each other. "Kimi?" Ella guessed.

I just shrugged and threw the bags into the room.

"We'll have to mention this to Kin." Ella told me seriously.

"After dinner?" I pled with my eyes, and Ella rolled her eyes to relent.

I wasn't necessarily used to having someone to eat with every day. After decades of making food and eating with whomever happened to be in the dining room, I was still growing accustomed to planning out meals with individuals. Aside from Ella's mother, we often met up with Kimi and Tony for dinner, but occasionally we would see Kin, Jancarlo or someone else we knew. The People of the Storm who lived underground together were like a giant family. We ate meals together, hung out, and did most things together. But with actual biological family members present, like Kin and Kimi, Ella and her mom or even myself and Nathaniel, they would occasionally have private family meals. Until recently, Nathaniel was usually in the mountains so I only got to see him occasionally. It wasn't until we discovered the power-suppressing rings that he had been able to reside underground at the base with us, so he was still more comfortable being away from everyone. I joined Ella and her mom more often than not, but there were times that Evelyn rightfully insisted on a meal with just her and Ella.

"We haven't made dinner plans. We didn't expect to be back so soon," Ella said. Knowing Evelyn was still assigned to the front desk, I wrapped my arm around Ella's waist and gave her possibly the most suggestive look I had ever given a woman. My mind drifted to the idea that Ella and I could possibly have a quiet intimate dinner with just the two of us, but she shattered the thought.

"Maybe we should invite Heather to dinner," she said, slightly apologetic. "She doesn't know anyone here. It might be a good opportunity for her to meet others and get more comfortable." So, with promises that we would have an intimate dinner later, we headed to Heather's room to invite her along.

I've learned a few things about cooking over so many years, so I threw together some fish and rice, allowing Ella and Heather to chat while making a simple salad. Ella was beautiful and smart, but when it came to food, I definitely had more experience. Back in the old days when I married my first wife, it was everything to know if a woman was a good cook, but it had been easy for me to keep up with the times and get past it. I appreciated Ella's great mind and strong personality rather than her homemaking skills.

I made extra, like I always do. I had hoped to eat with Nathaniel, but we saw him at the desk in the lobby after he spoke with Jancarlo. Ella had brought a plate to her mom and invited Nathaniel to join us as well, but he grumbled about being around people before making a brief apology and calling for Boris to take him back to the mountains. Ella, Heather and I sat down to our food just in time to see Tony slouch through the double doors into the dining area. I immediately beckoned him over.

At Heather's wide eyes, Ella said, "Heather this is Tony. Don't worry, past his rough appearance, he's a really sweet guy."

"Rough appearance" was putting it mildly. Tony was enormous, bald, muscular and extremely intimidating if you didn't know him, even with the current sad puppy look on his face.

Once Heather seemed to be able to swallow her food again, I asked Tony, "Is Kimi coming too?"

Tony's face scrunched up, "I don't know." He hemmed. "I don't think so." He stared forlornly at the table as Ella gave him a plate of food.

"What's going on, Tony?" She asked him sternly.

He shrugged his shoulders and stabbed a fork into his food. "Let's just say," he glanced over at Heather who sat quietly chewing. "I don't think Kimi feels the way she used to."

"She's had a lot on her mind lately. We all have." I tried to come to Kimi's defense, but I also knew she was acting strange.

"Is there anything she's done in particular?" Ella asked.

"She stood me up again the other night." Tony said through a mouthful of fish. "When I asked her about it, she said she just forgot. She's not even making excuses anymore." He shoveled in more food as if it would help him feel better.

"That doesn't sound like her," Ella said. She seemed as if she were trying to find something wrong with Kimi, but I couldn't think why. Kimi was one of her dearest friends here, and one of mine as well. I tried to give her the benefit of the doubt.

"Doesn't sound like who?" Kin had come out of the kitchen behind us with a thick shake in his fist. He sat down next to Heather with a brief acknowledgement to her.

Before I could say anything, Ella answered him. "Kimi," she stated. "Has she been acting strange to you?"

Kin shook his head then took a long draught of the shake. When he stopped drinking, he had finished off a good fraction of the tall glass. "I haven't seen very much of her lately, actually." He turned to Tony. "What did she do?"

"Nothing," Tony shook his head. "It's not a big deal."

According to Ella, Tony was extremely self-conscious and probably would let Kimi's weird behavior slide, but Ella stepped in to ask Kin for him. "She stood him up." She said with a quick glance at Tony who didn't meet her eyes. "I imagine she just forgot, but it just doesn't sound like something she would do."

"You're right," Kin said. "Tony, we haven't talked much lately, but I know Kimi would never do something like that on purpose."

"Or maybe she's just changed her mind about me." Tony muttered as he raised his glass to take a drink.

"That's not right either." Kin shook his head and took another sip of his own drink. As he set it back down he explained, "See, I talked to Gretchen about this one time, a long time ago. When SP-"

"SP?" Heather interrupted.

Kin smiled in her direction. "Sorry, Storm People, SP."

Heather nodded, and Kin continued. "So, when SP have strong feelings about someone or something, it takes a lot to change it. All the processes in our bodies and minds move slower; we lose weight slower, we gain weight slower, we age slower, we mature slower, and we fall in and out," here he motioned at me, "of love slower."

"That's why it took me so long to get over my first wife," I pointed out.

"Right," Kin answered then took another drink. When he finished, he said, "It hasn't been that long, Tony. I don't think things would have changed too quickly."

At the sound of this, Tony's eating slowed down. As his face began to lift, the subject of conversation herself walked through the doors.

When Kimi entered, I noticed two things different about her. First, she had a shiny metal headband holding back her jet-black hair. I had never seen her wear her hair any way other than either down or in a ponytail. I had certainly never seen her put accessories in her hair.

The second thing I noticed was a small round mirror hanging from a chain around her neck. As with the hair accessories, I had never seen her wear jewelry before either. It dawned on me she had been wearing it when I saw her earlier as well. The mirror triggered something in my head, but after a moment of not being able to understand why, I put the thought aside. Maybe later it would come to me.

"Hey, Kimi," Kin called to her. She turned slowly, almost hesitantly to come over to us. "We were just talking about you."

Now, I don't know what my face might give away, but I prayed I didn't have the deer-in-the-headlights, guilty look everyone else had. I was about to aim a swift kick at Kin under the table, but he stood up to greet her, adding, "Yeah, I just told these guys it's been way too long since you and I had a good sparring match."

I felt the tension leave the table so I could meet Kimi's face again as her eyes narrowed maliciously at Kin.

"Come on," Kin goaded her, "I think you might need a reminder of who the older sibling is, don't you?"

As she stood there silently, Kin chanted something in Japanese, dancing around her with a sing-song voice, an obvious taunting from their childhood days. He looked so ridiculous, the rest of us couldn't help but snicker. Unfortunately, I think Kimi thought were laughing at her because her jaw began to clench and unclench as he danced around. Kimi's eyes narrowed so much I wasn't even sure they were still open until finally she yelled, "Fine!" She crossed her arms over her chest. "Name the time and place."

"Same as usual," Kin answered standing up straight with a huge grin on his face. "First thing in the morning, practice arena."

Kimi stepped up to Kin toe-to-toe. "I'll melt you," she whispered. On that pleasant note, she stormed out the door again. That's when I noticed one more difference. She had her black knit hat sticking out of her back pocket. It was a hat she requested shortly after Kathryn's arrival with the SP over fifteen years ago. The hat had my powers in it. When donned, it made the wearer invisible. I had given the same type of item to Kin about the same time and Ella shortly after she joined the Storm People.

It wasn't odd, necessarily, for her to have the hat, but she rarely had it on her while at the base. She brought it with her on most of our missions, but I found it strange for her to carry it with her now when she ought to be nipping into the kitchen for a bite to eat.

"Well," Kin said lightly as he plopped down again next to Heather, "if that doesn't bring her out of her funk, I don't know what will." He grabbed his drink in one hand and put the other on Heather's shoulder. Standing up to leave, he announced to the group, "Come and watch. I could use a cheering section." He raised his glass to us before he slipped out the door.

Chapter FIVE

Ella, Tony and I had stayed up quietly talking about the situation in the dining room. Heather had wandered away after dinner in the direction of the practice arena, and we didn't see her for the rest of the night. Tony wanted advice, as if I had any to give. Ella was much more helpful. She had given up a life on the surface and her goal of being a psychiatrist to join the Storm People here at our base. I often wondered if that was a very good move for her. She was great at connecting with people, the way she had with Heather. With her powers to read minds, she could figure out exactly what was bothering someone and why without them saying a word. She didn't read the minds of the SP often, though.

When she first came to us, she gave herself rules to live by. Her main rule was not to read the minds of her friends and associates if they knew her powers. When she connected to my mind, she settled on the surface so she would only receive what I intended her to hear.

The exceptions to her main rule were few, but I knew she used her powers when she sparred with others, and she was getting to be a really good fighter. Another exception was when she scanned anyone coming into the base. Jancarlo saw it as very necessary for our safety. Ella tried not to pry too much, but she would check unknowns before they would be allowed access to the base. But while dealing with friends, like speaking with Tony, she stayed out of his mind and let him express his feelings rather than thoughts.

The next morning at 0600, I threw on some clothes and dashed out the door. "First thing in the morning" around here was six, but I doubted if they would be ready to start at that time. I usually slept until seven or eight, but I made an exception today.

I was surprised to hear firm voices coming from the hall ahead of me. I was even more surprised when I recognized Ella and Kimi's voices. They sounded like they were keeping their voices low so no one would hear. I know I shouldn't have done it, but I threw my net over myself and stopped around the corner to listen.

"…. other people." Kimi was finishing her thought.

There was a pause then Ella said softly, "Kimi….you know I would never…"

Her voice trailed off as if Kimi knew what she meant. "I'm not talking about just you." Kimi pointed out, but I caught the fact that she still included Ella in her point. "You never know," she continued, "There might be others. It's just a safety precaution."

"Yeah," Ella answered even softer.

"I gotta go," Kimi mumbled then I heard her tread down the hall.

I pulled my net off and turned the corner to see Ella stuck halfway between shock and rage. I had never seen her like that before. "What was that about?"

"I'm not sure," she muttered with her eyebrows pressed together.

"What happened?"

"I'll show you." I knew what she meant, but still was caught off guard at the anger in the memory she shared.

In my mind, from Ella's point of view, I saw Kimi walking down the hall. *Notice,* Ella told me in my mind, *she's walking* away *from the arena.* Ella greeted her with a cheerful hello and mentioned she was coming to watch the match.

Kimi seemed annoyed by the comment, but the moment quickly passed. Kimi made some excuse about going back to the kitchen to get some water.

Before she could get away Ella said, *I tried to contact you last night. I couldn't find you anywhere.*

She waited for an answer, but Kimi just said, *Sorry.*

So, Ella tried another approach. *I like your headband. I've never seen you wear something like that before.*

Oh, yeah, Kimi hemmed again, *it's new.*

Ella decided to stop beating around the bush, *Is that the secret item Kathryn made for you yesterday?*

At this, Kimi stopped to stare at her seriously. She began to ask, *How did you...?* She stopped herself and her eyes darted around the hallway. *I guess no secrets are safe around you, are they?*

What does it do? Ella pressed her.

Nothing, was all Kimi would respond at first, but Ella gave her a knowing look and tapped her forehead. Kimi's defiance fell away because she knew Ella could find out for herself. *It has a dampening field in it.* She finally acquiesced. *It keeps out…other people.*

Ella took this as a shot at her. With all the anger swelling inside her, she remembered times she had promised myself, Kimi and others she wouldn't enter their minds without their permission, but mostly she just felt hurt that Kimi would insinuate she might take those liberties. She gently responded, *Kimi…. you know I would never…*

Kimi didn't backpedal much. She just added, *I'm not talking about just you.* Ella caught the same fact I had; she hadn't exempted Ella. *You never know…There might be others. It's just a safety precaution.* I had heard this part of it, but this time I watched as Kimi fidgeted more and more throughout the conversation. She made her excuses to leave, and Ella ended the memory in my mind.

She looked at me sternly. *She's had Kathryn make her an item to keep me out,* she said in my mind.

Whatever she's doing, I insisted, *we owe her the benefit of the doubt. Besides, it's not a bad idea for safety.*

Ella pursed her lips in indecision. *I suppose.* She finally relented. *But why would she* need *to keep people out?*

I don't know. Come on. I nodded my head towards the arena. *Maybe this will bring back the old Kimi.*

Ella took a deep breath. Once she gave me a weak nod, we walked together towards the gym.

When we passed through the gym, we saw a few others already seated on small boulders Tony must have arranged. There were even a few people that had not been part of the conversation in the dining hall but must have heard about the show. Jancarlo was among them. Ella and I sandwiched ourselves between Heather and Tony. Evelyn had opted to sleep in because she had been at the desk until late.

The arena was a large cavern we used for practicing with our powers. It was about four football fields long and four wide. Over five stories tall, it was big enough to house small hills of boulders piled together and spread randomly throughout, but there were no other weapons or tools present.

By the time we arrived, Kin and Kimi had already begun and were dancing around each other. They each had their hands wrapped, but they had no other protection. Kimi wore the silver band in her hair, that miraculously didn't seem capable of being dislodged. She had a tank top and black shorts and the little mirror she had taken to wearing was somehow secured to her chest as well.

I had seen the twins fight numerous times. Their style and grace always amazed me. I was no novice myself because I had learned much from both of them.

Just as I noticed a few small fires burning around the arena, Ella leaned over to Heather. "Have they already been throwing fire at each other?" she asked.

"No," Heather shook her head, "apparently Kimi was here early practicing. Those are leftovers."

I wasn't sure if Ella was in my head or not, but I projected my thoughts to her anyways, *That accounts for her walking away from the arena wanting to get a drink before they started.*

I wasn't too surprised when Ella answered me, *True*. That was all I could get from her before our attention turned back to Kimi and Kin who started throwing some serious punches now.

Even though they had no head protection, or anything else for that matter, they never pulled their punches. They both saw it as a sign of weakness in themselves if they requested it, but they were very good at playing it safe when working with others. I think it must have been a cultural element with them or possibly just an ego element.

Maybe it was just my imagination, but Kimi's style seemed to have altered slightly. She started out somewhat flat-footed, but bounced on the balls of her feet more as the fight progressed. The twins both knew multiple styles of martial arts and sparring, so I passed it off as her just toying around with something different to catch Kin unaware. It didn't work.

Kin landed a few good punches then laid a round-house kick into Kimi's stomach. I noticed Heather almost smiling as Kimi doubled over for a moment. Kin was completely indifferent to the fact he had knocked the wind out of his own sister and started taunting her all over again. Kimi waved him over to her. Once he was close enough, she caught him with a backhand that knocked him back just enough for her to get a sidekick into his gut.

Once they both staggered upright again, they pounced on each other. If it had been boxing, I would've given the round to both of them. I struggled to keep up with the myriad of techniques until Kin dropped down to sweep Kimi's legs out from under her. She landed on the flat of her back, but instead of knocking the air out of her lungs like it should have, she simply rolled to the side and kicked Kin in the head as he ran in to jump on top of her. That's when the fight went to the ground.

The fact that these two could withstand such blows was testament enough of the training they had endured, but after a few minutes of rolling, escaping, and trying for multiple submissions, they started to get serious. Kimi stood several times, attempting to get the fight from the ground to standing. She must have really wanted to take out some frustration, forcing the fight to standing so she could punch and kick.

I knew the match couldn't last much longer at this dangerous pace. Kin threw Kimi into a nearby boulder at one point when she tried to bring her heel down on his head. She took the rock in the small of her back and her face crumpled in pain. I knew both Kin and Kimi could go see Gretchen when they finished, but I worried they might be pushing things a little too far just for ego's sake.

Kin loped, slowly, over to Kimi and grabbed her arm. He wrenched it behind her back as both of them screamed. With effort, Kin said, "Who's the older sibling Kimi?" He repeated the question in Japanese, but Kimi's eyes flared in rage. Before Kin could brace himself, a massive serpent of flame roiled out from one of the fires still smoldering on the cavern walls. The flame engulfed Kin and changed from bright orange to brilliant white.

Kin immediately let go of Kimi's arm and stood with eyes wide open. Straining, he extended his arms out to the sides to separate the flames from himself. I knew the twins, as well as other fire manipulators, were fireproof to a point, but I couldn't be sure what that point might be. I assumed they could withstand fire similar to the temperature they themselves could create. I didn't know who, out of the two twins, could create the hotter fire.

Kin made some good headway with the white flames when Kimi got her second wind and renewed her attack. As he endeavored to withhold the flames, she kicked him in the gut and face numerous times. Kin finally brought his hands in to deflect her persistent fists, but that meant he must ignore the fire.

When it seemed Kimi ran low on energy, she head-butted Kin in a last attempt to engulf him in her inferno once more. It worked. Kin clutched his nose with blood dripping from between his fingers and slowly sank to the stone floor as Kimi's fire consumed him again.

I saw Heather lurch forward out of my peripheral vision, but Ella quickly slapped a hand on her knee. "I know what you want to do," she said quietly to Heather. "But I promise if you did, Kin would be just as upset about it as Kimi would. Besides," she glanced quickly at her then back to the twins, "you would never survive the heat."

I surmised that Heather had been contemplating transporting into the fire and transporting Kin back out. Ella was right. Neither of the twins would ever forgive anyone for interfering in their sparring match, even when they took it too far. The only one they would tolerate it from thundered, "ENOUGH!"

Jancarlo stood a few boulders away from us. The arena held its breath in silence as Jancarlo lowered his voice. "Enough, Kimi."

She had her lip curled back in a snarl, but her face slowly melted back into her usual casual severity. She straightened, steadying her breathing. She raised one eyebrow at Kin as her fire drifted back to the wall from which it came. A wicked grin touched her lips. While Kin stooped, she stepped closer to him. "Does this mean I'm the older sibling now?" she hissed.

Without a word, Kin dropped his hands to his sides, splashing blood everywhere, and stormed out of the arena.

I had never been one for violence. Both Kin and Kimi had insisted that my peaceful ways would get me killed someday. Having watched them spill their own sibling's blood so freely, I couldn't see how it would keep them alive. I was unnerved with how the match ended. Something didn't feel right to me, but I assumed it was my distaste for the manner in which the twins solved their issues.

The spectators slowly filed out of the arena. Behind me, I heard Heather tell Ella, "Well, I certainly don't feel like having breakfast anymore."

I turned to say something about none of us having an appetite, but I saw Tony through the glass in the back half of the gym and stopped in my tracks. Ella followed my eyes. The gym had a great view of the arena beyond. We watched Tony slowly approaching Kimi. We couldn't hear what was being said, but after a short exchange, Tony left Kimi behind. It didn't seem as though they had said anything rude or mean, but Tony's face was creased in painful resignation. Ella and I exchanged a curious glance but turned back around quickly before Tony could see us watching. Not that he would have noticed with his head hanging down so low.

We moved sluggishly down the hall lost in our own thoughts. Before I took stock of our surroundings, Ella opened the door to her room. I followed her inside and sat in a chair at her desk.

Jancarlo had used his rock moving powers to add and attach a room for Evelyn, and even a living room/dining area for them to share, like a normal apartment. With her mother still asleep, we must have both subconsciously wandered straight to her room like we used to do before Evelyn arrived.

We sat in silence for a few more minutes before I heard Ella's voice in my head, *I just can't believe that person is really Kimi!*

She said it forcefully enough in my mind that I flinched a little in shock. The fact she said it in my mind meant she thought we might be overheard if she said it out loud. *Who else could it be?* I asked her, unsure of her answer.

I don't know, she relented, *but it's not Kimi.*

I was about to ask her what she meant along with a whole slew of other questions when one of the stones on the panel of gems on her wall began to glow. The panel was an intercom-type system Kathryn and Jancarlo had recently installed almost everywhere on the base. Each precious stone had Ella's powers embedded in it. When touched, it would link your thoughts to the twin stone and whoever's mind that touched it. Since electronics didn't work for us, we had tried other intercoms in the past, but none of them functioned properly. Until Ella showed up, we just shoved written messages under doors or visited each other face to face. I had to admit, it was much more convenient this way.

I happened to know the gem glowing linked to Gretchen's office. Everyone had a link to Gretchen's office in case of a medical emergency. That probably added to her business these days.

Ella saw it glowing and, rather than cross the room to touch the gem like the rest of us had to do, she must have reached out with her mind. She was the only one who could remotely connect to the intercom this way. She could listen in on others' conversations if she wanted to as well but had promised Jancarlo and others she would never do it unless absolutely necessary. We all trusted her implicitly.

Her eyes glazed over for a minute with the silent conversation. When she blinked around at me, I heard in my mind, *Jancarlo wants us to come to Gretchen's office immediately.*

Without another word, we both swept down the hall. I think we knew what was going on. Kin must have been in Gretchen's office. I just hoped he was ok.

Chapter SIX

We opened Gretchen's office door without knocking to see Kin sitting on the vinyl couch by the wall. Jacob, the hiker, was nowhere to be seen. Gretchen sat next to the couch holding Kin's hand. It might have been a strange sight if I hadn't known how Gretchen's powers worked. She could heal the body just by being in contact with the skin. Kin sat expectantly like he had been waiting for us to come in the door.

Jancarlo leaned against Gretchen's desk with his back to us. When we came in, he turned. "Thanks for coming, you two. We need to have a silent conversation." He nodded to Ella and turned back to Kin.

We all heard Ella say in our minds, *Go ahead.*

Tell them what you told me, Kin, Jancarlo said.

I don't think that woman is Kimi, Kin answered firmly.

I felt a smack on my arm and turned to Ella who said, *I told you so!*

I rubbed my arm better. *What makes you guys so sure?* I asked.

Kin answered, *That's not the way Kimi fights. I know her style inside and out. She pulled some moves I've never seen before. Besides that, she didn't create fire, she only threw it. It wasn't anywhere near the temperatures I've felt Kimi use.*

Are you using this as an excuse for her beating you? I know it was heartless of me, but I had to ask.

I let her beat me. I knew Kin would never throw a match unless absolutely necessary, so I knew it must have been important to him. *I had planned on doing it in the first place to help Kimi feel better, but once we got fighting, I realized she's not my sister. I almost took her down but decided to let her take the match this time so hopefully she'll be cocky the next time we meet. She won't know my full capabilities.*

Whoa, whoa, whoa, I had to speak up. Ella nodded her head in agreement with what Kin had said, as if Kimi was now the enemy. I had to stop this insanity! *Kimi is beyond suspicion.* I asserted. *She hasn't done anything but use a different fighting style, and you turn on her?! Is that all it takes to start fighting amongst ourselves?*

Kin's right, though, Ella let her voice be heard. *Kimi has been acting really strange. Avoiding interaction with everyone, standing Tony up, and getting Kathryn to make that headband! What does it take for you to be suspicious of someone? Yes, we should give her the benefit of the doubt, but one person can only cross so many lines!*

What headband? Jancarlo asked Ella.

A metal headband that repulses powers, specifically, mine. I can't read her mind or even contact her mentally. Ella narrowed her eyes at Jancarlo. *She told Kathryn you sanctioned it.*

I did no such thing. We all stood in stunned silence, scrutinizing each other.

Did you ever find the mirror? Ella asked Kin. After our last fight with the Shadow, when Devin Ross died, we found a small mirror hanging on a tree near the fight. Noah, the man who can communicate with and control animals, said he thought he saw Eva Winford, Ross's girlfriend and partner, in it, but no one else had seen anything. It was a diamond shaped mirror no longer than a man's palm, but we were certain it had someone's powers in it. We had brought it back to the base with us in order to inspect it, but found nothing. Only a day or two later, it disappeared before Kathryn could examine it.

Kin shook his head. *You think this could have something to do with her?*

Possibly. Ella answered. Eva had disappeared that same night. We had yet to hear anything about her. *Kimi has been wearing a mirror. Could they be linked somehow?*

We won't know unless we find it, Jancarlo said.

Is there any way someone could have possessed her somehow? Kin asked. He nodded his head towards Ella and said, *Ella, you took possession of Bam Bam. Devon Ross was able to use some kind of mind-control on the people in the Amazon. Is it possible that some other mind-reader can take possession of people? Have you ever tried it?*

I tried it once. I nodded in agreement and had to stifle a grin. We had been playing around with her powers at one time, and she had tried to make me do something against my will. I just kept telling her, "No," in my mind. She glanced at me from the corners of her eyes while a grin played on her lips as well. *We're pretty sure I can't control humans, just animals and only strongly influence them at that. I think I could only control Bam Bam because he was previously an inanimate object. I really just replaced the animation with my consciousness. But I can't do that with humans.* She returned her gaze to Kin. *I've given it lots of thought and some experimentation. The powers Ross used in the Amazon must have been a mix of mind reading and power blocking. As far as I know, Ross is the only one that could do it. It wasn't super-powerful. It could definitely wear off or the person being influenced could fight it and force it out of their minds, like Namal did. At this point, I believe Ross made Perry Anderson give him that ability. And, to be honest, I think Kimi would easily be able to fight it off as well.*

I'm betting, I added, *Ross wouldn't have allowed anyone else to have that ability. He wouldn't want anyone to use it against him.*

I'm sorry, Kin, Ella finished, *I highly doubt anyone is controlling Kimi.*

Silence ensued until finally Jancarlo cleared his throat. *But she still hasn't done anything that would be punishable.* He said with finality. *Anyone has the right to ask Kathryn to make items for them, stand people up, and fight using a different style.*

But she lied too. Ella insisted. *She lied about you giving permission for Kathryn to make something for her.*

Kathryn has every right to use her skills how she chooses. Yes, she lied to Kathryn, but that's something that Kathryn will have to deal with. Other than acting suspicious, Kimi has done nothing to warrant any kind of reprimand. Jancarlo answered back just as firmly. We stood in silence for another moment. I was relieved Jancarlo stood up for Kimi but even more surprised the two people turning on her were the two people closest to her, other than her boyfriend. *Having said that,* Jancarlo interrupted our ponderings, *I'm going to give you permission now, Ella. If I ever start having similarly strange behavior, you go to Kin. If the two of you merit it, you can inspect my mind to see if I'm the same person or if something else is going on. Are we agreed?* He looked at Kin, who nodded, and back to Ella again, who nodded as well, although they both cast their eyes down. We all knew the severity of the situation to force them to take those extreme measures. *Ok then,* Jancarlo stood up to his full height. *We'll keep eyes on her. Watch her closely, but don't do anything to set her off again. If something is going on, she'll have to make the first move.*

"Onto other business." He said out loud. An obvious signal for the mind-reading to end. Ella gave a small, reluctant nod. Jancarlo opened his mouth to speak, but before he could say anything there was a small knock on the door, and it creaked open slowly. We all stood quietly, on edge from the recent conversation, but relaxed when Heather peeked her blonde curls around the door.

"I just came to see how Kin was doing," she almost whispered.

Kin cracked a grin and waved his hand for her to come in. "I'm fine. Thanks, Heather." He nodded to Gretchen. "She can heal just about everything." he said.

As he finished speaking, Gretchen came out of her trance, yanking her hand off his. "I wouldn't have so much work to do if we didn't insist on trying to kill our own people. And your own sister, nonetheless!" She growled at him. "I'm going to go see if Sheila needs any help fixing Kimi up." She pointed a stern finger at Kin who just sat with half a grin on his face. "You are NOT to spar with your sister again for at least a month. I'm forbidding it! I need a break! You had four broken bones, including your nose and internal bleeding that would have killed you in another couple hours! I don't even want to talk about all the infections seeping into your system!" She continued with a steady stream of complaints while she brushed past Heather out the door. Just before the door closed, she pushed it open again to stab an accusing finger at Jancarlo. "And YOU should have stopped that madness sooner!" She yelled then slammed the door behind her.

Heather stood with her eyes wide open in shock from Gretchen's outburst, but the rest of us were used to beratings from the good doctor. She often accused us of trying to overwork her or kill off each other and ourselves, if she wasn't claiming we were bumbling fools. The rest of us sat there trying, unsuccessfully, to keep grins off our faces. Heather finally relaxed seeing how we took the rebuking.

Jancarlo spoke up once the door was firmly shut. "You're just in time, Heather. I was wondering if you would be willing to attempt a recovery mission." The way he said it sounded so important that Heather squared her shoulders and lifted her chin.

"Absolutely," she said. "What do we need to recover?"

"Well," Jancarlo hesitated a bit, "the item to recover is kind of large. I'm not sure how much you can transport. I heard about the car." He nodded his approval. "But Bam is a little bigger than a car."

"Who's Bam Bam?" she asked, then added, "Other than the obvious one."

"Bam Bam is a giant rock man." Kin supplied.

"We kind of inherited him when his maker disappeared." Ella told her. "He stays in the Rocky Mountains for now."

"We can't have him sitting up there for someone to find, but we haven't had a means to get him back here until now." Jancarlo finished for her. "I would like you to see if you can bring him to the arena. He'd be great for practice. Do you feel comfortable with trying that?"

"Yeah," she answered, "I think I can do it."

I watched as Jancarlo's eyes flickered back to me and I got a sinking feeling. I immediately started shaking my head behind Heather before she could turn. I did not want to be stuck babysitting this little mission.

Unfortunately, Jancarlo wasn't going to let me off the hook. "I hoped you would accompany her, Liam, just to make sure everything goes smoothly, and invisibly, if necessary."

When Heather turned to face me, I stopped the shaking, quickly composing my features into a willing smile. "Sure," I answered, but I knew it didn't sound very convincing. "But what about the new recruit I heard you talking about on the phone yesterday."

"Don't worry about that." Jancarlo waved me off. "I'm sending Evelyn. The new person is a water mover as well."

Evelyn had recently taken over the job of bringing the water we needed into our underground base when Adam, our previous water mover, had gotten too old to be young anymore. She kept bad water out and good water flowing smoothly, among other things. But another water mover would be a higher priority than sitting at the front desk. My chance to get out of the babysitting trip wouldn't work. I just nodded my head through tight lips and fallen face.

"Great," Heather spoke up. "When do we leave?"

"Immediately," Jancarlo said. Then he turned to Ella. "Ella, would you be able to let Heather know where they're going?" After she nodded, he added, "Then I have another job for you."

"Oh?" Ella cocked her head to the side.

"Kathryn should be able to make you that translation device today. You might have to work with her and Sophia later to make sure it works. But for this morning, would you mind working with Jacob? He's having a really hard time controlling his new abilities."

Ella, of course, agreed to help. I have to admit, I got a little uncomfortable with Ella working alone with macho, rugged, Jacob. He was much more her age than myself, and I had to concede he was better looking, but I let the negative feeling pass.

Ella turned to Heather, putting a picture in her mind of our destination. Heather nodded to let her know she got it, then they both turned to me. Ella squeezed my hand. She knew I didn't like to kiss or show public displays of affection. "See you when you get back."

"Good luck with Jacob." I said, but in my mind, I added, *Dinner later?*

Always. She gave me her usual answer as she nodded.

I turned back to Heather. "Ready to go when you are."

She gave me half a grin, and I put my hand on her shoulder. She nodded to Jancarlo and Kin before we disappeared, saying, "See you later."

The air shimmered around us like steam off a pavement in summer which gave the illusion of warmth, but when we solidified, I was reminded with a chill of the difference in altitude of our destination. We stood in a wooded, mountain area, but I didn't immediately see the cabin. We were in the right area. The trees and mountain peaks were familiar. I had been here a number of times visiting Nathaniel, so I knew the place pretty well. I glanced around to find the cabin behind us nestled in the forest. We were in the right place. I breathed a sigh of relief when I saw it, knowing nothing had gone wrong.

I pointed out the cabin to Heather, and we headed through the trees. "I wonder how we ended up over here?" I said it out loud, but I didn't think Heather would yet have an answer.

However, she responded with, "I'm not sure. The picture Ella put in my mind had Bam Bam in it. Maybe I was off because he's not over there."

I pondered that for a moment. I wasn't really sure how the transporter's powers worked. Even if I had been, powers worked differently for each person, so they are mostly learned by experimentation.

I didn't think about it for long. Once we got to the cabin, I realized storm clouds hung overhead, although storm clouds were usually present whenever I came here. We emerged from the trees, and I saw the large depressions in the ground around the cabin, indicating Bam Bam's presence. I also noticed the windows to the cabin flung open.

The cabin "windows" were nothing more than doors in the walls that could swing open. They held no glass because when Nathaniel was around, the glass constantly shattered from lightning strikes.

"Nathaniel?" I called out as we approached the cabin.

I heard movement in the cabin but no response. Maybe I wasn't being cautious enough. Then, my grandson Nathaniel, poked his shaggy grey head out the front door. As uncouth as Nathaniel came off at first sight, I knew he was extremely well educated and had a small fortune at his disposal. He claimed, since I was his grandfather, it really should belong to me, but it was family money from his father's side, and his mother was my daughter, the daughter I never met. However, he did use the funds to help the People of the Storm whenever they needed it, which thankfully wasn't all that often.

We chatted with Nathaniel for a few minutes. I introduced Heather and explained our purpose in coming. "Where's Bam Bam?" I asked.

"He's down at the lake, getting some fish." Nathaniel said. "I don't mind being with the SP underground, but I certainly miss the fresh fish."

"We could bring some back to the base with us," I said. I did love fresh mountain trout as well. That was one of the treats I got when I would visit Nathaniel before we learned how to tame his powers.

"We'll see how much he brings back with him." Nathaniel turned to Heather. "I've learned you have to be very specific with Bam Bam," he said. "He doesn't really understand sarcasm or turn of phrase. Once I told him to jump up because he was sitting down and, boy, did he jump! He shot well over the trees. When he landed, it sounded like thunder. I would know." He mumbled the last.

Heather enjoyed hearing about Nathaniel's adventures. She good naturedly listened to him drivel on. Eventually, we heard Bam Bam plodding through the trees. When he came in sight, his hands were cupped seamlessly together. In the bowl he formed were a half dozen fish and enough water to keep them alive.

"He's a good fisherman," I conceded.

"In here, big guy," Nathaniel yelled while pointing to a rain barrel next to the cabin. The fish landed in the barrel with a huge splash. "Sure you don't want to stay for a bite? Nothing like fresh grilled fish." He offered us again.

"Maybe another time," I answered. "Jancarlo is expecting us back."

We had only been waiting about twenty minutes or so, but I figured we needed to get back right away. Besides, I was eager to be done with my babysitting assignment.

As I threw my net out over Heather and Bam Bam, I said good-bye to Nathaniel then pulled the net tightly around the three of us. I gave Heather the go-ahead, putting my right hand on her shoulder and my left on Bam Bam's arm. The air swirled around us, and I saw Nathaniel give a half-hearted wave before he disappeared.

I thought we were doing fine at first because the commotion around us started getting dark, like we were going to reappear in the underground cavern we call home.

But we ended up with the breathless sensation a little longer than I was used to. I wanted to ask Heather what was going on, but I didn't have any air in my lungs. Finally, the mountains reappeared around us, and I took a deep breath. Dropping my hands, I asked Heather, "What happened?"

She looked just as baffled. "I'm not sure," she said. "I felt some kind of resistance. I couldn't end up on the other side. I don't know what it was, but I couldn't get us into the arena, so I brought us back here."

"Ok, maybe you're just still figuring out how to use your powers." At least she could think logically while in transit and keep us from solidifying in solid rock or something else dangerous. "Give it another try. Let's see if it happens again."

She gave a small bob of her head, and I grabbed hold of both her and Bam Bam. This time she took a deep breath, and her eyebrows came together in concentration. The forest around us swirled together in a green blur again. It took a second longer than usual, but the massive arena cavern eventually formed in front of our eyes.

As soon as we reappeared in the arena, I let out a sigh of relief. But my relief was short-lived as we were encircled by an immense blazing wall of fire.

Chapter SEVEN

I immediately crouched in front of Heather, searching the surrounding area. The flames were as tall as Bam Bam with his fifteen foot plus height. Drops of sweat appeared on my forehead immediately from the heat. Much as I tried, I couldn't see anything through the blaze.

"Who's there?" A voice yelled over the roar of the flames. "Show yourselves!" I recognized Kin's voice.

I remembered my net was still stretched over us and quickly removed it. "It's Liam!" I yelled back. "What are you doing?!"

As soon as I spoke, the flames died down but remained in a small circle around us. Bam Bam could easily step over them, but I knew Kin could also melt him where he stood if he tried it. "Is anyone else with you?" Kin asked seriously. Something had to have happened during our short absence.

"It's just me, Heather and Bam Bam." I turned to Heather whose face burned bright red from the heat. I still couldn't see Kin, but I knew he also owned a hat with my powers in it.

"But is there anyone else with you?" Kin asked, lowering his voice. "Can you sense if there was anyone else you were covering with your powers? Heather, could you sense anyone else transporting with you that shouldn't have been?"

I couldn't think of why he would be asking these questions, but I figured it was safest, with Kin, to answer them. "I always know exactly who I'm covering and where they are when they're covered. There's no one else with us."

"Heather?" Kin asked.

I nodded to Heather for her to answer him.

"From the few times I've done it," she answered, quivering, "I can tell who I take with me. I didn't sense anyone else with us."

The fire around us extinguished completely, leaving us free to move around. I instructed Bam Bam to sit by the arena wall, and I approached Kin as soon as he took his hat off.

"What was that all about?" I demanded in a low voice. I didn't like to get upset about anything in front of a woman if I could help it, much less a child, (I know, I know, I'm old-fashioned that way) but Heather was both.

"Easy, Liam." Kin held his hands up in front of himself. "We had an escape. We had to lock down the base while you were gone."

I calmed down, but only a little. We had security in place to make it impossible to transport in or out of the base, but we hadn't activated it yet because we didn't have a reason. I still didn't like being attacked without warning or provocation.

"Jancarlo knew we were bringing Bam Bam here. Why didn't he put it in place after we got back?" I asked. I noticed Heather listening to both of us carefully.

"Wiki escaped." He answered. "You took longer than expected, so we put up the shield, but dropped it after the first attempt to get in. That was you, wasn't it?" He questioned both me and Heather.

We both nodded and Heather added, "I felt something pushing me away, so we had to try again."

"Good to know it works." Kin said earnestly. "Jancarlo should be putting it back in place now. Come on." He jerked his head toward the door to the gym and we followed him out.

Once in the hall, Heather matched our strides down the hallway to the lobby. Walking next to Kin, she watched him tuck his hat into his back pocket.

"You're like a ninja with that thing, huh?" she said quietly.

"That's how the ninjas *really* do it." He winked at her.

She stopped in her tracks, quietly exclaiming, "I knew it!"

"Good job bringing Bam Bam back, by the way," Kin told her as she ran to catch up to us. "Your powers are impressive. Keep honing them."

We turned the corner into the lobby area to find a ring of people with Jancarlo in the middle. He held his hands over his head, facing the ceiling, looking a little like Atlas holding up the ceiling from a distance. The difference was that Kathryn had her hand on his arm. Both of them had their eyes closed and their faces compressed in absolute focus. A moment after we got there, they both lowered their arms and opened their eyes. I knew it took a long time to entirely wrap the base in the protective shield. They had previously wrapped it from the bottom up, but left several places unprotected. Jancarlo didn't want to alienate the other transporters, but they all knew we would be putting up these defenses sooner or later. The only place they would be leaving unprotected was the clearing room behind them.

Jancarlo surveyed the crowd gathered in the lobby. "I'm glad so many of you could make it here." He announced to the group. He obviously had Kin or someone else gather the entire group living underground while he worked to secure it. Now was the time for the announcement. "We've had an escape from the high security holding cells. We're not sure what happened or how he got out, so we're putting security measures in place to avoid another attack. We do know that it happened within the last two hours, so we will be asking everyone for their whereabouts at the time. No one will be able to transport in or out of the base unless you go through the security clearance room, there." He pointed toward the small room with the glass window. "We'll work on putting in more transporting areas to keep the disruptions to a minimum, but if you have any problems or concerns, feel free to talk to me or Kin."

While he spoke, I found Ella and her mom in the crowd and sidled up next to them. She glanced at me and said, "I'm going to be really busy for a while."

"No kidding." I answered her. "How'd it go with Jacob?"

"He seems like a very nice young man," Evelyn put in.

Ella rolled her eyes then filled my mind with memories of weights flying around the gym and rocks floating through the arena. "He's powerful but extremely chaotic," she said. "If he could get his mind under control, he would be a powerful ally, but until then, he's very dangerous." She put a memory in my head of her getting a barbell dropped on her foot. She was with Gretchen getting healed when the alarm sounded.

"I also got this," she added, holding up her left wrist jingling a charm bracelet under my nose. For a moment I thought Jacob had given it to her, and I was about to protest, but she said, "It's my translation device." She indicated the many different colored rocks hanging off the bracelet to make the tinkling sound. It sported easily thirty or forty stones of various mediums cut into little donuts, but no two rocks were alike.

She admired her new bracelet. "With this, I can read anyone's thoughts and memories no matter what language they're in," she said. "I can even read yours if they're in Irish." After a moment, she looked around at the crowd. *Do you know who escaped?* She asked in my mind.

Wiki, I answered her. *Kin told me after he attacked us in the arena.* I pushed the memory of the fire surrounding us and Kin asking if anyone was with us, into the front of my mind.

Wiki, she said with distaste in my mind.

Evelyn's eyes bounced between us as we spoke silently. She knew we were discussing something and waited for Ella to explain. Before we could, Jancarlo beckoned Kin, Ella, Tony and me to join him in the conference room. As Evelyn followed us, a quick glimpse bounced between her and Jancarlo. As a father/grandfather I knew what it meant. It said, "If it involves my daughter, it involves me."

Heather watched us walk away. The last I saw was her and Jacob eyeing each other with suspicion before she turned her back on him.

The six of us walked swiftly to the conference room. Jancarlo held the door open for us to join him inside, but before he closed the door he said, "Ella, find Kimi as well."

"Right," she nodded slowly, but her eyes darted to Kin.

"Are you sure we should?" Kin asked in a low voice.

"She's part of the security team." Jancarlo said firmly. "We can't leave her out of the loop."

We sat for a minute in silence with the door open. Finally, Ella shook her head. "I can't find her anywhere," she said. "It must be that headband of hers."

Jancarlo swore forcibly and punched a finger to the intercom on the wall. He put his finger on gem after gem, but after half a dozen tries, he said, "We'll have to catch her up later." He closed the door all the way then turned a knob next to the door. The knob activated a host of powers in accordance with the room. When turned all the way on, our conversation could not be heard or eavesdropped upon in any way. The only way to end the effect was to turn the knob off or open the door.

"Before we start, Jancarlo," Kin said,, "did anyone have eyes on Kimi when this happened?"

Tony nodded, saying, "She was teaching a class in the gym about an hour ago."

"So, she's disappeared since then?" Kin said.

"What do you mean, 'disappeared'?" I asked him, somewhat short. I knew he was suspicious of Kimi, but I wasn't ready to believe anything was wrong. It couldn't be true.

"I mean," he said with a matching edge to his voice, "she's not where she's supposed to be, and she's not responding the way she's supposed to." The way he glared at me actually made me worry he might get mad at me. Kin was not the type to be messed with.

At this point, Jancarlo stepped in. "The problem we're here to discuss is Wiki." he said as his eyes volleyed between the two of us.

"Remind me who Wiki is," Evelyn spoke up.

"Wiki," Jancarlo answered, "was one of the Storm People. A powerful transporter. But he worked with Devin Ross to try to kill all of us. He's been in a holding cell downstairs since Ross died."

"Wiki's not a problem," Kin said. He glared at me a moment longer then turned his attention to Jancarlo. "Wiki has always only watched out for himself. The only reason he joined up with Ross was because Ross promised him dominion over the SP. Otherwise, I doubt if he would have done anything about his anger. I don't think he'll give us any trouble now that he's gotten away from us. He'll just crawl into a hole somewhere and hope we don't find him."

"I'd have to agree with Kin," Ella said. I got the feeling she agreed with him on more than just one item. "He's out for number one. He always has been. He's not going to chance getting tangled up with us again."

Tony bobbed his head. After a moment of awkward silence, he asked, "Do we know how he escaped? Did he have help? Did he damage anything?"

Kin shook his head. "I went down to the cells for a routine two-hour security check. His cell was empty. No forced exit. No one saw him or anything out of the ordinary, and he had been present at the previous two-hour check. Even the ring from his neck was gone. There's only one way out of the detention area down his hall. It would've taken him past the posted security team. They didn't see anything, and they're very reliable." He sighed. "No, he had to have transported out or had someone else transport him out."

"The only other transporter around is Heather." Ella said. "I've been in enough of her mind to know that we can trust her. She'd never do something like this."

"We know she wouldn't, Ella." Jancarlo said. "Neither would any of the other transporters. They've all practically disowned him for what he did."

"So, the only option left is for him to have transported himself out?" Tony asked, clarifying.

"It seems the only likely option." Jancarlo stated flatly. "Maybe the rings don't work as well as we thought they did. Maybe the ability to capture someone's powers has limited timing, like Gretchen's stones. I'll talk to Nathaniel to see if he's experienced anything odd with the rings. Liam, you can join me." Looks like I would be getting my grilled fish.

"Kin," he said turning to him, "go back down to the holding cells, and check the cameras." Kin started to protest but Jancarlo waved him off. "I know they don't work great but see if you can glean anything from them."

What Gretchen calls "residual lightning" in our makeup messes with everything electronic or computerized, including the security cameras pointed down the halls to the holding cells. They usually just show static, so they're more for show than anything else. I'm sure Kin had other ideas of how to get information, but he would do as Jancarlo asked then discuss it with him in private later.

Jancarlo turned to Ella. "Ella, check the memories of anyone working in the detention areas around Wiki's cell. See if you can find anything unusual. Do it in one-on-one interviews, so they know what we're looking for. We want to be as open as we can with the security team. Tony, find Kimi. Let her know what's going on, and see if she has any insights. Tell her to report to me as soon as she can."

"Jancarlo, about Kimi-," Kin tried to interject.

"I know your concerns, but she was in plain sight of others when this went down. The last thing we need to be doing is turning on each other. I'm choosing to trust that Kimi is still Kimi, maybe just dealing with something is all. I'll keep your concerns in mind, okay? But in the meantime, she's still a valuable member of this group. Understood?"

Kin nodded, but the tightness in his face spoke volumes.

"For now," Jancarlo continued, "we keep all access to the base restricted. Keep our eyes, ears and *minds*," he tilted his head to Ella, "open. That's all."

Chapter EIGHT

Nathaniel, it turned out, had never experienced anything odd with the power-suppression rings nor had anyone else. That information was both comforting and disconcerting. Jancarlo joined us for freshly grilled fish in the mountains, but without any more answers than he already had. The rings worked and they worked well.

Nathaniel decided to stay in the mountains a little longer. He wanted to be out of the way and not cause any more stress. We left him with a ring, should he need it, and a communication bracelet for when he decided to come back. I would've stayed with him, but I wanted to be near Ella.

It also turned out that I wasn't really needed much of anywhere, unlike Ella. Kimi was rarely around where anyone could find her, and Kin and Jancarlo would hole up in Jancarlo's office trying to figure out how Wiki escaped. Even Tony kept to his room or the gym and wasn't great company. The trout in the mountains turned out to be one of the last few times I ate dinner with someone else.

In what felt like work to simply keep me busy, I was paired up with Gretchen again to gather new members and sometimes train them. We had been paired up for quite a while before Ella came along, so we were used to working with each other, but I still missed having Ella as my partner. I often caught myself trying to talk to Gretchen in my mind only to remember that she couldn't hear me.

Over the next few days, time with Ella was limited. When she wasn't sitting at the lobby desk clearing people to come and go, she was working with new recruits that Gretchen and I brought in and conducting personnel interviews of security and others. Ella and I tried to spend as much of our evenings together as we could, and as much as Evelyn allowed—which wasn't very much. But between Evelyn and the excessive workload, over the course of a week, I saw Ella only once and we didn't eat together at all.

One night, about a week after Wiki's escape, I found her dragging herself into the quarters that her and her mother shared. "Rough day?" I asked to get her attention.

She could only nod.

"Do you want something to eat?" I asked, hoping I could coax some time together.

I'm too tired to eat, she answered in my mind.

Is everything ok? I asked back.

No, she said, *everything is not ok. I just found out that Kimi was in the detention area right before Wiki escaped. Kin and I saw her back for a split second in the cameras. I also had to dig through Jack's brain to see it, but it was there.* After a moment of hesitation, she added, *It was suppressed.*

Suppressed? I asked in shock. *Like what Devin Ross did to the people in the Amazon?*

Similar, she said, *but not nearly as powerful. Different somehow. Like Jack was trying to suppress it himself. Like he was learning how to hide things from me.*

That's certainly not good, I said.

It gets worse, she said. *Several of the prisoners have the same block on their minds. Some have a block in areas so strong that I barely recognized it. I almost thought it was just an empty space between thoughts. If I didn't have this much experience, I definitely never would have even noticed it.*

How could that have happened?

I don't know, she groaned. I knew she was rapidly getting used to having all the answers all the time. I could feel her anxiety seeping into her words in my mind. *I don't know if they've had this block the entire time I've known them or if it's a recent addition in their minds. The only way I'll get any answers is if they tell me or I break through the block. But it's like pounding my head against a wall either way.*

I'm sorry, was all I could say before Evelyn appeared at the door.

"Hello Liam," she greeted me with indifference. The attitude was becoming more prevalent for some reason.

"Hello," I said, trying to ignore it. "I was just inviting Ella to get something to eat, if you'd care for anything as well?"

"No, thank you," she said without any consideration. "It's late. Ella," she said bringing her daughter the rest of the way through the door while at the same time cutting off not only my view but also any access to their quarters, "why don't you go lie down."

After Ella threw me a wistful glance and slipped away, Evelyn turned to me. "She's had a lot on her plate, Liam," she said, concern and fatigue creasing her otherwise youthful face. "I'm worried about her. You can certainly understand that."

"Of course, I—"

"I know," she interrupted, "you want to be with her and she wants to be with you. But I think it would be best for her if she uses what time she has to rest. Don't you?"

"Evelyn," I mustered my courage, "have I done something wrong? Is there a reason you don't want me to be around Ella?"

Evelyn's shoulders dropped as if in relief. I realized she was probably relieved to be able to say something out loud. I suddenly trembled at what she wanted to say.

"You haven't done anything in particular, Liam," she said, not unkindly. "I just know what young men want from young women. You've been married for crying out loud. You have a child, and you have—"

I held up my hand to stop her before she said something that would embarrass both of us. "Are you saying you think I'm too old for Ella?"

"In a way," she said. "I know physiologically your ages are similar, but I also know that you know what you want. Ella has plenty of time to decide what she wants. I don't want your need for…companionship, to sway her own discovery. Does that make sense?"

I nodded. "You want her to date other people because you think I need…to date her."

Evelyn shrugged.

"I don't *need* anything from her, Evelyn," I said, making sure to keep eye contact to get my point across. "I was on my own for a long time. I didn't date anyone for decades. I care for Ella, and I simply *want* to be with her."

"Well," she said, "perhaps you haven't given her the chance to figure out if she *wants* to be with only you."

I could only drop my jaw before she closed the door in my face.

Another week went by with tensions mounting. Hardly a smile could be seen, and everyone watched each other closely. People kept to their own business without much conversation. Many people got cleared to leave and stay on the surface under whatever guise they could manage instead of enduring the constant scrutiny.

Gretchen had been busy as well, so Jancarlo asked me to begin visiting new lightning strike victims with Evelyn. I hoped it might be a way to show her my professional side, but we hardly spoke. We were civil and professional, but even the people we came to see could sense our awkwardness. We appeared in the clearing room together two weeks after Wiki's disappearance.

"I'm meeting Ella in the dining room," Evelyn said as we walked into the halls.

Trying not to sound too eager, I said, "I'm hungry. I can make us all something."

She must have been extremely tired because she nodded. "Sure," she said with a little reluctance.

Following a few steps behind, I entered the dining room in time to see Heather coming out with one of Kin's health shakes in her hand.

"Don't tell me you're drinking those things now," I said to her, pointing to the shake. "That's not food."

She shook her curls. "No," she said. "I'm just getting it for Kin."

"He asked you to do that?"

"No," she said again, "I just know that he takes one this time of day, and I thought I would get it for him. I've watched him make them, so I know how to do it."

I had to shrug it off as she disappeared down the hall. When I searched the dining area, I saw Evelyn sitting next to Ella who was laying stretched out on a bench.

"Are you okay?" I asked, sitting on the opposite side of her.

"Yeah," she nodded, removing the arm she had over her eyes. "Just exhausted. I've been working with new people and checking everyone that comes in. I didn't come to check you guys because I knew you were coming back and not many other people come through these days." She lifted her head. "How did it go?"

"Fine," Evelyn and I said at the same time.

After a few awkward back-and-forths of: "You tell her", "No, you go ahead", Ella just snapped, "I'll do it myself!"

Evelyn and I sat rightfully abashed while Ella dug through our minds to see the man who had been struck by a downed electrical line after a car accident. We set up an appointment for Gretchen to heal him before we left. He would not be manipulating water for the rest of his life.

"Oh good," she muttered, covering her eyes again. "I won't have to dig through someone else's mind. I never realized how exhausting it is."

"How is it going with Jacob?" Evelyn asked, as Tony lumbered through the doorway.

"Good," Ella said, perking up to watch Tony slouch through to the kitchen. "He's doing a lot better and helping out more."

"Can he go up to the surface yet?" Evelyn asked.

"I don't think so," Ella said, while Tony banged some cabinets in the kitchen. "They haven't pronounced him dead, but his face isn't in the news much anymore. Once things calm down, Jancarlo said we can replant him back into his life if he wants. We're just waiting for the go ahead."

We all watched without a word as Tony again loped back out of the dining room doors with a large jar of peanut butter and a spoon in his catcher's-mitt sized fist.

"I guess he's not doing so well," I said once he left.

"No," Ella said sitting up. "I haven't looked into his mind at all, but everyone can tell he's miserable. He and Kimi haven't spoken for quite some time. He won't talk to anyone else, and all I see him do is work out or grumble around in the kitchen for odd things to eat. Yesterday, I saw him walk out of the kitchen with a bottle of ketchup and a head of lettuce."

We all shook our heads and I stood up. "I'll make us something to eat," I said and slipped into the kitchen.

As I set vegetables on the counter, my heart stopped a moment when I saw Kin poke his head around the other door into the kitchen. I glanced around myself then narrowed my eyes at him. "Everything okay?" I asked.

"Are you alone?" he asked in a whisper.

I nodded then turned back to my chopping as he slipped through the doors. When he came to stand beside me, I asked, "What's with all the cloak and dagger?" I knew things were tense, but I had never seen him this on edge.

"I'm trying to avoid Heather," he said in a whisper. "I mean, I'm a ninja. I have an invisibility hat, and I have experience eluding transporters, but she keeps popping up wherever I am. I don't know how she does it."

"She's not that bad, is she?" I knew she had been hanging around him a lot, but I didn't know how things were for him. Kin and I didn't hang out much. I was good friends with Jancarlo and confided in him quite a bit, but Kin and I had never really had that type of relationship.

He rolled his eyes at me dramatically, then before I could stop him, he scooped up two fists full of the carrots I had chopped for the stew and dashed them over to the blender. Dumping the carrots in and grabbing more stuff out of the refrigerator, he said, "She won't leave me alone. At first it was cute. I'll admit, I liked the attention. But she's so young, and she won't stop asking me about Japan. She's been helpful, yes, but it's starting to border on stalking."

I just grinned and shook my head. Heather was sweet and in desperate need of attention, but Kin and Kimi both couldn't tolerate someone who wasn't all business. Although you couldn't tell, she was also about 40 something years younger than Kin. Besides, I knew he had a wife back in Japan. Although she believed him to be dead, Kin would never dare do anything contrary to that relationship. He took "until death do us part" to the extreme.

We made our meals in silence. Just as he poured his disgusting shake into a tall glass, Heather appeared behind us, and the shake toppled from his hand to splatter across the counter. I tried to hide my laughter in a hearty "Hello" to Heather.

"It's a good thing I already made you a shake," Heather said, producing the previous beverage.

"Ah," he said, pushing the spillage into the sink. "Thank you."

She set the shake on the counter next to him until he finished cleaning up the mess.

"Is there anything I can help you with?" she asked as he picked up the second glass.

"No," he shook his head, "I was just going to work on some paperwork. Very boring stuff." He tried his best to be polite but shake her off his trail at the same time.

"Why don't you help me with my stew, Heather?" I offered.

When she turned to me, I saw a grateful Kin mouth, "Thank you" behind her before he slipped past us out the door.

I set Heather to work chopping more vegetables while I browned the meat. "You've been helping Kin out a lot, huh?" I asked her casually.

"Whenever I can, yeah." She answered me. I could tell she would rather be hanging out with Kin, but I tried to engage her in conversation.

"Are you okay?" I asked as she slowly chopped more carrots.

She shrugged. "I miss my family."

I hadn't expected that. I turned the meat in silence then finally offered, "You're a big help around here. I know everyone is happy to have you."

She chopped again for a minute then stopped and said in a low voice, "You want to know a secret?"

I gave her my full attention but was careful not to make any promises not to tell anyone. I couldn't promise that because Ella usually found out everything anyway.

"Ella already knows," she said, reading my mind.

I nodded. "Go ahead." I gave her a conspiratorial grin.

"I can transport to someone just by thinking about them."

My eyebrows popped up. I had never heard that one before. "So, you can transport to a person, instead of a place?"

She nodded with a small grin on her face. "If I can concentrate on a person clearly enough, I can transport to wherever they are. I don't have to know their location."

That explained how she kept finding Kin so easily. "What if they're going to the bathroom?" I asked jokingly, turning my attention back to the dinner preparations.

Heather's eyes widened, "I hadn't thought about that."

"With so much power, you have to set your own boundaries." I couldn't count how many times I had told Wiki the same thing. He was careless with his powers to his and others' detriment when he was younger. He kept appearing in the middle of crowds or restricted areas. It wasn't until he got older that he started reigning himself in more, but it was probably also the fact that the novelty of it had worn off. Ella had picked it up pretty fast, but she had been much older when she got struck.

"I guess I should think about that stuff." Her smile fell slightly as she turned back to the vegetables.

"It all comes with time," I assured her. It was true. She was new at this, and her growth wasn't going to peak for quite a few years now, but eventually she would get the knack of how things worked.

Seeing as Heather helped, I invited her to join us for dinner later. It had to simmer on the stove for a while, so I had planned to get a workout with Ella before dinner. Evelyn left to give Jancarlo the report from our excursion, and I invited Heather along with us. I hoped to keep her out of Kin's hair, if he'd had any. Reluctantly, she followed along muttering something about watching us.

When we got to the gym, Tony was there lifting weights. Of course, he was always there these days. He helped out around the base as much as he could, but working out was his way of dealing with his disappointment over Kimi. When we came in, he called Heather over to spot for him. I asked how in the world she was going to do that, she told me she simply transported him out if he needed help, which he never did.

While Tony added weights to his bench press bar, Ella walked in with distraction creasing her brow. When she met my eyes, a brief vision of Kimi walking down the hall to the detention area flashed in my mind. The memory was so flooded with suspicion I was taken aback.

Ella's eyes wandered from mine to Tony for a moment, but she joined me at the treadmills. Tony made no movement to show that Ella had shown him anything, so I assumed she didn't. She said a short hello to Heather then jumped on the machine next to me.

Once we were both in motion, I heard her in my mind as I expected.

Kin is down in the detention area, so he should be able to keep an eye on her.

I thought he was going to do paperwork. I figured it was just an excuse for Heather, but Ella confirmed it for me.

She's never where she's supposed to be anymore, Ella said. She had told me all this before and we had hashed it out many times, but she continued to keep me updated on everything Kimi.

Why are you so suspicious of her going down to the detention area? I tried not to push through the bitterness accumulating inside me at the idea of everyone following Kimi around like a criminal. I tried to see it from Kin and Ella's point of view, but I just couldn't comprehend it. We had too much history. I wouldn't even have Ella in my life if Kimi hadn't helped me heal. No, there was no way Kimi was an enemy. I don't care how many feelings she hurt.

I don't trust her being near the prisoners. Kin tries to keep her out of there as well. After a pause she added, *Besides, she said she would come work out with me. It's been ages since she sparred with anyone.*

Well after what happened with Kin, can you blame her?

Yes, she added stubbornly, *I can. It's her job to make sure everyone is in peak security condition, and she's been avoiding it.*

Silence passed between us for a few minutes. I stewed over Ella's lack of trust in our closest friend. She stewed over my lack of trust in her.

"Would you guys stop doing that." I heard Tony mutter from his bench press.

"Doing what?" I asked.

Without stopping his lifting, he said, "Heather and I are getting annoyed that you guys are having a silent conversation without us."

Sorry, Ella said, including Tony and Heather. *We were just discussing…things…*

I knew she didn't want to bring up Kimi again for Tony's sake. Luckily, Heather changed the subject for us.

Can I ask you guys something top secret? She said. When we all nodded, she continued. *The other day I was traveling with Boris, and I don't think he was supposed to say anything, but he mentioned that every People of the Storm base has a secret transportation device or area. He said I might have to make one for you guys if you don't already have one. Is that true?*

I stiffened and sensed Ella's tension on the treadmill next to me. Of course we had secrets like that. Of course we had a secret rock in the arena, covered and guarded, that we could use to get to and from anywhere in case of emergencies. We assumed the other Storm People had the same things. We had had it since before Wiki's time. But no one had used it or spoken of it for a long time. It was supposed to be a secret that only Jancarlo, Kin, Kimi and I knew about. Once Ella came along, I only assumed that she had discovered it as well, since she knew every other secret of our base. But how Boris knew and why he would mention it, I had no idea.

We, um, don't usually discuss such things, Ella eloquently hemmed.

Especially, I added, *with transporters, considering you don't need it.*

So, there is such a thing? Tony asked.

Ella and I shared an awkward glance while we both considered what to say.

Gratefully, the doors to the gym opened, and Jacob walked in. I didn't know him very well other than our first short encounter, but I had never been so happy to see the guy. Ella and I greeted him as he sat down on a weight bench next to Tony on the opposite side from Heather.

Heather casually eyed him while his back was turned, but Ella and I both saw it and threw conspiratorial grins at one another. Ella introduced Tony and Heather to Jacob, adding that Heather could spot for both of them.

"How is she going to spot for me?" he said bluntly. I'm sure he didn't mean it to be as rude as he made it sound, but not addressing her directly exacerbated the insinuation. In another day and age, I would have demanded he apologize for being so rude.

Narrowing her eyes slightly, Heather responded with the same intonation. "I'm a transporter," she pointed out. "I can transport Tony out from under the weights if they fall on him."

"Don't you just transport the weights too?" Jacob asked flippantly as he prepared his own weights.

"I transport what, and who, I want," Heather shot back at him.

As much as I wanted them to get along, I left them to work out their own differences. It was just as well because Jacob responded, "Doesn't matter anyway. I'm not here to work out *those* muscles. They don't need much work," he added with half a grin. She just rolled her eyes away from him. "I'm here doing a homework assignment."

He surprised me by jerking his chin at Ella in acknowledgement. She tilted her head to him slightly then turned back to focus on her machine. "Don't push it too much. Try to take it slow." She told him.

My machine sped up as jealousy squirmed through my chest.

She didn't look at me, but in my mind I heard, *You knew I was working with him, Liam.*

I tried to turn my thoughts back to my own workout as I responded, *At least he seems to have some respect for you.*

It took my knocking him out a few times for that much to happen. I covered a laugh with a cough and laid jealousy to rest while she continued, *He's an arrogant, immature, egotist. Heather has every right to her distaste. Keep in mind,* she peered at me from the corners of her eyes, *that I have not delved into his mind very much. He might be as sweet as Tony deep down. All I know of him is very superficial. If I had taken Tony at first glance, we wouldn't have the friendship we have today.*

Of which I'm also jealous, I sniffed. *I shouldn't have to share Tony with anyone.*

Ella couldn't hide her smile as she laughed silently.

The next hour passed with Tony and Jacob competing to see who could lift the most weights. Heather ended up transporting Jacob out from under almost twenty-two hundred pounds when the weights threatened to come crashing down on top of him. He asserted that he hadn't needed her help, but Ella quietly told me Heather had saved his life. He was just too stubborn to admit it.

After the weights competition, the men took to picking up objects and people. Jacob had the advantage because, although they might not weigh the same, some things were awkward for Tony to pick up with just two hands. Jacob could use his powers to pick up multiple large objects.

I informed the ladies that dinner would be ready soon once the weight-lifting pair moved to the arena. They wanted to see how much they could pick up while working together. A practice that might be good for both of them, but I saw little benefit for myself as a spectator. Thus, I made my excuses to leave.

Once we were in the hallway outside the gym, Heather really let us know how she felt. "My gosh," she said, "I thought we would never be rid of him. He's so cocky!"

I winced inwardly. That word still caught me off-guard at times. Heather continued her rant of Jacob's many character flaws until we finally sat down to dinner. With her back to the dining room doors, she didn't see Kin walk by, notice her sitting with us, then speed past the doors and out of sight. I found the entire situation rather ironic.

The next day I found myself, once again, paired up with Gretchen to meet another new member of the Storm People. It was more pleasant than I expected. He was an older farmer from out in the middle of Tennessee, and his new powers allowed him to shift light. We shared everything with his wife because he insisted on not keeping anything from her. The seasoned woman never batted an eyelash at the display of our powers or the course of the conversation.

When we left the couple, they were gracious and seemed at peace with their turn of events. Gretchen healed both of them of many maladies and, although grateful, they insisted they were going to continue as they had always lived. We told them if they ever needed us, not to hesitate to call for assistance. We left them the phone number of one of the new therapy centers because they didn't need any more assistance getting their lives back to normal. I couldn't help but harbor a hope that someday Ella and I could live in a similar circumstance, placidly growing old together.

After meeting with the couple that morning, we transported back to the clearing room at midday. A thrill ran through me when I saw Ella sitting at the desk. She smiled at me. "How did it go?" She asked.

I glanced up at the ceiling with just my eyes, indicating that I would show her. I recalled the memory of telling Mr. and Mrs. Anderson of our unknown powers and their even-keeled acceptance of the Storm People. I also pushed through to her a memory of them standing in their front doorway seeing us off. They held hands, so content with life, even after such a traumatic incident.

"Aw," Ella cooed, "that's so sweet."

Gretchen excused herself to head back to her office as I joined Ella at her desk. Before I could sit down, Ella said in my mind, *Could you do me a small favor?*

Always, I said with a grin, playing on her favorite response to me.

She hesitated a moment, biting her lip. Watching her do it just made me want to do anything possible to make her happy. I had a feeling I knew what she wanted but waited for her response anyway. Finally, she said in my mind, *Kimi just came by here on her way to the arena. Kin wanted me to keep an eye on her while he had a conversation with Jancarlo. There's no one in the arena I can watch her through. I just wondered if you could slip in there to see how, or what, she's doing?*

Do you want me to go in invisibly? Or can I talk to her like a normal person? I asked her dripping with sarcasm, but I would succumb to whatever she wanted at this point. I tried to keep my question firm so as not to betray my weakness for her.

However you like. I'm just curious what she keeps doing in there.

All right. I answered. I peered down the empty halls before swiftly touching my lips to Ella's cheek. She gave me a sly grin, and I thought she might know of the hold she had on my actions at the moment.

Reluctantly, I turned from the desk, but my heart shot into my throat as I was startled to see Heather standing in front of me, quiet as a ghost and on the verge of tears.

She wasn't there to see me, though. She stared intently at Ella behind me. Ella peered around my shoulder as Heather sniffled with desperate pleading in her eyes. I watched her chin twitching and a couple tears stumble down her cheek for a moment while my eyes bounced between them. They had a short, silent conversation, then without even glancing at me, Heather ran into the clearing room and disappeared.

I cocked my head at Ella. She was only supposed to let people go in and out of the base for business cleared by Jancarlo, but she avoided my eyes. "I'll tell you later," she muttered. I just shrugged it off as girl-stuff and slouched down the hall to my assignment.

I figured I would keep my net off. I could always use the guise of searching for Kimi to invite her to dinner. I hadn't done it for a while, and I figured it was well overdue. Who knows, maybe if everyone's tempers had cooled off, we might even be able to get some kind of reconciliation out of her. How very wrong I was.

Slipping in the arena doors, I called out to see if she really was in there working out. I didn't see any fire bursts or flames immediately and thought she might have left or be working out in one of the adjacent rooms. The sheer size of the arena made it impossible for me to tell if she was in there at all.

I walked among the mountainous boulders strewn across the practice floor, vaguely in Bam Bam's direction. I figured I could at least ask him if he had seen Kimi. I yelled again hoping for any response from anyone. As I came around a smaller boulder, I saw a fireball erupt in front of me. I ducked back behind the rock just in time.

"Kimi!" I yelled while crouched behind the boulder. "It's me, Liam. Hold your fire!" Instead of the slow and cautious peek around the corner I knew Kimi would expect of me, I threw my net over myself then launched from behind the rock far enough away that a second fireball would go past me. It never came, but I rolled as quietly as I could. Landing in a crouch on my feet, I looked up to see Kimi and the former Shadow member, Perry Anderson, who was supposed to be locked in a cell alongside his compatriots. Perry Anderson, the man who could manipulate the ability to gain powers through man-made electricity. The man who could give himself and anyone else the powers they wanted. The man who thought of himself as a god. Quite possibly the most dangerous Shadow member in the holding cells and probably the world. His metal ring to suppress his powers lay on the floor at his feet. He and Kimi took hold of the secret transportation rock in the alcove. The same rock only a handful of Storm People knew about because it wasn't locked under the same security as the rest of the base. I watched in horror as the air shimmered around them and they disappeared.

Chapter NINE

I raced back down the hallway to Ella. When she saw me running, she stood up and stared at me wide-eyed. Half a second later I heard, *What happened?*

Without answering her, I pushed through the single image of Kimi and Perry disappearing with the transporter. Ella's mouth dropped open only to snap shut a moment later with her jaw clenched.

As I ran past her on my way to Jancarlo's office I said, *You were right all along. That can't be Kimi. Find someone to cover for you, and meet me in Jancarlo's office.*

I bolted past her to the opposite hallway. I didn't bother knocking, just swung the door open wide. Jancarlo sat behind his desk leaning back and staring up at the ceiling. Kin sat casually in the chair opposite Jancarlo's desk. I could tell I was interrupting something but had more pressing matters to announce.

"I just saw Kimi and Perry Anderson disappear in the arena with the transporter," I blurted out to both of them.

Their relaxed faces melted away. Kin jumped up from his chair growling, "No." He glanced back at Jancarlo. "I'll check the prisoners." He blasted out the door before he was even done speaking.

I watched him leave then turned back to talk to Jancarlo, but he raised his hand to stop me. "Wait until Ella gets here."

"She already knows," I said.

Jancarlo nodded and I realized she was probably already in his mind. "But she's bringing Tony too. We need to have this conversation in private." We waited only a minute, but it seemed like an hour. Jancarlo got up from his chair to pace back and forth across his office, a habit I had seen many times from him while under pressure.

Finally, Ella and Tony turned the corner into the open office door. With confusion, Tony asked, "What's going on?"

"Ella," Jancarlo said simply.

A split second later we all heard, *Please include Kin in the conversation if he's not moving around too much.*

I'm here. Kin answered.

Good. Tony close the door. While he did so, Jancarlo addressed me. *Liam, why don't you show everyone what you saw.*

It only took a moment to push the memory through to everyone else. I simply showed them Ella asking me to check on Kimi then the confrontation in the arena. As he saw Kimi disappear with Perry, Tony's jaw clenched and his teeth ground together. Try as they might, everyone could not keep their anger from seeping into each other's minds.

Kin, Jancarlo said, *lock down the two clear areas. No one goes in or out, no matter who it is.*

On it, Kin answered. *I'm heading to the front desk now. I'll grab my four best people and station them at each entrance.*

Ella, Jancarlo continued, *get Heather in here. We'll need her to help us hunt down…* Jancarlo stopped pacing when he saw Ella staring up at the ceiling like she had eaten a lemon.

Um, Ella's lips curled in on each other as she evaded the order. I remembered Heather disappearing out of the clearing room. Heather wouldn't be able to help anytime soon.

What's wrong? Jancarlo asked sternly. If looks could kill, I was sure Ella would be pushing up daisies.

I let Heather leave, and I don't know where she went or when she'll be back. Ella said it rapidly like she was hoping no one would hear her if she said it fast enough. Unfortunately, everyone heard.

Can you contact her? Jancarlo asked. *Do you know where she went?*

Ella shook her head. When Jancarlo stared her down, she added. *She was really upset, and I knew she needed some time away. I can only contact her if I know where she is. I'm sorry.*

Jancarlo just heaved a sigh at this then resumed pacing.

We could try to contact Boris again, Tony said.

Boris can't do what Heather can, Jancarlo said. I guessed that Heather had told him what she could do about transporting to a person as well as a place. *Without Heather it would just be a wild goose chase. They could be anywhere.*

What can Heather do? Tony asked.

She can transport to a person if she concentrates on that person, without knowing where they are. Ella said.

Tony's eyebrows almost escaped his forehead. *I guess that would come in handy,* he said.

There was silence for a few minutes while Kin contacted extra security teams to cover transport stations then posted extra guards to patrol the detention cells as well.

Finally, Jancarlo stopped pacing. *Ella,* he said, *contact Boris or any of the other transporters. Make finding Heather and bringing her back top priority. Liam, go with her so she can transport anywhere they need to without interrupting anything. Tony, help Kin secure the prisoners. I want you two to make sure all the rings are in place* and *in effect. Change their cells around so anyone transporting in will find them in the wrong places. Let's not make this easy.*

We all nodded our consent and set off in different directions. Ella and I headed back to the front desk where Evelyn had taken over for her. I could still see the pillow lines on her face, but she was alert as ever so Ella must have explained the situation to her.

Without a word, Ella stood over her mother and reached her mind to the console displaying five or six dozen gems. As her mind touched a gem, it glowed with a soft light. She scrunched her lips together then shook her head, "He's not responding. He must not have it on."

"Try someone else," I suggested. There were a few transporters in the world, and we currently had contact, through the gems, with five of them. One was Boris, in

Russia, the other four were in Africa, Europe, Argentina, and China.

She touched the gem for the transporter in Africa. Turning her eyes back to me, she said, "He's on a mission right now." Without waiting for a response, she moved to the next in line, the transporter in Europe. I didn't particularly like Theresa, but I figured we were desperate enough to use whoever would help us.

The gem glowed for a minute longer than the others before Ella said, "She's on her way."

As we watched the clearing room, I leaned closer to her. Under my breath, so others couldn't hear, I asked, "Couldn't you have tried Quincy or Tali first?"

"I was just going in order. I don't know who put them in *that* order." She whispered back to me sharply.

Theresa appeared in the clearing room, and the two guards who stood there lit up at her presence. Indeed, she had a most contagious perk in her every action, but often times that joviality got her and anyone with her into trouble.

"Dar-ling!" she shouted in her thick Russian accent once she stepped out of the clearing room. She spread her arms wide as if to hug both of us with a wide grin on her face. One would have thought she had just been invited to a party the way she acted. She threw off her fluffy fur coat into the waiting arms of one of the guards to reveal black faux-leather pants and knee-high boots to match with a tight-fitting, low-cut white sweater top. I noticed Ella's eyebrow lifted slightly at the sight, but I winked at her, and her face smoothed out again.

Instead of approaching both of us, Theresa swept me into a tight embrace. I was used to her personality and had warned Ella many times of her continued advances, although they were seldom ever sincere. She flirted with every man she met which usually brought our group unwanted attention and an occasional jealous attack. Her fiery red hair bounced around her shoulders as she kissed me on both cheeks. "I knew I vould hear from you soon, my love. It vas only a matter of time before ve vere brought together again."

"Theresa," I exclaimed as I tried to extricate myself from her iron grip, "this is hardly the time for such talk."

"I vill never give up, my sveet." She pinched my cheeks together then turned to Ella with her own raised eyebrow.

"I'm sorry, Theresa," Ella said, ignoring the cheery behavior and stifling a grin, "but I'm going to have to check your thoughts. Just to make sure it's really you."

"Of course, my dear." She answered only partly to Ella but returned her eyes to me. "Just don't look too close at de memory of Liam and me on assignment in Rome," she said with a wink at me.

I rolled my eyes at her, but she still didn't relinquish her grip on my hands. She stood staring at me in silence as Ella probed her mind for any hint she might be a traitor. I noticed Evelyn watching closely from the desk as well. Luckily, I knew Ella would be extremely thorough in her case, so I was able to withstand Theresa's coos as she stroked my cheek lovingly.

The trip to Rome was nothing for Ella to be jealous of. Often, when on assignment with Theresa, she would make me act like we were married even though she could easily have been taken as an older sister, if not my mother. "Vee must play de part, my luh-ve," she would whisper to me, then she would make me kiss her in public. I think she enjoyed looking like a cougar with a young man on her arm. She knew I hated it, but she also knew I would keep up pretenses. In Rome, she got very carried away, and I chastised her for it later.

Good to know. Ella said in my mind when I recalled the memory of the harsh conversation we had following the incident.

My pleading eyes fell to Ella as I asked if she was finished.

"I'm afraid it's really her," she said out loud, earning a scornful glance from Theresa, which Ella happily ignored.

Quickly changing the subject, I said, "Why don't we check Heather's room for any idea of where she might go?"

Without a backward glance, Ella hurried down the hall leaving me to deal with Theresa. I tried to throw a "help me" glance at Evelyn as well, but she studiously ignored us as we followed Ella. Theresa finally let go of my hands as we walked but kept steadily by my side. "So vhat is it you need of me?" Theresa asked.

We should probably have this conversation silently, Ella said in both of our heads.

Theresa stopped and threw both her arms out as if to brace herself for an earthquake. Her eyes devoured the walls. "Vhat vas dat?" She questioned the ceiling.

Ella spun around to face her. *That was me, Theresa. Please keep walking.*

"I knew you vere a mind-reader," she finally addressed Ella, "but I had no idea you vere capable of such dings." She glared at Ella's back with such fear I was proud Ella could throw a curve ball like that at her.

We haven't gotten around to telling everyone about it, Ella answered her.

"Do you prefer silent conversations, den?" Theresa asked while following her down the maze of halls.

Ella stopped again but didn't face her. "Yes," she answered out loud, "especially when they have sensitive information in them." At this she glanced at me then turned back around to approach Heather's door.

I took that as a warning to explain things to Theresa. "Just concentrate on pushing your thoughts out to Ella and me," I said. "We'll hear what you say and not much else."

So, are you two going to explain vhat is going on? Theresa asked.

Of course, I answered her. *Heather was cleared to leave right before we had a prisoner escape. She was upset about something, and we don't know where she would have gone. We need to find her.*

Vhy do you need Heather? Theresa's eyes bounced between Ella and me. Ella pulled out a card she had grabbed from Jancarlo's office and slid it into the slot for Heather's room. Normally, the door would open to Heather's thumb print and not allow anyone else, but this card was for security purposes only and would allow us to enter without her thumb print.

She doesn't know. Ella told me.

Know vhat? Theresa's eyebrows were dangerously close to her eyes. I had seen that scowl on her face before, and it was the reason I usually just did whatever she wanted.

Heather has special transportation abilities, I told her. I explained Heather's extra special powers and the need to find Kimi and Perry Anderson while Ella rummaged through Heather's room looking for information.

I don't know vy Jancarlo is so easy on dose Shadow people, Theresa said. *Franco heals dem vid-out dem even knowing about it. He easily plants somevon in de hospital vhenever an accident occurs. Dey don't even know dey had any po-vers by de time our people are done.*

You know Jancarlo won't do that, I said while inspecting a few dozen postcards pinned on Heather's wall over her desk. I pulled the thumbtack out of one to show it to Theresa. *Can you take us to some of these? Maybe Heather would be here.* The postcard I showed her was a beach in Fiji. I remembered it as the one Heather had had when we first met her. It was the same beach she had accidentally transported to with her bed.

Theresa sighed heavily and plucked the postcard from my hand, glaring at it as if it had done her a great personal wrong. Returning it to the wall, she said, *She von't be at dat one if dat's vhat you vant.*

Ella and I looked at each other then at Theresa while she scrutinized the postcards. Ella's eyes narrowed and lips compressed together, but before she could respond, I tried being more diplomatic. *Do you know where she could be?*

Until that moment, I had forgotten Heather had spent the past few weeks being carted around the world with most of the other transporters. That must be where all the postcards came from. Theresa had most likely spent plenty of time with her and might even have a friendship with her. Of course, it was hard for me to imagine Theresa could be friends with any other female.

I have some ideas. She shrugged. Removing half a dozen postcards from the wall, she said, *Let's start vid dese.* She pushed them into my hands and walked out the door.

When I showed them to Jancarlo and told him our plan, he pointed out the same thing I noticed. Upon closer inspection, we recognized all of them to be tall buildings and landmarks.

"She likes to look down on dings," Theresa told us as if it was common knowledge. "I took her to most of dese places with our light shifter, Anna Marie to keep us invisible. Vee had some vell-deserved 'girl time' looking down on de men."

We spent the next hour or so transporting to the places on the postcards, checking out the Eifel Tower, Mount Rushmore, and the Empire State Building. According to Theresa, these had been her favorites. Also according to Theresa, Heather knew her way to the European People of the Storm base and knew where they kept their stock of invisibility hats. She thought maybe Heather had borrowed one in order to do her introspection in private. I tried to throw my net out as far as I could to see if I could sense her underneath, but we still had yet to find her.

We were at the Statue of Liberty when I heard Jancarlo's voice in my mind. *Liam, can you hear me?* Good thing I had grabbed a communication bracelet before we began our search.

We had been staying in contact via Ella's powers, so we all heard him. Ella answered, *We're all here, Jancarlo. What's up?*

We have a report from Henry at the White House, Jancarlo said. Henry was one of the Storm People with the power to lift objects. He was with the Secret Service in order to protect the president. Many things the general public never heard about were reported back to us. Henry had personally thwarted quite a few attempted assassinations. Many presidents owed him their lives.

Henry says someone appeared on the top of the White House. Security has been alerted, Jancarlo continued. *He thinks it's Heather because she's sitting somewhere inaccessible to mortals.*

Sounds like von of de spots on de list too, Theresa interjected. *Ve'll be dere in a moment, Jancarlo.*

Thanks.

From the crown of the Statue of Liberty, above the viewing windows, Ella and I put our hands on Theresa's shoulders. Theresa's eye sparkled with a wicked gleam. Before the air around us started to shimmer, she batted my hand aside making me fall into her waiting arms. Ella just rolled her eyes at Theresa's behavior but couldn't finish her sigh until we solidified on the roof of the White House overlooking the south lawn.

Luckily, no one could see us. I made sure my net secured the three of us. We turned around to see half a dozen Secret Service men approaching Heather.

The scene was picturesque. The setting sun glistened on the tips of the blooms still clinging to the end of summer. Heather sat on the corner of the White House roof peering into the Rose Garden in full bloom, but with all the beauty surrounding her, her face hung low and her eyes burned the color of the sunset.

Fortunately, being unarmed, she didn't pose much of a threat. We could still claim she was just lost from a tour group or something, but they would have no record of her coming in the door. On the other hand, the corner of the roof she perched on had a direct view of the Oval Office across from the garden. I was happy to see all the men had their guns in their holsters, but they still treated Heather with extreme caution even though she had tears in her eyes and her long blonde curls partially covered her face.

"Miss," one of the men said, approaching her cautiously, "you're not allowed to be here. You need to come with us."

"And what will you do?" Heather mumbled to him. "Break my heart too, most likely."

I started to stretch out my hand to Heather, preparing to make her disappear, but Ella put her hand on top of mine. *She can't disappear right in front of them.*

But they'll arrest her, I insisted. *What else are we supposed to do?*

Ella gazed pensively at Heather for a moment then pursing her lips, she turned to Theresa. *Theresa, go talk to Heather. See if you can talk her into coming back with us.*

By myself? Theresa asked incredulously. *She's not supposed to disappear, but it's ok if I suddenly appear and get arrested too?*

Ella reached behind her and pulled out her precious flat cap. Handing it to Theresa she said, *I want this back. Maybe you two can have a good long chat about how horrible men are while you're in a high security cell.*

Theresa nodded slowly then pushed the cap on her head. I withdrew my net from Theresa, as now she was invisible to everyone. *Don't vorry, Liam,* she said in our minds. *Vhat I say vill never change how I feel about you, darling.*

We're going to have to be out of contact with you, but I need you to drop us off first, Ella said to Theresa. *If you need us, you'll have to come get us.*

Vhere am I taking you? Theresa asked with skepticism.

To the president.

Chapter TEN

When we materialized in the Oval Office, the president was not behind his massive Resolute Desk.

Don't worry, Ella told Theresa. *Get to Heather before she takes off again.*

Good luck, Theresa said in our minds. Even without seeing her face, I could hear in her tone that she had finally adopted a more professional attitude. *I'll go deal vis the easier von,* she insisted then was gone.

Now what? I asked Ella.

I'll find out where he's gone. She closed her eyes, and I watched as her eyes twitched underneath her lids. Finally, she opened them. *He's in one of the inner rooms close by. They moved him there as a precaution. Henry's outside the door.*

I waved my hand in front of me and, bowing slightly, said, *Lead the way.*

We slipped out of the Oval Office into the hallway when Ella claimed no one was looking. The door swung without a sound. Good thing the White House staff kept their doors so well oiled. To the left, four Secret Service agents stood in front of a door. One of them was Henry.

While the other three men were obviously in the prime of their lives in health and fitness, Henry seemed to be easily in his sixties, but his shaven head hid the emerging gray hair. The rippling muscles made it apparent he could handle himself against even these strong young men. I happened to know he occasionally made a point to train with Kin, Kimi and Tony. He had a strong squared jaw, and his mouth curved down in a permanent frown. Creases between his eyebrows gave him the look of deadly seriousness, although when off-duty, he was extremely kind and easy-going.

Even though he looked older than the younger men, I'm sure they would have been surprised to learn just how long Henry had been around. He may even be a little slower than them, but his powers to lift objects made up for his lack of speed by allowing him to fly as well. Just being around him made me feel like confessing to something. I'd always been glad he was on our side every time I saw him.

We crept down the hall towards the guarded door, then I heard Ella say, *Henry, we're here. Ella and Liam. We need to talk to the president.*

Do you need to go inside? If the sound of Ella's voice in his head surprised him, he didn't show it. He didn't move a muscle while they conversed.

It would be best. Ella answered him.

Henry's ridged posture finally broke as his eyes swept the hall. He turned to the man next to him to ask in a rich baritone, "Did you hear something?" The man shook his head and glanced down the hall too. "I'm going to check the president," Henry announced. Then he turned, opening the door behind him with his left hand so his back pressed against the door. He made sure to swing it open wide enough for us to slip into the room beyond.

The small office had at least ten people inside, but none of them appeared to be security staff. They all had pens and clipboards, folders and papers. The president must have insisted on continuing his work with the minor threat of a young girl on the roof of the White House. There were no windows in this room, so they must have deemed it safe enough.

"Is everything okay, sir?" Henry asked when half the group turned to him.

The president peeked up from the computer he pecked at. "Yes, Henry," he answered. "Everything is fine." He was a tall, lean man with distinguishing patches of gray over his ears. Although he was a good-looking man, the burden of the office he held weighed heavily on him. It showed in the added lines on his face and bags under his eyes, though he had only been in office for less than a year.

We're in, Ella told Henry. Henry nodded in response to Ella and the president then shut the door. *Although I don't know how we're going to stay undiscovered.*

We're going to have to tell the president to make everyone leave, I said, knowing something of her plan and also knowing it would be best to let her take the lead. She was going to have to do some quick thinking and lots of mind probing. The rest of us couldn't handle the overload of information without losing our minds completely.

I'll stay over in the corner out of the way, I said. Leaning in to squeeze her hand, I brushed my lips to her cheek. *Good luck. If all else fails, we can all disappear into thin air.* I retreated into the corner to watch the show. Ella kept me privy to most of the conversation.

For a moment, there was nothing. I knew she had come out of my mind to dig through the president's mind for fodder. Finally, I heard Ella call his name in my mind. She used a soft, slow taunting tone. With such a stark difference from the other voices around us, it stood out like a clown bursting into flames in the middle of the room.

Stewart. She called him by his first name to immediately convey authority.

The president could hear the glaring difference as well. He looked up with confusion on his face. "Yes?" he said out loud, his eyes bouncing between the people in the room. A few people glanced at him with questioning faces, but none of them answered him.

Stewart, don't talk out loud. The people around you will think you've gone crazy. I really don't have time for that right now. Ella sounded patronizing. *Just think what you want to say. I'll hear you.*

The president hurriedly switched off the computer monitor. Then putting his face in his hands, we heard, *Who are you?*

Ella was busy dodging around the many people in the room. *I'll explain in a minute, but first you need to tell the people in the office to leave you alone.*

Why should I do that?

Because we need to have a private conversation, and these people will notice if you're silently staring into space. Like I said, she insisted, *I don't have time to have someone thinking you're crazy.*

Fine. He answered.

At that moment, one of his aides decided to lean over. "Are you okay, sir?" he asked.

The president looked up at the other man. But in the same moment, Ella picked out of his memory the different phrases he could use to tell the aide he was under duress.

Ella shoved the memories into his mind. I'm guessing he had been considering using one. *I wouldn't do that if I were you. You see, I can just knock you out and move on to the next person in line that can help me.* Her tone again sharpened as she barked at him internally. *Just get them out!*

He finally relented to his fate. "I'm fine, Eric," he said. "I'd just like a little break." He sat up straighter, saying to the room in general, "Could everyone please give me some privacy for a few minutes?"

He watched them go with guarantees he would be fine and back to work in a couple minutes. Once the door closed behind the last straggler, Ella sent me an image of Henry helping the woman close the door. I knew she meant he would be watching out for us as well.

Ah, she said, *that's much better.* She kept her voice relaxed. *Now we can hear ourselves think.*

I had to stifle a snicker at the pun. The president, on the other hand, was not amused. "Now will you tell me who you are?" he asked out loud to the seemingly empty room.

I told you, Stewart, Ella answered, *say it in your mind. We wouldn't want anyone to hear us.*

Okay. We could sense his irritation. *But you had better have a good explanation for why I just sent all my people away. And if I don't like it, I'll call the Secret Service in here and see if you like bossing them around.*

It won't do you any good to make empty threats, Stewart. Ella smoothly replied. *Do you remember being told of The People of the Storm?*

We all sat in silence with bated breath. The president had been told of our people upon entering office, but he was to deny he knew anything about us. Most of the presidents never had anything to do with our people…as far as *they* knew. We dealt with our own problems and being told about us sounded like a high school prank. It needed no telling that they quickly forgot such a far-fetched tale. Most presidents didn't believe it until they met one of us.

When he took his time answering, Ella got restless. *Let me help you.* She quickly pulled up the memory of him doing his first walk-through of the White House with the last president.

Former President Collins said, "There are these…people. They call themselves The People of the Storm… They supposedly have special powers…I don't know if you'll ever meet them, but hopefully not…They keep pretty much to themselves." The new President Stewart Brandon had no idea one of us worked for him.

He took a deep breath as the memory ended. It could be somewhat disconcerting when someone used your own mind against you. The color drained from his face, and his hands started shaking.

Now do you remember? Ella asked with a stern tone.

Yes, I remember. His eyes darted around the room.

Go ahead, Ella said in my mind. *Let him see me.*

Reluctantly, I drew my net off her slowly. She didn't seem intimidating at all. A young, teenager in a t-shirt and cargo pants with her hair pulled back in a smooth braid. She had no weapons, just a multi-stoned charm bracelet on her wrist. She reclined on a small couch by the wall. But when the president looked at her, she glared back at him with ice in her eyes. I had never seen Ella be so intimidating with just her eyes.

"I guess we can speak out loud now. I'm Ella," she told President Brandon. "I'm one of the People of the Storm. The girl on the roof is one of our people. I'd like you to have her released. They probably have her in custody by now."

"Why should I do that?" He answered her tersely.

"Many reasons."

"Name three."

"One, because we could just disappear as easily as I appeared in here, making you and your staff look very ignorant. Two, I could easily, by myself, render everyone in the building unconscious then walk out the front door with her, making you look even worse. And three, because I'm sure you want to keep our existence a secret, as much as we want you to, in order to maintain the harmony between our people." As she said it, she stared him down, and I noticed him swallow a few times. "These are your choices of how to handle the situation, Stewart."

The president came out of his reverie. Blinking his eyes, he shook his head slightly. "You want me to turn her over to you?" Ella's chin dipped to her chest. "How do I know you're to be trusted?" He lifted his chin and tried to stare back at her. "Is the girl a criminal? What do you want her for? Why did she show up on the White House roof?"

"The girl is innocent." Ella sighed, absentmindedly fiddling with her bracelet. "She got her heart broken, and she wanted to get away to think. She likes to see things from above. She really loves the garden here, and I have a feeling she wanted a little attention as well, since she wasn't getting it from the one person she wanted." At this she looked back up at him. "She means you no harm. She has unique powers, which is how she got up there in the first place, and we need her help with something internal."

"She's been here before?" the president asked.

"Yes," Ella said. "Several times, I believe, and you never even knew it. Like I said, I think this time she just wanted some attention."

Ella stood up and slowly walked towards the president. "As for my being trustworthy, ask yourself this. If I can seize complete control of this building by myself, why would I ask your permission to have the girl first? If anyone's worth of *trust* should be in question here, it's yours."

The President's breath caught in his throat as Ella continued. "I know every…" She paused, and he jumped as if electrocuted. "…little….misdeed, and….not-so-little…mistake…..you have ever made,…Stewart." She sneered his name. I didn't see the images Ella put in his head with each pause, but the president's face twitched with almost every word she spoke.

Grimacing as if his head hurt. "Are you blackmailing me?" he asked.

She grinned and leaned over the desk to him threateningly. "Hardly. I want you to know that *I'm* trusting *you*, which is more than you deserve." Ella turned away from his desk. "We weren't going to bother with you until this little incident, but now I'm not even sure if we should have a professional relationship with you. Afterall," she paused as she pushed one last image in his head. He actually dropped his head away in shame. "You don't seem to know the meaning of honor."

After Ella let this sink in, she started on the attack again. "Our people have been more help to this country than you can even imagine, and you presume to question *our* motives?"

At this, the president looked up at her, "What have your people done for this country, other than infiltrate my office?"

Ella lifted an eyebrow at him. "Call Henry in here." When the president made no move to talk to anyone, she said, "Never mind, I'll do it." She looked at the president then allowed her eyes to flicker to the door. I knew Ella had no need to use any part of her body for her powers to work, but she wanted the president to be aware that she was doing something without his knowledge or approval.

Henry, please come in here a moment. I heard Ella contact both of us in our minds.

The door opened, and Henry came in, closing the door behind him.

"Henry is one of our people, Stewart." Ella announced. Henry glanced at her out of the corners of his eyes, but I think it was more at the use of the president's first name than the revelation of his origins. "Henry," she continued, "how many presidents owe their lives to you?"

"Four," Henry answered succinctly.

"And how many assassination attempts have you upset *by yourself?*" she asked while watching the president's reaction.

"Forty-two," came the response.

"How many for this president alone?"

"Four, so far." Henry answered with the confidence of a soldier. The president's jaw went slack at the answers.

"Thank you, Henry." Ella said it as a dismissal, and Henry left the office. Then she turned back to the president, staring down at the most powerful man in the world. "So, Stewart," she said, "how are you going to repay our people?"

"I had no idea." He blinked at her stupidly.

"Of course, you didn't." Her tone softened only slightly. "Henry is good at what he does, isn't he?" The president could only nod in response. "And you want to keep him on your staff, don't you?" Another nod. "We want to be your allies, Stewart." Ella sat back on the couch. "The choice is yours."

Stewart again came back from his thoughts and cleared his throat. "Henry," he called to the door.

Henry's face again appeared in the door. "Yes, sir?"

"Go get the girl. Bring her in here." Stewart ordered.

"Right away, sir," Henry said with a nod, but before he closed the door he glanced back at Ella.

Henry, Ella told him before he left, *Theresa should be with her.*

He nodded slightly and closed the door.

"Let me introduce you to my associate, Liam." Ella said, gesturing in my general direction.

I abandoned my comfortable spot leaning against the wall to stand exactly by her hand. Pulling my net off myself, I said, "Nice to meet you, Mr. President."

"Have you been here all this time?" he asked, slightly taken aback. I just nodded slowly. "It seems your people are more powerful than I assumed."

"Powerful though we may be," I told him honestly, "all we want is amity."

"We have that in common," he said with a fierceness in his eye.

"Sir," I figured I should be the good guy and give the man a little respect. I could tell Ella didn't like him for all his dirty secrets. "Our people will be at your service should you ever need us, but a friendship should be two ways. Don't you agree?"

"Of course," he answered.

After another minute of awkward silence, Henry knocked on the door, and the president invited him in. With a wide sweep of the door to allow Theresa to enter as well, he ushered Heather into the room.

Heather was shy and morose, but at least it seemed she hadn't been crying anymore. Interestingly enough, she didn't come across as too star-struck at being in the office with the President of the United States. She muttered a quiet hello to us and stood in front of his desk.

"So, this is the 'threat' to my security?" Stewart asked, surveying Heather.

"You might be surprised by what she's capable of, but none of it is, or ever was, directed at you," Ella answered for her.

"Why the White House?" the president directed his question to Heather.

She tried to hide under her heavy eyelashes. "I like the Rose Garden."

The president nodded. "It's my favorite too."

Without warning, Theresa whipped off Ella's hat and thrust it into her expecting hands. "Vell," she announced boisterously, "if no one is going to introduce me, I'll do it myself." She gave a graceful curtsy then swung her leg up on the desk to perch herself in front of the president. "I am Theresa Michalowitz," she said with the air of a performer, "transporter extraordinaire at your service. And you are much better looking in person, Mr. President," she added with sly narrow eyes.

If nothing else, Theresa was good at lightening the mood. The president cracked half a grin and shook her hand gently. Then standing up from his chair, he circled in front of our group. He stopped in front of Ella. "You're right." he said. "A friendship should work both ways. Does this mean you'll keep my secret if I keep yours?"

Ella narrowed her eyes at him. "Your secrets are yours to divulge, not mine." He nodded, "As for our people…" she grinned up at him and almost whispered, "no one would believe you anyway."

He nodded again, and his shoulders seemed to drop as if a burden had been lifted from them. "I'll move back to my office to take the focus off this one." He turned to Theresa, "I'll assume you have your own discreet way of leaving?"

She smiled at him. "Of course, darling."

He stepped past us to the door but turned one last time to face us. "I hope we can work together with a little more trust next time," he said.

"This should help," Ella said. He nodded and left.

"Vell, he vas lovely," Theresa exclaimed cheerfully.

Rolling my eyes at her, I threw my net out over our group. A moment later, the room was empty.

Chapter ELEVEN

Theresa took us back to the base under Georgia. After a few private words with Heather, she told us she was leaving. "Unless you can t'ink up some other excuse to keep me here?" she said while waggling her eyebrows at me.

"Fresh out," I said.

"Ah, vell," she shrugged, "it vas fun vhile it lasted." She stepped back into the clearing room, throwing two exaggerated kisses with her hands. "Until next time, my pets!" She pointed at me, winked and was gone.

I heaved a sigh of relief and turned to see Ella smirking at me. "What's so funny?" I asked, narrowing my eyes.

"Nothing," she answered shaking her head. I was so distracted I barely noticed Evelyn following us down the hall. We stepped into Jancarlo's office.

Heather sat in a desk chair with her face bowed. Her eyes weren't as red, but she wouldn't meet anyone's gaze.

"You do understand how important you are to us now, don't you?" Jancarlo was saying.

"Jancarlo," Evelyn stepped forward. "As a mother, I don't think we need to worry about any of this at the moment."

"What are we supposed to be worrying about?" Jancarlo snapped.

"Sleep," Ella answered. "It's late and I think we could all use some rest and then come back to the problem of Kimi in the morning."

Heather cast her eyes to Ella. She didn't seem overly concerned by Kimi's disappearance, just grateful that Ella didn't focus the conversation on her own. I assumed Ella or I or someone would explain what had happened and why we had to go looking for her.

"She's right," Evelyn said. "Come on, Heather. I'll get you something to eat."

She put her arm around the young girl and steered her out of Jancarlo's office. Ella followed, and I reached out to her. "I could make something, if it would help?"

Ella shook her head and said the scariest thing a man could hear. "I think we could use a girls' night."

Early the next morning I fell in with the three women in the hall on the way to the conference room. They spoke in whispers and giggled a lot before they noticed I was there. Ella drifted away from the other two to slip her hand in mine and peck me on the cheek when no one was looking.

As we entered the conference room, Ella said, "She's quite taken with you, you know." I glanced at her confused. "Theresa," she answered my questioning stare. "I'm going to have to keep an eye on her thoughts." She raised an eyebrow when she said it but slipped away from me. The conversation quickly ended as I saw the shadow on Evelyn's face when Theresa's name came up.

Pursing my lips, I filed away all the responses I would give Ella (and probably Evelyn) concerning Theresa. The woman was infuriating, but I knew I would never hear the end of it from Ella about how much she doted on me.

When we came into the room, Kin and Tony sat on one side of the table with their heads close together whispering. From the tone when we came in, it sounded like they were arguing. I couldn't fathom why Tony would still think Kimi was herself. Even I didn't believe it anymore. Kin knew her better than anyone. No one should have questioned his judgment, as I had come to realize.

Sitting across from them, Ella hesitantly asked, "Are we interrupting something?"

"No," Kin answered turning himself away from Tony. "We're discussing who should be going on this little assignment."

"I want to go," Tony expanded, "But Kin doesn't think it's a good idea."

"Neither do I," Jancarlo said firmly as he walked in the door. Heather and Evelyn slipped in quietly behind him then sat next to me across from Kin. I could see Kin trying to make eye contact with her, but she deftly avoided his gaze. "There are a lot of us who want to go on this rescue," Jancarlo continued, ignoring the tension between the two, "but I only want two people going."

My eyebrows dropped as I thought about it. Heather had to transport to Kimi. I could keep her invisible, and I was strong enough to carry or restrain Kimi if need be. I assumed he was talking about me, but got shocked out of my plans when he said, "I want Heather to transport Ella with her."

Although there were only a few of us, we made a lot of noise with our simultaneous objections.

"She's my sister!" Kin yelled. "I'll get some answers out of her!"

"What are they supposed to do if there's trouble?" Tony said, rising from his chair, tension rippling across his face.

"It's too dangerous for just the two of them!" I put in. "We don't even know where they're going!"

Evelyn seemed like she wanted to argue but couldn't solidify the words. Unfortunately, she just wanted to protect her daughter, who could protect herself very well.

The arguments continued while Jancarlo tried in vain to regain order. Fed up with the chaos, Ella jumped up and pounded the table with her fists. "Be quiet or I'll knock you all out!" she yelled over our voices. I opened my eyes wide in surprise, but she pointed at me sternly adding, "You too."

She seated herself again. "Thank you, Ella," Jancarlo said. Then gesturing to her, he asked, "Now does anyone think she can't handle herself?" After a moment of uncomfortable silence, he continued, "I know we all want answers, but I don't want to risk anyone unnecessarily. Ella has her cap," He motioned to Kin, "I hoped you could lend yours to Heather."

Heather's eyes only strayed to Kin for a moment while he continued staring at Jancarlo. Then she found a profound interest in the table, her hands, her chair, the wall and anything else around her. Kin gazed at her. "Of course." He wasn't about to pass up a chance to make amends with her. I'm pretty sure Jancarlo would have insisted on it anyways. That made me expendable.

"As for trouble," he continued, "Well, Ella can take care of herself and Heather pretty well, wouldn't you agree?" When he said it, Jancarlo stared directly at Tony. The first time Ella and Tony had sparred, she'd used her powers to take him down. Even though he towered a good foot over her and weighed several stones more than her, he was always at her mercy. He probably recalled that embarrassing match while he nodded his head dejectedly. That made him expendable too.

"As for getting answers out of Kimi…" Here Jancarlo turned to stare Kin down, who decided Heather's fascination with the table was contagious. "I think Ella has the best chance of getting to the truth succinctly. Don't you?" Only glancing briefly at Jancarlo, Kin let his head jerk down once. That took Kin out of the equation as well. Jancarlo stood up straight. "I'm glad we're all in agreement." He said, "Kin, get your hat for Heather. Meet us at the clearing room. They'll leave immediately."

Having all been cowed, we shuffled out of the conference room. Ella followed next to me as we headed back to the clearing room. "I thought he would send both of us," she said quietly.

"No," I shook my head, "Jancarlo is right. It should be the fewest amount of people possible."

Hearing this, Evelyn slipped past us, hurrying back to the front desk.

I decided in that instant to put my petty feelings aside and be bold. Ella was now leaving on a dangerous assignment to who knows where, for who knew how long. I hated leaving her, but I hated it worse when she left me. I grabbed her hand and pulled her off to the side of the hallway. A recessed doorway added a small amount of privacy. Peering deep into her eyes, I whispered, "Be careful."   "Always," she whispered back. She put her hand to my cheek, and I leaned in close to kiss her firmly. After a minute, she pulled away to stare at me seriously. "You act like this is the last time I'll see you." She put both of her hands on the sides of my face. "I'll be fine," she said.

I couldn't seem to shake my foreboding feeling. Eventually, I succumbed to the fact that we had others waiting for us, so we proceeded to the lobby. Relinquishing Ella's hand, I watched her walk into the clearing room with Heather.

"Remember, Heather," Jancarlo told her through the window as the women stood side-by-side in the small room. "Focus on Kimi. Find her wherever she is, then come back quickly for reinforcements."

She nodded in acknowledgement, and both women donned their invisibility hats but didn't disappear. The effects of the room made it possible for me to see Ella wearing the flat cap my brother used to wear when we would go into town after harvest with our father. She looked cute in it. The sight made me nostalgic but anxious at the same time. So many things could go wrong. She winked at me as she put her hand on Heather's shoulder, then they both disappeared.

Chapter TWELVE

The next few minutes were excruciating for me. I leaned against the lobby desk then moved to the couch. I paced around the coffee table then perched in an armchair all in just a few minutes. When I finally walked behind the desk next to Evelyn, she imitated a New York accent and muttered, "Sit down, sonny, you're makin' me noi-vous."

I mumbled an apology then went to sit by Jancarlo on the couch. Before I could settle comfortably, Heather reappeared in the clearing room, by herself. I bolted to her with Kin and Tony close behind, but she stared past us at Jancarlo without leaving the room. "We appeared in a cave. We're not sure where. We didn't see Kimi, but Ella said she would go look for her so I could come back to report. I'm going back to see what else we can find. No one else seems to be there."

"Ok." Jancarlo said. "Both of you come back as quickly as you can."

Heather nodded then disappeared again.

"Nothing?" I said to Jancarlo while Kin and Tony returned to their seats. That didn't sound right. If Heather had been concentrating on Kimi, she should have transported straight to her. I had no idea how her powers worked or if there were any counteractive powers preventing her from getting to Kimi, but hopefully Jancarlo would see fit to allow me, Kin or Tony to find out. "Maybe me or Kin should go with her when she comes back," I suggested with high hopes.

Jancarlo watched Kin. He was sitting on the armrest of one of the chairs making fireballs in the air above his hand. He seemed as distracted as the rest of us, not really paying attention to the fires as they twisted around his hands.

Looking back at me, Jancarlo lowered his voice. "I would send Kin, but Heather doesn't want to work with him right now." I shrugged my acknowledgement, and Jancarlo continued a little louder. "If they don't find anything there, I'll let you guys check it out too, okay?"

I nodded slowly then went back to wait on the couch.

It seemed an eternity before Heather and Ella finally appeared in the clearing room again. We all raced over to the room as they exited, but both women wore solemn expressions.

"I don't understand," Heather muttered. "She should have been right there." She pulled the hat off her head and pushed it into Kin's hands without a word to him.

Ella watched her walk away until Jancarlo asked her for a report. "I don't know what happened," Ella answered. "There was nothing but a maze of tunnels. We searched as far as we could, but all we found was this." She indicated the small round mirror hooked on a chain. It was the same one Kimi had been wearing the past few weeks, but now Ella had it around her own neck.

We exchanged glances with each other, amazed that our only hope had failed. Finally, after a few minutes of thought, Jancarlo said, "Everyone brainstorm more options. We'll regroup and find another route to follow at 0700 in the conference room. Ella, I'm not sure where Heather wandered off to, but grab her and get to my office. I want a complete report, now."

Ella started to slowly follow Jancarlo to his office, but I hurried to intercept her. "Would you like to brainstorm over dinner when you're done?" I asked her quietly, leaning close to her ear.

She seemed to stiffen slightly but relaxed just as quickly. Giving me a small smile, I expected her usual answer, but she said, "Sure, why not?" Only pondering the difference for a moment, I agreed to meet her in the cafeteria after her report.

I quickly sautéed some onions and peppers with chicken and found some tortillas to wrap them in. I made quite a lot since Tony and Kin hovered over me the whole time. We all spoke in low tones flooded with anxiety about what had happened. Tony was convinced Kimi had changed her mind about not just him but all the Storm People in general. Kin brushed off his ideas as quickly as I did. Kimi would never abandon our people. She was loyal to the death to friends and family, the same as Kin and many other Japanese Storm People I had met. She had no reason to turn against us. I began to entertain and expand on the idea that someone else was in control of Kimi when Jacob came in to join us.

Kin and Tony filled Jacob in on the specifics of the day's excitement while I gathered garnishes for the meal. I decided on a meal I could throw together quickly so it would be ready when Ella got back. We were just helping ourselves when both women walked in the door. Heather lifted her chin slightly when she saw Kin sitting at the table too, but she casually sat with Jacob on the other side of the table from him.

I dished up a couple of plates for both of them before I sat to eat. Ella took a bite of the fajita then inspected it quizzically. *What's wrong?* I asked her in my mind.

She glanced up at me while she chewed a little more then said, "This would be even better with a little jalapeño." I had never known her to be much of a cook, but maybe she had learned a thing or two from the café where she used to work.

"I'll try that next time," I said.

The two women spent the next hour telling and retelling everything that had happened in the cavern. Although there wasn't much to retell, they answered the same questions over and over again. It was pitch black, which for us meant the women could still see a little bit, but it was still extremely dark. There was nothing but stone passage after stone passage. "Around every corner was another passageway," Heather said at one point. "If I didn't know I could transport out at any moment, I would have been afraid I would get lost."

"A couple of times, we did get lost, remember?" Ella said.

"Oh, yeah," Heather bobbed her head. "I would say, 'Let's try that passage,' and Ella would say, 'We just came from there.' It was crazy."

"At least you didn't run into any animals or anything," Kin said.

"Or another Bam Bam," Tony added.

We hung around after all the food was long gone. Kin was the first to leave. He said he would be able to brainstorm better while working out, so he headed for the gym. After that, the group broke up in different directions. Jacob offered to help me clean up the cooking dishes, so we headed back into the kitchen. As Ella got up to leave, I touched her on the shoulder to get her attention. *Can I come over when I'm done?* I asked her in my mind.

She stared at me for a second with creased eyebrows. Shaking her head, she rubbed her forehead. "I'm sorry, Liam. I'm really tired. Can you just say it out loud?"

I glanced down the hallway to the lobby desk. Evelyn watched us carefully. "Never mind," I said, giving her arm a squeeze. "Go get some rest. I'll see you in the morning."

She smiled warmly. "Thanks." She sighed and turned to walk away.

The next morning proved as fruitless as the previous day. We had no new ideas of how to find Kimi, and the passage Heather and Ella had discovered remained just as empty. Kin, Tony and even Jancarlo insisted on Heather taking them there. Ella went along as well. I, however, did not get a chance to see the empty cavern passageways. I was never much for spelunking, but I also had to bring in two more people to add to our numbers.

When Kin wasn't interrogating Ella and Heather about the caverns, he was checking to make sure we had plenty of supplies in case of an attack. Now that two prisoners had escaped, along with the possible defection of Kimi, it appeared to everyone to be more of a plot. Kin wondered aloud if we'd been too quick to assume Wiki wouldn't be a threat. He also checked on the other Shadow prisoners more often than the routine two-hours.

Not surprisingly, Kimi never came back. After a few days, Kin redistributed her duties. "She must have known you saw her when she disappeared." He told me at one point. "She would know better than to show up here again."

I couldn't argue with him, and I didn't want to. I had my own problems. I wasn't seeing much of Ella anymore. Jancarlo kept her busy, among other things, trying to pry information from the minds of our prisoners. She was dedicated as always and spent a lot of time down with them.

She wore Kimi's necklace everywhere she went. I noticed Tony didn't like seeing the reminder, so I mentioned she probably shouldn't wear it around him. But she shrugged off the suggestion, saying, "I'm just trying to figure the thing out."

Almost a month after Heather had joined our community, our people were in turmoil. Again, we were on edge and speaking in whispers to everyone. Having more than one escape from what is supposed to be a high security area doesn't exactly exude confidence. But after the second escape, I didn't have Ella's support to lean on as much. It was easy to see how Tony had become so cynical, and I took comfort in working out with him. It was the only thing that seemed half normal. Ella and I never ate together and barely spoke, she was always off on some assignment or another.

Another week passed, and I didn't even see Ella in the halls anymore. Three more days, and I only received messages through her mother of which assignments she was currently working on .

After the fourth day of not even seeing Ella's face, I finally went to Jancarlo. He and I were pretty good friends. I had confided in him when I first fell in love with Ella, and he had helped me work through many things in my life. We had known each other a long time. I wanted to get it off my chest and complain that he was overworking her.

"I don't know what you're talking about," he said.

His answer surprised me, I knew he wouldn't purposely keep Ella from spending time with me or lie about it. I had knowledge of the goings on with the Storm People that many others didn't because I had been with the American Storm People for decades. So, I knew he wouldn't do things and not tell me about them. When I listed the many assignments she kept working on for him, his jaw clenched, but his eyes softened, "I haven't given her any assignments like that," he said quietly.

"Searching the prisoners minds?" I asked. "Searching for Kimi's mind in the cavern? Working with the new recruits?" As he continued to shake his head to my questions, I started rising from my chair without knowing it.

When the implications of what he wasn't saying hit me fully, I was already on my way to the door.

"Wait, Liam." Jancarlo called me back before I reached it. "Let's think about this." He stood and began his trek across the floor while talking to me, carefully watching his feet. "The last time we had some suspicious activity, I did nothing. Then another prisoner escaped, and the suspicion was warranted." He stopped, chewing his lip. "We're going to have to look into this, but I'm not sure how. Normally, I would ask Ella to check it out for me, but obviously she can't."

I nodded in agreement. "We'll have to go old school, Jancarlo."

"Don't get caught," he said to me seriously. "If she's not doing anything wrong, she won't be happy with you for it."

I gave a quick jerk of my head then practically ran out the door. Before I even cleared the door, I pulled my net tight over me. I jogged down the hallway not bothering to conceal the pounding of my feet on the floor. When I came to Ella's hallway, I slowed to a lighter step so as not to warn her of my approach. According to Evelyn, Ella was going to be searching more people's minds, but she was going to do it from her room. I listened at her door carefully and silently for a full two minutes. I didn't hear any movement inside. She wasn't there.

Kimi's room. I ran down the hall a little more subtly this time, approaching Kimi's door carefully. I knew

I could make the room door disappear to see inside the room, but if I could see through it, then so could anyone on the other side. It was too risky a move to make right now, so I leaned over to listen at the door again. This time I heard Ella's voice inside. Why was she in Kimi's room? Were they working together? Maybe Ella had found Kimi, and Kimi had convinced Ella to help her. I had to work to slow my breathing enough to hear anything being said. I only heard one voice, Ella's, and I only caught snippets. "…Afraid of her…easier than Kimi…Liam….getting information is quicker…" When I heard my name, it caught me off guard for a moment, but I quickly regained my concentration. I had to. It sounded like she was on the phone with someone, but Kimi didn't have a phone in her room that I knew of. After another minute of not hearing what was being said, I decided I would need help.

Heather was in the gym running on the treadmill when I finally found her. A few other people were there as well, Jacob being one of them. I kept myself invisible, and no one noticed the door open by itself. I knew she wouldn't be able to hear me if I tried to talk to her, so I walked up and switched the treadmill off.

She stumbled, shook her head and began checking the machine. As she leaned over to look underneath it, I whispered in her ear. "Heather, it's Liam. Don't draw attention to me."

She jumped when she heard me, bumping her head on the display. Glancing around warily she whispered back, "What are you doing?"

"I need your help," I said. "Come out in the hall with me." She quietly agreed and gathered up her stuff.

She ignored Jacob who gave her guff about not being smarter than a treadmill, but soon we were outside the gym together. I threw my net over both of us. When I appeared, she glared at me. "What's this all about?" I was reminded again of her mother when she said it.

"I need you to transport me to someone," I said. "But no one can see us."

"Ok," she said closing her eyes. "Who?"

"Ella."

She opened her eyes and stared at me incredulously. "Why don't you just go talk to her?"

I pulled her out of the way as Jacob poked his head out the door. He looked left and right then went back into the gym. "She's acting suspicious," I explained to her in a low voice. "Jancarlo told me to follow her. She was supposed to be in her room, but she's in Kimi's room talking to someone. I just want you to transport me into the room so I can hear the conversation."

"Ok." She relented.

I put my hand on her shoulder, and we started to disappear. To my horror, we solidified back in the same spot.

"What happened?" I asked her.

"I don't know," she answered, scrunching her eyebrows tightly. "I'm being blocked somehow. It's like when I tried to transport back to the base when they put the security in place."

"Maybe the security field is blocking you," I said. "Let's try from the clearing room."

Knowing that the room would negate my invisibility net when we stepped inside, I had a short conversation with Nathaniel, stationed at the desk. He didn't seem to care much about what we were up to. He knew he could trust me.

Once we were in the clearing room, I turned back to Heather with my hand on her shoulder. "Okay," I said, "let's try this again."

"I'm just transporting to Ella, right?" she asked again.

I gave her a nod and we disappeared.

I expected to reappear in Kimi's room. I had seen the room a hundred times and knew what to expect. Instead, we appeared in a cavern. "Where are we?" I asked.

After a moment of thought, she quietly answered, "That's weird. This is the same cavern we transported to when we were searching for Kimi."

"Are you sure your powers are working the same way?" I asked as I inspected the tunnels cautiously. I was suddenly worried we wouldn't be able to get home.

"Not anymore," she whispered.

I finally had the chance to see what everyone else had described to me. Never-ending stone passageways that all looked the same. Next to me, Heather started to shiver. She was still wearing running shorts and a tank top, and the cavern was very cold.

"Why don't we go back and let you get some clothes on?" I suggested. "Then we can try again and see if we end up in the same place."

Heather nodded, and I put my hand on her shoulder again. We jumped back to the base and set off quickly to her room. I didn't bother leaving my net on us. When we got to her room, she grabbed some clothes out of her closet and headed into the bathroom. "I'm going to contact Jancarlo." I informed her as she closed the door.

I walked over to her jeweled console next to her door and put my finger on the first gemstone on the panel. Concentrating on pushing my thoughts out of my mind, I said, *Jancarlo.*

I knew he would have to notice the gem on his own console glowing, but I waited only a moment.

Yes, Jancarlo answered.

Jancarlo, it's Liam.

Go ahead, Liam.

Ella wasn't in her room like she told me she would be, I explained to him. *I heard her voice in Kimi's room, but couldn't make out much of what she was saying, so I asked Heather for help. We tried to transport to Ella, but we ended up in the same cave where Kimi was supposed to be.*

That's strange, he answered, contemplative.

We're wondering if there might be something wrong with Heather's powers, I said. It was infuriating that we should hit this bump in the road now. I tucked away my frustration and tried to focus on what needed to be done.

Why don't you have Heather do some simple jumps before you try again? Heather should have a bracelet to contact me if anything goes wrong. Let me know what happens.

Got it. I took my hand off the console as Heather reappeared in a long sleeve shirt and jeans with her hair pulled into a ponytail. She fastened the indicated bracelet onto her wrist.

"Jancarlo says you should try a few simple jumps first, just to make sure everything is okay," I said.

"That's what I think too," She said. "Maybe I just can't jump to a person anymore."

"Maybe," I said. "Maybe you can try to jump to Jancarlo, since he knows what's going on."

She nodded her head, and I put my hand on her shoulder. As the air shimmered around me, I hoped we would solidify somewhere normal then wondered if I should have made us invisible. But my concerns were unwarranted. We reappeared in Jancarlo's office with him and Kin staring up at us.

Seeing Heather glance quickly away from Kin, I said, "Well I guess that worked. Why don't you try to take us somewhere else." To the bewildered men I said, "See ya."

With a nod, we transported out of the office and into the lobby. I nodded to Heather and she confirmed that this is where she meant to go, then something struck me.

"Why don't you see if you can just transport us into Kimi's room? You've seen it before, right?" I asked.

"Briefly," she shook her head. "I only saw a small part of it. If the image in my mind is indistinct or incomplete at all, it might not work."

"Do you think you can try?"

She was pensive for a minute then said, "I'll try."

I wondered if I was pushing her too much. Putting my hand on her shoulder, I secured my net around the pair of us.

When we reappeared in Kimi's room, I almost sighed with relief. Heather seemed pleased with herself. I took stock of the room and noticed the shower running in the adjoining bathroom. Ella was taking a shower in Kimi's room for some reason. This was getting weirder and weirder. I whispered praise to Heather as we began to investigate the room.

There was a phone sitting on the desk. I pointed to it and told Heather in a whisper, "Kimi doesn't have one. Neither does Ella."

"I wonder where it came from." She stepped closer to inspect it and gestured to the necklace with the mirror charm on the table next to it. "So, it's definitely Ella in the shower, but why couldn't I transport to her?"

The questions bubbled over. What was going on here?

At that instant, the shower shut off. I pulled Heather harshly away from the table to the other side of the room from the bathroom door. "Whatever you do," I breathed in her ear. "Don't make a sound….no matter what."

She just nodded in return. We waited a few minutes. Finally, the door to the bathroom opened. Deep down, I had known all along who it was, I just needed it confirmed. With dark, russet skin and almost black hair streaking down her back, I recognized her. She was only an inch or so taller than Ella and Kimi, but she had a long, pointed nose between small black eyes. Once wife of Raphael Winford…lover of Devin Ross…self-proclaimed enemy of the People of the Storm. It had been her all the time. It was Eva Winford.

Chapter Thirteen

Stepping out of the bathroom with a towel wrapped around her, she went straight to the table where she picked up the mirror necklace. As soon as she put it on, her image shifted back into Ella. I had a hard time containing myself. Eva was a dangerous woman, and I had to find out what she was doing here. As I watched her pick up some of Ella's clothes to put on, my teeth ground together. She stopped what she was doing and, with Ella's eyes, carefully scanned the room.

Heather shook my arm, but I couldn't even look at her. She could have been choking and dying, but I only had eyes for the woman pretending to be Ella. In an instant, the room around me disappeared as Ella stepped toward me with narrowed eyes. We reappeared in Jancarlo's office.

"That's why you couldn't transport to Ella or Kimi, because they're somewhere else entirely!" I seethed. "It's been Eva all this time!"

"Eva?!" Jancarlo and Kin erupted from behind me.

"Who's Eva?" Heather asked.

I finally pried my eyes back to her, pointing at the empty space in front of me as if the woman still stood there, "THAT was Eva!" I bellowed. I slumped into a chair and cradled my head between my fists. "She's been somehow using that necklace to create the illusion of Ella and probably Kimi too. She's been impersonating them for who knows how long!"

"But who IS Eva?" Heather asked the men behind me.

Kin answered her, telling her all the atrocities Eva had been accomplice to with Devin Ross. He told her of the two of them plotting to kill the Storm People ending with Nathaniel. Eva's powers made her capable of giving a shadow of life to inanimate objects, hoping to use them against the Storm People. She had initially been the one who created Bam Bam. With time, she had gained the additional powers of fire throwing, which made it perfect for her to impersonate Kimi, and lifting objects, although the latter powers were not as powerful as the previous.

While Kin explained who she was, I sat brooding. How could I have been so stupid? Ella had been right all along about Kimi. Now she was gone. But where? In the cave?

I jumped out of the chair, knocking it over, and pointed to Heather, "Your powers are still intact," I insisted. "Take me back to the cavern. Ella and Kimi must be there somewhere!"

"Kin," Jancarlo said as we all ran to the door, "keep an eye on Eva until Liam can locate Ella and Kimi!"

"On it!" Kin barked as he slapped his black knit hat on his head.

Once we were back in the cavern, I inspected the walls carefully. They seemed solid enough. I turned to Heather hopefully. "You already investigated these caverns," I said, "but Eva must have taken over Ella's form shortly after you arrived. Then Eva redirected you the entire time." She nodded and I continued, "Where did the real Ella go when you first separated and you came back to report to Jancarlo?"

I watched her with impatient eyes as she peered down the dark passageways. Finally, she closed her eyes and held her arms out swaying them slightly as if dancing.

Her eyes popped open, and she pointed to the passageway directly behind me. "That was the one she was going down when I left." She said it so confidently I mustered some hope. "It's also the one she kept me away from every time I tried to go back to it."

I turned, but I couldn't see more than a few yards down the passageway in front of me for the darkness. From what I could see, there was nothing there. "How close do you usually transport to a person?" I asked her as I felt along the wall on my right.

"Usually, within feet, but I think it also depends on the distance I *envision* them when I transport."

I spared her a short glance but continued to edge along the pathway then stopped after we got more than twenty feet down the hall. There was nothing but empty darkness in front of us.

"I'm never more than ten feet away from them," Heather insisted, watching the passage the way we had come.

"I believe you," I said. Stepping to the opposite side of the tunnel, I put my arm out to keep Heather from approaching. "Stay back."

Reaching my net out, I grabbed a section of the wall about five feet in diameter and made it disappear. The resulting "hole" looked like Bam Bam had just knocked a chunk out of the wall. Staring in, we could detect a small opening on the right, further toward the way we had come. I moved my net down the wall section by section as we watched to see what would appear on the other side. The gap gradually opened up, and to our shock, we saw Ella! She was slouched, unconscious in a small cell, her hands over her head chained to the wall. A rag was tied around her head. She had no clothes on except what seemed to be a dirty bed sheet tied haphazardly around her like a toga. A dark metal ring clamped around her neck that I knew kept her from using her powers.

As we stared in silence, her leg twitched and her chin came up. Her eyes fluttered open for a moment in my direction, but then she slipped back into unconsciousness. Instinctively, I jumped forward to reach out for her, momentarily forgetting a wall was still in front of me. Heather tried to stop me right before I jammed my hands against the wall.

"We'll have to find a way around to the door," Heather said as I pulled my net off the wall in front of us. "Obviously, it must be that way." She pointed down the hallway we had been exploring. "Why else would she keep us from it?"

This time, instead of being cautious, I tore down the hall as fast as my vision could keep up. The sight of Ella chained to a wall had lit a fire in my mind. Nothing would quench it until she was safe again. Only a few more feet down the hall, we found a hidden passageway. It seemed like just more rock, but Heather, going about the search more methodically than I was, laid her hand on it and almost fell through the opening. It reminded me of the Shadow's hidden passageways in their old base, having spent too much time there, I knew exactly what it was, and dragging Heather with me, we shot through the illusion.

Sure enough, a row of rugged looking rooms with rock columns for bars greeted us. One room held Ella like we had just seen her, propped against the wall, and in the cell next to her lay Kimi.

Kimi was much worse off than Ella. Not only dirty and unconscious, she also sported cuts, bruises and dried blood all over her head, face and arms. Her once smooth face was pale, her cheekbones jutting out abnormally far. Dark circles encompassed her partially open eyes, and her hair hung in clumps around her head. I noticed she had the same toga-type sheet wrapped around her, but her feet were chained as well as her wrists. If I knew Kimi, it was because she had put up much more of a fight. How long had she been here? The only hopeful sign I saw was the shallow rise and fall of her chest.

Neither of them stirred when we approached. As I stood grinding my teeth, Heather hesitantly touched me on the arm. I had half-forgotten she was even there, and I startled. "We need to go back for help," she said timidly. "I can't transport into the cells."

"You go back," I said a little harsher than I meant. "I'm staying. Go back and get Gretchen or one of her healing stones," I added a little gentler unable to remove my gaze from the two suffering women.

Heather nodded. "I'll be back as fast as I can." Before I could say anything else, she was gone.

I looked down at Ella in the small stone cell. We had been in a situation much like this before, and I wished it could have been me in there instead of her. I whispered her name softly and crouched down to see her better. "Ella," I said repeatedly, "can you hear me?" Eventually her head twitched toward me. "It's ok. We're going to get you out of here." As I said it, I took ahold of one of the stone bars in front of me. The bar was so thick I couldn't fit my hand all the way around it. If the rooms had a dampening field, as I suspected since Heather couldn't transport into them, then we would have a hard time removing them.

As I inspected the cell and bars, I felt something on the other side. A little awkwardly, I moved the object hanging there. Holding it to the side of the bar so I could see what it was, I realized it was the back of a small diamond-shaped mirror. I inspected Kimi's cell and found the same thing. Both mirrors were hanging on the opposite side of the cell from the two women. They were also the same thing Noah had seen Eva in briefly, ages ago, after our fight with Devin Ross and his followers. I had a hard time believing Eva hung them there for the prisoners' vanity.

I tried to solicit a reaction from both Ella and Kimi, but both remained largely unresponsive. Ella would occasionally turn at the sound of my voice but made no motion to answer me.

After what seemed like an eternity, I heard voices in the passageway we had come from. Heather jogged casually through the opening with Evelyn, Tony, Jancarlo, Gretchen, Nathaniel recently returned from the mountains, Kathryn, Jacob, Migan and Brendan, who were two fire throwers from the security team. I didn't know them very well, but I was glad to have them. Jancarlo instructed Migan and Nathaniel to station themselves at one end of the hall while Brendan and Jacob were told to take up guard duty at the entrance they had come through. I wondered briefly where Kin was but then assumed he must be dealing with Eva.

"Ella!" Evelyn choked as she ran to the cell holding her teenage daughter. I felt immediately guilty for not having contacted her or thought to contact her once I knew her daughter was missing. Then I felt worse for also thinking that somewhere in the back of my mind I probably didn't let her in on the problem immediately because she didn't realize it for herself first.

Jancarlo glanced over at the women and inspected the cell doors, as I had, while I told him what I had found. "Tony," he called after I told him all I knew, "see if you can break or move these bars."

Tony stepped up and the rest of us moved out of his way. His powers of super-human strength would certainly be able to get the job done any other time, but I wasn't sure if the dampening field would hinder him. As I predicted, he couldn't move the bars. Frustrated, he stepped out of the way as Kathryn came forward.

Kathryn's powers were complex at best. I knew she could touch someone and take all or part of their powers away from them, and I knew she could duplicate someone's powers and place them in objects. But she could also amplify powers or copy her own powers creating similar dampening fields. Working against someone else's powers or against someone else's dampening field might or might not impede her, I wasn't sure.

She stepped up to the rock bars and placed both her hands on them. Bowing her head and closing her eyes, she stood perfectly still while the rest of us held our breath. Finally, she sagged back from the bars. "That's a weird sensation," she said. She took a breath and stood up straight to wave at Tony. "You should be able to move it now."

While Kathryn moved over to the cell holding Kimi, Tony stationed himself firmly in front of Ella's cell. With a deafening rumble that shook the walls, he lifted free the entire wall with the bars attached. He stepped to the side and, carefully maneuvering around everyone else, put the bars against the opposite wall. As soon as he was out of the way, Evelyn and Gretchen rushed into the cell. I hesitated a moment then pushed in behind them.

They knelt on either side of Ella, so I slipped next to Gretchen. Gretchen touched her arm softly as Evelyn gently tried to lift her head. Next door, Kathryn had worked her magic, and Tony noisily removed the door into Kimi's cell. "She's being drugged with something," Gretchen said. Her eyes glazed over as she connected with

Ella's body to search it for answers. "She should be fine, but I'll have to work with her." She blinked rapidly and focused back on Evelyn. "Physically, she'll be ok."

I nodded. "Go check Kimi," I said, taking her place. Evelyn's eyes snapped to mine. For a moment, they burned with anger but immediately shifted back to Ella.

As Gretchen darted out of the cell to post herself next to Kimi, Kathryn stepped up to me. "Liam," she said gently. "The chains also have a dampening field in them. I need to remove it so Tony can get them off."

Reluctantly, I let go of Ella and moved back. I knew if I touched Ella, the chains or Kathryn while Kathryn removed the field, she would probably take my powers from me. Evelyn did the same on the other side. When Kathryn let go of the chains, the dark metal ring also dropped from Ella's neck. Then Tony stepped forward and, with a finesse I hadn't known he possessed, pinched the metal chains around her wrists, prying them apart like peeling an orange.

I caught her before she could fall to the floor completely. Without asking Evelyn's permission, I scooped Ella into my arms and ran to Heather in order to flee the stone prison.

Chapter FOURTEEN

"I should have been consulted," Evelyn fumed. "I'm her mother." She and Gretchen sat perched on Ella's bed. Gretchen held Ella's hand with her eyes closed and her head bowed, blocking out the world and the conversations around her. Evelyn sat with her hand on Ella's foot using her water moving powers to push fluids into Ella, like an I.V. drip, at Gretchen's request.

"To be honest," Jancarlo said, "in that situation I had no idea who I could trust. Liam brought it to my attention so we kept it between ourselves but acted on it immediately."

Evelyn's withering gaze swept me again, but I ignored it. "Next time something like this comes up," she hissed, "I insist on being informed."

"Noted," Jancarlo said, but I think we both understood that he would do as he saw fit no matter what she, or anyone else, insisted.

"Someone," Jancarlo turned to me, "went to a lot of trouble to restrain them. There were separate dampening fields in the walls of the room, the chains and the rings around their necks. Normally I would think it was overkill, but with Kimi and Ella, I guess too much is never enough.”

“Do we have any idea what she was doing?” I asked.

“No,” Jancarlo said. “We’re hoping we’ll get more answers when Ella’s up for it.”

“How’s Kimi doing?” I asked.

Jancarlo sighed, “Gretchen woke her and got her moving and as furious as she always is. She’s resting and having some time with Tony and Kin.”

I had brought Ella straight back here after we got her out of the stone cell. I assumed Tony had taken Kimi back to her room as well, but I hadn’t seen her yet. Gretchen had deemed Kimi’s need greater and spent a long time healing her. Not that I minded. Ella was, indeed, in better shape than Kimi, but I figured my place was at Ella’s side. I had spent a lot of time waiting for Ella to wake up in the past, but this time we desperately needed answers.

While we had been busy freeing Kimi and Ella, Kin had had a knock down fight with Eva. He must have really been taking it easy on her when they sparred under her guise of Kimi because he easily subdued her. Of course, he’d been invisible at the time as well. I guess he wasn’t willing to take any chances of her getting away. Now, Kin hovered outside her cell, in his hat, keeping a very close watch on her.

Tony wasn’t leaving Kimi’s side. According to Jancarlo, he was hesitant to believe it was the real Kimi, but he still wanted to be there for her when she woke up.

As we sat in silence, Gretchen worked her magic on Ella. After a few minutes Ella's eyes finally flickered open. She took a deep breath and bolted upright in bed.

"Kimi!" she said as Gretchen tried to calm her. "I found the real Kimi!" she exclaimed.

Evelyn helped Gretchen keep Ella from jumping out of bed. "It's okay, Ella," Evelyn said. "We got Kimi back too."

"Too?" she asked. Then her eyes settled on the bed, and she realized something was wrong. "What happened?"

"You were both kidnapped by Eva," Jancarlo said. "We found you both unconscious in a cave somewhere." He gave her a minute to think then asked, "Do you remember anything?"

She shook her head. "I'm sorry. The last thing I remember is seeing Kimi locked up in a cave." Ella turned her big eyes to Jancarlo. "She must have ambushed me."

"Explains the massive contusion on the back of your head," Gretchen said.

"Ella," Jancarlo said, "are your powers intact?" He tried to appear casual as if not wanting to alarm her, but the seriousness in his tone told the real story.

Ella stared at Jancarlo, but I assumed they were communicating in their minds. He nodded. "Good," he said. "We need to have a meeting as soon as possible. Are you up for it?"

Ella looked at Gretchen who said, "I've done everything I can. Normally, I would advise you to rest, but this is pretty serious. You'll have to make your own call as to how you feel."

"I'll be okay." Ella nodded, then added, "But I'm really hungry."

"Kimi was too," Gretchen said. "I'm guessing Eva didn't feed you much, but she must have kept you hydrated somehow. For you, it's been a week or two. For Kimi, I'm guessing it was much longer." She stood up to leave. "I'm supposed to go work on her some more after she's eaten, but you should be fine, especially after some food and water. Let me know if anything comes up."

"We have yet to get a report from either of you," Jancarlo said as he and Gretchen headed for the door. "Let's meet in the conference room in half an hour. Good to have you back, Ella." He nodded to her then opened the door for Gretchen.

After they left, I turned back to Ella. Evelyn kept her eyes anywhere but on me. "I'll go make you something to eat."

"Wait," Ella said, "I'll come with you."

"Ella," her mother pressed, "you should rest. Liam can get you something."

"No," Ella shook her head. "I want to get up. I just need to use the bathroom, and we can go to the kitchen."

"I'll let your mother help you," I said. "I'll go ahead and start on something."

I slipped out of the room before Ella could stop me and before Evelyn could force me. I could tell Evelyn wanted to be alone with her daughter.

At a young age, my mother had instilled in me that anyone who had been through something traumatic must eat something to calm the nerves. In fact, my mother always fed everyone any time she possibly could. Food was medicine, as important as air, and ever present in our lives. Through the years, I had tried to honor her memory by doing the same.

I made a few quick roast beef sandwiches because I knew Ella loved them. I put a small side salad with it on the table just as the two women walked into the dining area.

"I'm okay," Ella insisted as we waited for her to sit. "I feel like I just woke up from a nap. I'm fine."

"You haven't eaten for ten days," Evelyn said. "I won't feel good about you moving around until you have something in your stomach."

Before we knew it, a half hour was up, and the food was gone. As we stood to leave, Ella turned to her mom. "You don't have to come to the meeting, you know," she said. "I'll tell you all about it later."

Evelyn's eyes narrowed slightly. "You really think I'm going to let you out of my sight after that?"

Ella turned at me for help, but I shrugged. "I'm not making her leave." I earned something of a cross between a smile and a grimace from Evelyn, so Ella shook her head as we all turned toward the conference room.

Entering the conference room, we saw everyone already present. Kimi sat next to Tony, who seemed pleased and determined all at once. He gave me a short jerk of his head in acknowledgement, but I felt like it was also a sort of thanks. I made a beeline for Kimi and hugged her tightly. All the color had returned to her skin. She still seemed gaunt, but the circles under her eyes had disappeared as had the cuts and bruises. She was never much for affection, we had always had that in common, but I was beside myself with relief at having both women back and whole again. Ella followed my lead and gave Kimi a hug as well. For her part, Kimi tolerated it, but only briefly.

While we exchanged pleasantries, Jancarlo closed the door and turned the knob on the wall next to it. Kin was there, sitting next to Heather, who seemed to have accepted the fact that he still existed. Jacob and Gretchen completed the group and we all took our seats.

Jancarlo called us to order immediately, "I had you all come here to get a report directly from Kimi and Ella so they don't have to repeat it to everyone." He held out his hand to Ella first. "Ella, start us off, please. Tell us what happened to you because Kimi's report will be a little longer."

"Like I told you before," she said softly, "I don't remember much of anything. Heather and I split up to look through the cavern when we appeared there. I found the passageway because I had my hand on the wall as I walked and found Kimi chained in a cell. I called to her a couple of times, but she was unresponsive. I started to leave to get Heather. I don't remember anything after that. I woke up in my own room a little while ago." She seemed uncomfortable and gave a small shrug as an ending.

"That's fine, Ella." Jancarlo said. Then he turned to Kimi. "How about you?"

"The last time I remember being at the base was just a couple weeks after Devin Ross had been killed." She started to say more, but she couldn't continue for the murmur that ran through the room.

"You've been gone *that* long?!" I asked in a low voice. It had been about three months since we fought the Shadow leader in the mountains. Jancarlo quieted us, and we all sat in stunned silence.

"Yes," she continued. "Eva must have jumped me when I came back from sparring with Ella one night. That's the last thing I remember. I was getting ready to go to dinner with Tony." Tony didn't seem too shocked at the revelation. I assumed that was the night she stood him up for the first time…and for good reason. "There were a few times," she said, "when the drugs she gave me wore off. I could see a small mirror hanging on the other side of the cell from me, against one of the walls."

"I saw the same thing in both of your cells." I said to the group.

"I could see Eva in it most of the time." She nodded to me. "I think the circle necklace she wore projected the image of whoever was in the diamond shaped mirror. I could see *her*, but you guys saw *me*."

"That would make sense," Jancarlo said. "When her cover as Kimi was blown by Liam in the arena, she must have regrouped back at Kimi's cell. Then she ambushed Ella when she showed up so she could assume another identity and get back to the base."

"A few times, I was able to reach the mirror and knock it down, ruining her disguise." Kimi said. "She told me no one saw her change, and she got back to fix it before she was discovered, but I had to try. That's when she added the chains to my legs."

I could see Tony's jaw muscles tighten. He glared down at the table to try to hide his anger, but I also saw Ella watching him carefully.

"She did feed me occasionally," Kimi said. "Every couple weeks or so, as far as I can guess. Most of the time I was unconscious. The only other times I was conscious she would beat me and question me about the location of some very particular gems. I told her about the gems in Kathryn's office, but she said these gems were different, much larger and with strong powers in them. I had no idea what she was talking about, so I couldn't tell her anything. That's pretty much all I can remember." She fell silent and the entire room was so quiet you could hear Tony's teeth grinding.

Along with the clenched jaw, I saw Tony's fist balled so tightly his fingernails were probably drawing blood. Kimi reached over and lightly placed her hand on top of Tony's arm. Immediately his fist uncurled and his jaw slackened. He also seemed to start breathing again.

Jancarlo's head slowly moved up and down while his eyes bored into the table. "Obviously," he said with slow enunciation, "we need to get the answers from someone else." He looked up at Ella. "How are you feeling, Ella?"

"Like getting some answers," she said with narrowed eyes.

"Good." He gave her a conspiratorial grin. "You're with me." Jancarlo headed for the door. "The rest of you, meet back here in the morning."

As the group began clearing out, Tony and Kimi had some quiet words together. I instinctively followed

Ella. "Liam, Evelyn," Jancarlo stopped us at the door, "you don't need to be present for this."

Evelyn's eyes burned into Jancarlo. The only other time I'd seen a look like that was when my brother and I had let the neighbor's cows loose as a prank. When we came home, our mother already knew what we'd done. She gave us one look, and we turned around to present our backsides to be warmed with her wooden spoon. She never yelled at us. She conveyed everything from that one gaze. Evelyn did the same, raising an eyebrow then following her daughter.

I watched the display then matched the attitude – although I didn't think I would ever be able to pull off the eyes. "You don't think I'm going to let Ella out of my sight, do you? You know me better than that." I pushed past him and fell into step behind Ella and her mother.

Jancarlo walked beside me but suddenly spun around in the opposite direction. I turned in time to see Tony's massive hand on his shoulder. Tony glowered down at Jancarlo, "I'm coming."

"Tony," Jancarlo started to say, "I really think you should…."

"I'm coming," he interrupted. Letting go of Jancarlo's shoulder, he stalked past Jancarlo and pushed between me and Ella on our way to the holding cells.

"And here I hoped for a small group," Jancarlo muttered to no one.

Tony transferred - none too gently - Eva to the interrogation room. He stood in the room by the door, and

Jancarlo leaned close to the hand-cuffed Eva before leaving. "If you say or do anything we don't like or try to get away," he whispered, "I'll let Tony do whatever he wants to you."

Eva tried to be defiant, but we could all see the fear in her eyes when she looked up at him. She sat morosely in the chair avoiding Tony's gaze while Jancarlo, Ella, Evelyn, and I watched them from the observation room on the other side of the mirror.

Ella was already digging through Eva's mind getting as much information as she could. The only reason we had to bring Eva from her holding cell was because the cell had a dampening field around it, and Ella's powers couldn't penetrate her mind while she was in it. For the same reason, we also had to remove the ring from around her neck, but we were confident in our ability to keep her under control. Ella's eyes got a faraway glaze the same way Gretchen's did when she worked with someone's body. They could understand so much more on a completely different level than I could even imagine, and I admired them for it.

After ten minutes, Eva got fidgety. She squirmed in her rigid chair. She kept sighing or glancing anxiously at Tony. He didn't say anything or do anything at all, and it must have made her nervous. Suddenly, her face went blank, her eyes widened, and she confronted the mirror with terror. Fear turned to anger as she narrowed one eye at the two-way mirror. She realized Ella was the one getting the answers. Her jaw began to work as if chewing something. Watching Ella's face, I knew she was having a silent contest with Eva. Ella's eyes were wide but focused very far off, and her jaw was fixed. Suddenly, she snapped her eyes shut, I guessed in order to concentrate, but she didn't move a muscle.

Finally, Eva flinched away from the mirror. Her breathing increased, and her jaw worked back and forth. She flinched again and again as if from an unseen attack. Finally, she let out a small yell and threw her head back and forth.

"I guess Tony isn't the one you should have warned her against," I told Jancarlo quietly.

Jancarlo touched Ella on her shoulder. "If she's giving you problems," he told her gently, "just knock her out."

Ella opened her eyes, and I could have sworn I saw fire in them as she glared at him. "Why would I want to make it easy on her?" she said to him. I had never heard her be so vengeful before. She looked beautiful and dangerous all at once. It was very intimidating. Evelyn chewed her lip watching the exchanges.

But Jancarlo wasn't stirred. He rubbed her upper arm for a moment. "Don't make it worse," he whispered.

Ella sighed slowly and closed her eyes. Without another sound, Eva slumped in her chair, her head lolling to the side.

We waited while Ella devoured Eva's mind, taking in anything useful. After a few minutes of watching Ella shift from foot to foot, I got her a chair to rest in while she worked. I noticed Ella's multi-stoned bracelet on her wrist. While she delved into Eva's mind one of the russet gems glowed softly and almost imperceptibly.

It took another twenty minutes for Ella to finish. When she finally straightened in her chair, she said, "I'm not sure how much I can trust the information I've just seen. Someone has been tutoring Eva in hiding her thoughts." She shook her head slightly. "Besides, what I found is extremely...." She shook her head again and almost laughed. "Improbable." Still shaking her head, she muttered, "At least I found some directions for the caverns. I know where the cave system is located, but I'm not sure about the rest of it."

"Is that why you were struggling with her?" Jancarlo asked. "Was she trying to keep information from you?"

"Yes," she confirmed. "But she's not very good at it, and it's nearly impossible for any human to do it."

"How do you mean?" I asked. I wasn't sure what she meant by "hiding her thoughts."

"Think about it this way," she said. "Think of something you would want to keep a secret from me while I look into your mind. Then you have to try to *not* think about it and build a wall around it all at the same time."

"It's like saying, 'Don't think of ice cream,'" Jancarlo said. "Now, all you can do is think of ice cream."

It was true. Now I wanted ice cream for dessert tonight. "But if you say she wasn't very good at it, then why can't you trust what you found?"

"Because..." she hemmed, "it wasn't very clear, and it's just... impossible."

Jancarlo ushered us all back to his office once he gave Tony leave to shunt Eva back into her cell. I had a feeling Eva would wake up with a few new bumps and bruises.

For the next hour or two, Evelyn and I watched as Ella drew maps of the cavern system's tunnels for Jancarlo, pointing out illusions and other hidden passageways. The cavern in which they had been held was apparently hundreds of feet under the rock and ice of the North Pole. As she drew the cavern map, she added a room deep within the maze of passageways, but she would not specify the occupant of the room. She claimed she wouldn't believe it until she saw it and would, therefore, not report it until she knew it was true. Jancarlo insisted they needed to be ready for anything, but Ella refused to say more.

She also told us of the big "plans" Eva had for the People of the Storm. She had watched Devin Ross die and blamed Jancarlo, me, Ella and anyone else with a fern-shaped scar marking them as having been touched by lightning. But her plans had morphed from revenge on the Storm People to revenge on the world. She was willing to massacre millions of innocents to get her revenge. The plans Ella had come upon would have once made her weak in the knees. These she told us about. But she still claimed not to trust the source or the information gathered.

"Fine," Jancarlo finally relented in his questioning. "We'll get a couple of groups together and head there tomorrow. I'll see you in the morning."

We left Jancarlo poring over the maps Ella had drawn. He seemed no less likely to sleep than either of us. As we walked, I thought in my mind, *Would you like something more to eat?*

With you? She answered with a grin. *Always.*

Before anything could be said out loud, Evelyn turned. "No," she said, her eyes bouncing between the two of us. "I don't have to be a mind reader to know what you're thinking. Both of you." She included Ella. "It's getting late, and it seems like Jancarlo has plans for everyone in the morning." She took Ella's hand and steered her toward their conjoined rooms.

"Mom," Ella said, not unkindly, "you know I'll just be talking with him anyway."

Evelyn sighed. "Yes, but you'll do it from your bed. You need rest, and I'm going to insist on it. I'm sorry, Liam." She said to me as she opened the door. But somehow, I didn't see any guilt as she shut the door in my face.

As it turned out, we didn't talk much that night. After repeated interruptions, Ella eventually gave up on our conversation to have one with her mother instead. The next morning, she informed me she had tossed and turned all night. I had been no more fruitful in finding peaceful rest. I couldn't remember ever waking up so tired. I felt like I had already fought the next battle. I offered to make breakfast for the three of us, but Evelyn informed me that she and Ella had already eaten. I grabbed something quickly and ran into the conference room behind them.

It wasn't a small room, but it wasn't large enough for all the people crammed in it. Most of Kin's security team stood against the wall, roughly a dozen men and women. I knew all their names, but didn't know them personally. There were lots of added chairs around the table, and they were still filling rapidly. I tried to grab a seat next to Ella, but her mother beat me to it again. Jancarlo stood at the front, still studying the maps while everyone came in. I thought for sure he had memorized them by now, but he still gazed at them as if seeing them for the first time.

I joined Nathaniel against the wall in back when Sophia, the translator who had helped make Ella's bracelet, came in searching for a seat. I hadn't seen her in a while and learned, while we waited for Jancarlo to start, she had been working on the surface with the new clinic. Before we could chat too much, Jancarlo called us to order.

"I've called you all here in order to, hopefully, prevent another attack on the Storm People." A murmur ran through the room as Jancarlo let everyone react to the news. "It seems Eva Winford had some help while she infiltrated our base. While under the disguise of Kimi and Ella, she has been transporting back and forth to these caverns of hers, and she's been creating more rock monsters like Bam Bam."

At first there wasn't much of a reaction to the news. Tony finally said, "But it can't be that bad. I mean Bam Bam does whatever we tell him to. Can't we just tell these new rockmen not to hurt us? Or have Ella control them?" A few people nodded in agreement.

"Ella can't spread her mind through all of them and these rockmen have been specifically programmed to kill us. They won't stop when we tell them to." He paused to let that sink in. "They won't listen to anyone but Eva, Wiki or Perry Anderson." At this, Tony's eyebrows scrunched together in concern, and he listened intently. Seeing he had finally caught their attention, Jancarlo continued. "We're splitting up into three groups. Group one will consist of Kin, Kimi and whomever they deem necessary to be on their security team. This group will need to scout the army and gather any information they can before engaging the rockmen, if necessary.

"The second group will need to get the word out to all our people to come and help should a battle be waged. If Eva is so determined to slaughter so many people, everyone is concerned. Heather will transport all able bodies around the world to the other Storm People and drop off liaisons to enlist help. I'll be directing those efforts, although I'll be going along with the third group.

"The last group will consist of Ella, me, probably Liam…" here he looked at me with an expectant gleam to which I nodded, "and Evelyn." Evelyn also nodded, but shot her eyes to me afterwards.

I would go anywhere Ella went. Good thing Jancarlo finally came to terms with that. I wanted to know what was in this mysterious room as much as anyone, but most of all I wanted to know if Ella was in any danger.

"We," Jancarlo told the room, "will be investigating something else in the caverns. According to Ella, it might be dangerous and it might not."

At this, some of the people in the room got curious looks on their faces. All this mystery, and their leader was leaving in the middle of it? Not only was it not like Jancarlo, but they were looking to him for guidance and expected him to stay there with them.

"Heather, Kin and Kimi will be in contact with me and give me regular reports." Jancarlo held up his wrist to show the group the leather strap on his wrist with rubies embedded in the middle. The three others had the same straps on their wrists with gemstones to link their minds with Jancarlo's should they need to communicate with him. "You have your assignments," he said as a dismissal. "Good luck."

As everyone filed out, Jancarlo turned to Ella. "Are you ready to go?" She nodded in response, and Jancarlo glared at Evelyn and me. "And her entourage?" Slightly abashed, both Evelyn and I nodded. "Good," he said with a hint of annoyance in his tone. "I want to be back here as soon as possible to join up with Kin and Kimi's group. Let's get this over with."

Chapter FIFTEEN

Before long we stood deep in the caverns underneath the Arctic Circle. We were the first to leave the base. The others were assembling their groups and would leave when Heather got back from dropping us off. Before she left, Jancarlo gave her a few last words. "Be careful," he told her. "You are critical to the Storm People now. You, of all people, should be the most careful."

"I'll do whatever I can," she told him in return.

"I think I might have figured out a way for you to return to your family as well." He watched her reaction carefully. "If you still want to."

She betrayed no emotion. She just nodded and turned away. "I'll report as often as I can," she said right before she disappeared.

A chill ran down my spine once she was gone. We didn't have a way out without her or another transporter. Normally, I wasn't one to be afraid. After all, we'd faced danger before. But losing Ella left me reeling. I wanted nothing more than to keep her safe. I took a deep breath and squared my shoulders. This … this in front of us was what would keep Ella safe.

"We don't have any maps, do we?" I said, searching the passageways.

Jancarlo tapped his temple. "All right here," he said.

"Great," I muttered, realizing why Jancarlo had been studying the maps so intently.

We wandered in the caverns for a long time. While we walked, Jancarlo told us his plan for re-introducing Heather to her old life. It was a good plan. It wouldn't take much work, and the simplest plans usually seemed to work out the best.

"Ella, can you tell us any more of what Eva was planning?" Jancarlo asked as he felt his way along rocky crags in the walls.

I held Ella's hand as we dipped around rock columns and under dripping archways. Ella had glazed eyes as she watched the passageway maps in Jancarlo's mind. "She has thirty rockmen like Bam Bam," she said. "They can all throw fire and are especially strong. She'd been hoping to empty the holding cells before she started the attack."

"At least we stopped her there," I said, pulling Ella gently around a wall.

"I don't know," Jancarlo said. "She has Wiki freed; he could follow up on any of her orders, and we're all going a million different directions."

"But Wiki can't transport in without being seen," Evelyn said.

As I walked Ella under an archway dripping with freezing cold water, I noticed the water cascading away from Ella's sides. I knew Evelyn was using her water moving powers to make the trek more comfortable for Ella.

"That's true," Ella said. "Which is why, she's left orders for Perry Anderson to march all those rockmen and whoever else he has down from the North Pole and wipe the Storm People off the planet. I think she figures Perry can set her free or the prisoners can hit us from behind or something. I know Wiki has orders to continue trying to free prisoners and get inside the base when all the fighting starts."

"Do we know if she's aware that we can all just transport up there and stop her?" I asked.

"Yes," Ella said. "She knows all of our capabilities and our plans and she's passed them along to Wiki, Perry and…others."

"I think," Jancarlo stopped and sighed, "that had we listened to Kin and Ella, she wouldn't know much of anything about us right now."

We all stopped. My stomach tightened. Ella must have ignored the images in Jancarlo's head in order to meet my eyes. But I didn't see any anger or malice, just sympathy. "It's just as much my fault," I whispered. "We're all too trusting."

"Well, Kin was right," Jancarlo said, resuming his pace. "I should have been more suspicious and more cautious. Kin will make a good leader someday."

"Trust is a good leadership quality too," Evelyn said.

"At least now we can contain the damage to the areas around the pole," Ella said, changing the subject. "We can't allow Eva's army to move into densely populated areas."

Jancarlo and Ella stopped walking at the same time.

"What is it?" Evelyn said.

I turned and held a finger to my lips. "They're probably getting a report from someone."

After a moment, our group began moving again.

"Kin said that the Canadians are going to supply cold weather gear from army supplies," Jancarlo said as they resumed walking.

"Sounds like Japan is pretty ticked about Kimi's kidnapping," Ella said. "Everyone seems to be taking it as a personal affront because she and Kin worked over there for so long before they came to America. They're sending some big names. They're dropping everything to come straight here and assist."

"Same with lots of other countries," Jancarlo continued. "It's a good thing the People of the Storm don't follow country politics. It sounds like we're going to have good numbers."

"And how are we supposed to use those numbers?" I asked.

"Kin and I will have to discuss it more," Jancarlo said.

It sounded like Jancarlo was going to expound on the thought, but Ella reached her hand out and stopped him.

"We're here," she whispered.

We silently turned a corner in the tunnels. The stone hallway yawned into an enormous cavern. It was at least as tall as our arena but only a fraction of the depth. My breath caught when I noticed thousands of baseball sized gems littering the floor of the smooth cavern. Then my eyes shifted to the walls to see thousands more embedded in the rock surrounding us.

Speckles of light sprang from all the different shapes and colors as if producing their own light. Some glowed with their own brilliance to give the cavern more light than anywhere we'd been so far. Each gem was at least as big as my fist with many of them much larger. The largest ones were as big as basketballs. All of them had been cut with jeweled facets, so they couldn't possibly be mistaken for naturally created gems.

Although the gems demanded the most attention, upon closer inspection, I could also see veins of multiple metals twisting through the rock. The walls and vaulted ceiling were a cacophony of mosaic colors made of rocks, metals and gems.

As I stared in awe at the glittering décor, Evelyn asked Ella, "Is this what you couldn't believe existed?"

"No."

I turned to her in surprise but saw her eyes fixed on a large mound in the far corner of the cavern. The corners of her mouth turned down in a frown. "He is," she said.

I followed her gaze and was about to inquire further when the small hill began to move. Any words I might have uttered stuck in my throat as I watched a small portion of the hill separate from the rest. An enormous triangular head on a long, thick neck rose from the floor and turned to face us.

He had two bright yellow eyes on either side of his snake-like head, so he had to turn to the side to see us. I couldn't see any front legs, but I could make out two powerful back legs. He had a long snout with wide nostrils on the front and a barbed frill ringed around the back side of his head, like a triceratops, but much sharper and probably more deadly. In the dark, I couldn't specify his color, but he seemed to match the gloom and dull greys from the passageways we had just come from. He opened his mouth into what I supposed to be a smile exposing sharp pointed teeth and a forked tongue with which he tasted the air. "You've come." He said it softly, but his deep voice shook the entire room.

"Good Heavens, Ella," Jancarlo whispered beside us. I muttered something much more profane under my breath. "I can understand you not believing in this."

"Many don't believe in my kind any longer, Jancarlo." The monster almost hissed his name.

Hearing his name must have shaken Jancarlo to his senses. It was a good thing too because I was still ready to pee my pants. He gave his head a small shake, and suddenly, in my mind I heard Jancarlo's voice. *Is he a danger to us?* he asked Ella.

I don't know, she answered honestly. *I can't read his mind.*

"You can't read my mind, young one," the being spoke up, "because I have hidden it from you. There are few who can do it, but I have the means and the training."

"Do you have something to hide?" Ella asked bravely. She didn't seem at all affected by the creatures' presence or ability to speak and read our minds.

"Everyone likes to have their own little secrets," he whispered with a small, punctuated growl I took for a chuckle. His forked tongue slid over his lips quickly. The question of whether or not he might eat us finally forced me out of the fear enveloping me. I had to be ready for action.

I'm sorry, Jancarlo, Ella said in our minds, *but you'll have to ask him your questions.*

Jancarlo gave a small bob of his head and cleared his throat. "Who are you?" he asked in a firm voice.

At this, the beast snarled in some strange language. Jancarlo turned at Ella for any help, but she just stared transfixed at the monster. Shaking her head slightly, she said, "I don't have a translation for that."

"Nor should you," the beast countered. "It is an ancient language for my kind and has never been uttered by humans. When this earth was still young, I was among the very few of us struck by lightning." He cocked his head slightly to see Ella. "Did you think you were the only creatures ever struck?" He allowed her a moment to think about it then turned his attention back to Jancarlo. "I gained the ability to speak and think unlike most of my kind, but no, that was not my power. I also gained the powers of seeing the thoughts of those around me. Mind-reading, as you call it."

"But what are you?" I asked in a shaky voice. I hoped he might be more willing to talk than eat.

His mouth opened to his savage smile again. I think he was trying to keep me afraid of him. Although we stood at least thirty yards away from him, I could see the serration on the edges of his teeth. "We were once a great and handsome race stretching across the whole of the earth. We were all different shapes, sizes, colors and, yes, powers. The humans, when they began, called us many things. Lizards, Fire-breathers, Death, Flying Snakes, Killers." Here he laughed again. "My personal favorite. Some even worshipped us as Kings and Gods. But today you would call us 'dinosaurs' to your modern scientists and 'dragons' to those who still believe. Your scientists have only scratched the surface of our extensive reign. Yet much of our existence has been obliterated for all time. There is no word in your language for what we call ourselves. The closest I can translate would be 'made-of-fire.'"

The four of us stood frozen in shock. Only Ella had had any inkling of what was in this cavern. I felt somewhat unnerved she hadn't shared this information. After our initial awe subsided, the creature finally said, "You are Ella, a fellow mind-reader." He nodded his head at her with reverence. "Liam, the light-shifter." I got a short bob. "Evelyn, the water-mover…and Jancarlo…." Here the monster hummed, "… the rock-mover."

"You know our names, sir," Jancarlo found his tongue again, "But you have yet to give us yours."

"Those who put me here called me Captus, but my surname is Onus."

"How did you come to be here?" Jancarlo asked. "And how do you know who we are?" It was good of him to keep his wits as mine had drained out from my feet.

Onus sighed, which was no small action. He filled the room with hot, steamy air and a small stream of smoke escaped from his nostrils. "One question at a time," he said slowly. This being seemed to do everything slowly, or was my mind working in slow motion? "You asked how I came to be here. I would tell you the tale, but, being the fateful creatures you are, you would die of old age or starvation before I could have done with it. It is a thrilling tale, to be sure. But it must suffice to say, I remain the last of my kind, imprisoned in this tomb and forgotten in order to witness the extinction of my race."

He growled deep in his throat, and the temperature in the room seemed to increase a few degrees. "As to how I know who you are, the woman who calls herself Eva told me much about you."

Hearing this, Jancarlo squared his shoulders and set his jaw. This must have been why Ella didn't know if the being in this room was dangerous or not. She didn't know his allegiances. "Are you her friend?" he asked.

"Friend?" Onus questioned.

"That is to say," Jancarlo tried again, "are you loyal to her and her cause?"

"I don't know about loyalty," Onus hemmed again. "She came to know of me from Devin Ross and sought me out for help. I gave her what I could."

"You gave her assistance in return for her trying to find something for you," Ella spoke up. Shockingly, her voice remained steady, unlike my knees. But her tone transcended steady. She was mad.

Onus finally started moving his body. As he inched across the stone floor, the sound of scraping metal echoed through the cavern. What I had presumed to be his body I now saw were folded wings with razor sharp, four-toed claws on the middle joint which he used to walk. When he was only ten yards in front of us, he lowered his head and narrowed an eye at Ella. I wanted to inch away from him back into the hallway from which we came, but it would look really bad at this point because Ella stood her ground defiantly under his sharp gaze. "Yes, there is something I desired."

"A gemstone."

Jancarlo's gaze bounced between Onus and Ella. "What gemstone?" he asked out loud.

"You know what stone I speak of, Jancarlo," Onus murmured as he turned his head to gaze at all the gemstones surrounding him. Jancarlo's eyes dropped. I knew Jancarlo pretty well. We could usually read each other like a book. He knew I had fallen for Ella before I said a word, and I could always see through any façade he put on for others. I could now see in his eyes his attempt to hide his awareness. Ella seemed completely non-plussed. She was hard to catch off guard. I, however, had no idea what was going on.

Apparently, neither did Evelyn. "Jancarlo," she said, "what's he talking about?"

When Onus could see Jancarlo would not help with the conversation, he continued. However, he turned to address Evelyn. "You have, no doubt, heard of stories that Draconis…"

"Dragons," Ella interrupted. She was brave to do so, but Onus just nodded in agreement. "It's Latin for 'dragon.'" She clarified for us.

"Yes, dragons." Onus nodded. "You have heard that we collect treasure." At this, Onus reached underneath his belly with a claw. Pulling it out, he revealed a half dozen gems in green, blue and white that had been tucked under his warm abdomen. "These are a few of those precious rocks I have been able to attain so far."

He rolled them on the floor in front of us. They glittered between us like we were going to play some sick game of dodgeball. Jancarlo hesitantly stepped forward to look at them, eyeing Onus all the while. After a few tentative steps, he bent down and picked up one of the largest white gems. It was the size of a cantaloupe with severe facets encompassing it. When Jancarlo picked it up, the stone glowed with a faint light while he passed his hand over the smooth surface.

Onus watched without enthusiasm and continued speaking. "The dumb animals you call 'dinosaurs' didn't do this, obviously, but those of us with intelligence made something of a habit of it. We put our powers into those very gemstones." He glared at Ella, and his eye twitched down to her bracelet. "Much like your decoration."

Jancarlo continued to examine the large gemstones. If I didn't know he had access to much the same thing by his own powers, I would have thought the gems fascinated him.

"Over time," Onus continued while watching Jancarlo, "we built vast stores of our powers for everyone's use. We even tried to teach the simple beasts how to use them but never to any avail. Eventually, as often happens with these things, some of our kind got greedy. They tried to obtain more than their share of the stones. This is where your stories come from.

"However," he hummed again, "there have been certain gems I have been searching for. And, yes, I have been asking Eva to help me acquire these gems."

"What would you use them for?" Jancarlo asked while putting the stone back down on the floor.

Onus rumbled deep in his throat and lowered his head to the floor. I could have sworn a smile touched his lips again. He pulled his other claw out from under him. Although empty, he extended it toward the gems on the ground much the way I would when shifting the light. The same piece Jancarlo had been holding flew into the waiting claw of the monster. He gazed hungrily at it. His rumble got louder and louder until it stopped suddenly. "Revenge," Onus whispered with a growl and shoved the gemstone into his mouth.

Onus sat up straight, touching the top of the cavern when stretched out. He spread his wings on both sides of him and roared, "I will seek out and destroy the murderers who put me in this cage!" The walls of the cavern quaked around us, and we all braced ourselves. "I will be Conqueror! Mors populo tempestatem!" He wailed.

Torrents of flame belched from his mouth, illuminating the gem-filled cavern and saturating us with heat. As he bellowed, the gemstones rooted in the rock rained down throughout the cavern along with the rock containing them. I heard Ella scream and saw Jancarlo with his hands over his head. I didn't know if Onus knew what he was doing or might mean us harm, so I threw my net over us. Unfortunately, I couldn't keep the chunks of rock and gem from cascading down on us. "Jancarlo!" I yelled over the tumult. "Call Heather to get us out of here!"

"I already have!" He yelled back. "I've lost my powers! I can't keep the rock away from us!"

We huddled together in the threshold to the cavern and watched in horror as Onus tore a hole in the ceiling above him. Without glancing back at us, Onus pressed his wings swiftly to the ground and his body lifted. The hole he'd created opened wide enough that light poured into the cavern, dazzling our eyes and making us squint away. When I chanced a peek back at the scene, Onus was already well into the shaft opened to the sky. Another moment and he vanished.

His absence, however, had no effect on the gems and rocks raining upon us. With Onus gone, we turned to escape the way we had come, but before we could, a large chunk of rock fell on Jancarlo, knocking him to the ground. Heather appeared just in time to take us back to the base before anything worse could happen. We lay panting in the front lobby as I tried to make sense of the things we had just experienced. To add to my confusion, chaos reigned around us. People were everywhere.

Heather fetched Gretchen for Jancarlo while Ella and I crouched over him protectively. "What did he say?" he asked Ella. I could see blood in his mouth and wished Gretchen would come faster. "Before he left, what did he say?" he repeated more harshly.

"Don't worry about that right now," she told him sternly. "We'll discuss it when you're better."

He raised his head up slightly and locked eyes with her. "Tell me," he said, his voice rasping.

Ella closed her eyes and took a deep breath. "Death to the People of the Storm."

Chapter SIXTEEN

Gretchen rushed into the lobby, pushing past Ella to grab hold of Jancarlo's hand. Ella stepped back, allowing Gretchen to take her place then collapsed on the floor behind her. She put her face in her hands, but I could see her shaking.

What have we done? She asked in my mind.

I couldn't answer her. My hands threatened to tremble like hers, but I attempted to pull myself together. The best way to get my mind straight was to get to work. So, I turned to Heather. "Where's Kin and Kimi?" I asked.

"Their group is still scouting. I took them as close as I could, but they still had to travel a ways, and they're trying not to give themselves away. We should hear something soon."

We looked back at Jancarlo as he sat up off the floor, seething in anger. Gretchen still had hold of his hand, but he turned on her. "What happened to my powers?" he snapped at her.

Gretchen put on a poker face. "Never mind the head trauma and internal bleeding," she answered coldly.

"It seems your powers were drained away somehow. They're returning now, slowly. It had to have been something much like Kathryn's powers."

Jancarlo nodded vigorously but kept his lips squeezed tightly together. "The gem you picked up?" I asked. Jancarlo glanced at me still nodding then turned back to Ella.

She nodded back. "It must have been what he needed to escape. He must have seen us coming."

"Did Eva know any of this?" I asked her. I didn't want to accuse her of anything, but I would have thought she might see it coming.

"No," She shook her head and wrapped her hands around it, dejected. "He never told her any of his plans. He must have known I would see them."

"Who?" Gretchen and Heather asked at the same time.

Jancarlo asked Gretchen, "are you done with me?" He forced himself to keep his voice a little gentler. She nodded back, not questioning the man she'd chosen to follow. Jancarlo got up from the floor once Gretchen removed her hand. "We need to re-group and…." He stopped suddenly, wide-eyed. He stared off into the distance, and I knew he was getting a report from Kin.

Ella gaped silently as she stood up next to him. She reached out to Jancarlo as if for support, but she wasn't looking at him. She glanced over at me. Just as I started to wonder, a vision filled my mind.

I saw Onus flying out of a crater in snow-covered ground announcing himself with a jet of fire. I could feel the terror in Kin's mind as the horror rose above the trees.

What is it?! someone next to him asked. Kin tore his eyes away from the deep emerald, green beast in the sky to the view in front of him on the ground. In the distance, the gigantic rockmen Eva had created stood still as a forest of statues, dozens of them. A few stared up into the sky at the monster. Two humans lingered in the middle of the army. I assumed they were Wiki and Perry because they were half the size of the monsters but not afraid of them in the slightest.

This thing came out of nowhere, Kin told Jancarlo. *It can't be a coincidence it showed up here, can it?*

It's not, Jancarlo answered him. *Onus is a new acquaintance of ours. He's out to destroy the Storm People, and he's working with the Shadow group. I'm guessing Perry is in charge now. Is there anything else we need to know?*

They're marching soon. We only have a couple hours, tops.

I'll send Heather for you. Come back and get everyone outfitted for the weather. Once he said it, Heather appeared beside Kin. *Thanks, Ella. Let's regroup and set up some strategies.*

Got it.

The connection ended, and Jancarlo gazed around. He beckoned Boris and Theresa over, two of the many people gathered in the lobby. "We need cold-weather gear for as many as possible. Would you be able to scrounge up some more for us?" They looked at each other sideways but nodded to him. "We'll replace or repay it all," he added. "Bring it to the arena."

Jancarlo turned his attention to the entire gathering of people. "Unless you have a specific assignment otherwise, to the arena! Gather anyone else along the way."

Only a few minutes later, we had all gathered as directed. As much as I had seen this area filled before when we fought the Shadow group in here, it still amazed me how many people could fit. About eighteen hundred Storm People had gathered from all over the world. We didn't bother meeting in the conference room as everyone needed to know the information. Leaders from the different parts of the world met with a small group of us in the middle of the arena and helped organize their own groups in sections of one hundred.

The Canadians had already supplied some cold weather gear which was being given out to the group leaders and others. While we provided details of the emergency we faced, more cold weather gear appeared in the corner of the arena. I wondered who obtained it, but Theresa appeared while I watched her whipping off her invisibility cap. It was a beret after the fashion of the French army, so I assumed it came from the European stores. She saw me notice the gear and said, "Don't ask, darling. Just say 'thank you.'" She threw what she was holding onto the pile, blew me a kiss, put her cap back on and disappeared. I took her suggestion and went to find myself some warm clothes.

Once I was geared up, I turned to find Jancarlo and Ella talking while Kin relayed more instructions to the group leaders. Evelyn had geared up next to me then brought a heavy coat and thick pants to Ella. I grabbed some that might fit Jancarlo. While donning the gear, Jancarlo and Ella discussed how best to use Bam Bam.

"Heather can transport him, but he could still be turned against us," Ella said. "I can take control of him and fight more effectively from within him."

"But you can't use your powers while you're in control of him," Jancarlo countered.

"I think it's more important to have his strength," she insisted. "We don't know if I'll be able to do anything against the others."

"Would you want to leave your body here for safety while you're in control of Bam Bam?" Jancarlo asked.

"No," Ella shook her head. "I'd have no means to get back into my body should something happen to Heather. I'll use my cap and keep my body close by."

"I'll help hide her," Evelyn said, "and watch over her body."

"This would sound like a really weird conversation if I didn't know what you were talking about." I said as I handed Jancarlo boots.

It seemed like it took forever for everyone to be outfitted and final strategies hammered out, but it was finally done. Everyone stood in fur-lined coats and boots, snow pants and gloves, except, of course, the fire starters and a few others.

"We'll have five groups of three hundred each coming in at five different angles." Kin repeated the instructions standing in front of the largest group. "The first three groups will keep the rockmen busy then the next group will reinforce one area to punch a hole through, allowing the remaining group of three hundred to go after

Onus. Hopefully the second groups won't be seen or expected.

"Do not underestimate these beings because we appear to have the numbers. There are thirty-five of them at last count and they might be able to make more. Bam Bam took on more than fifty of our people until Ella stepped in, so technically, it's an even fight here. Plus, they have this Onus creature now. We don't know what he's capable of yet. From the last report, he's at least capable of breathing fire, lifting objects and reading minds. That makes him our most formidable enemy. Use all means necessary to extinguish both Onus and the rockmen."

Once everyone had their marching orders, we prepared to transport to the Arctic.

The Americans opted, with Bam Bam's help, to go after Onus because he was our responsibility. We had a group of two hundred with an additional fifty from Canada and fifty from Russia being our closest neighbors. Nathaniel was especially excited to have the ring off his neck to focus his energies on other beings. He didn't get to practice it often. Usually if he could focus the lightning he attracted, then he could keep it away from those he didn't want harmed. In this case, he would be focusing on Onus. Although we weren't sure if he would be able to do any damage, if nothing else, it would be a distraction. He would be keeping his ring attached to his belt in the hopes that we would be successful in defeating Onus and he could put the ring back on immediately.

The five groups transported to their places, using Heather's knowledge and Kin and Kimi's strategies for the best placement. They surrounded their target from different angles and spread out a mile from the rockmen. Each group had numerous powers at their disposal to use however they deemed essential. Our group transported in last and closest to the scene. Once Ella was in place overseeing the battleground, with Evelyn at her side, the rest of our group huddled nearby. Jancarlo, Bam Bam, myself and the others anxiously awaited our turn to act, spotting our target almost immediately. Ella from her vantage point would coordinate the attack, along with Jancarlo and Kin, for the time being.

Onus paced in a small circle in the midst of the massive stone giants. He was large enough that he seemed only slightly taller than the rockmen when on all fours, but we knew better. The ground where he paced was void of all snow and steaming in the cold dusk of the day. Wiki and Perry watched him from a cautious distance.

At the moment Ella passed on word from Jancarlo for the fighting groups to move in, the rockmen suddenly stood as one, as if at attention. Seemingly without being told, they faced the angles we would be coming from in groups of five or six. Without any word or signal, they charged toward our people.

Chapter SEVENTEEN

Ella, watching through other peoples' eyes, warned everyone to be on the defensive then large groups began transporting into the fight. All we could do for a few minutes was watch in torture. Group One, on the north, seemed to be doing okay when they first entered the battle. Boris had transported three hundred people at once smack into the center of the fight. He had argued for transporting all of us at once straight onto Onus's back, but we had scant knowledge of Onus and his fighting abilities, so the idea had been rejected. Group One, however, quickly took down one rock man by melting his feet with fire then cooling the melted rock into puddles. They did the same with another two, then three more giant rockmen. I started to wonder if Boris knew more than I realized.

My attention veered from Group One when I saw Group Three, the group coming from the south-west, quickly overtaken by the rock army. They had been confined to transporting in groups of twenty. If it had gone as planned, we would have had the element of surprise on our side, but the fact the enemy had been alerted worked against Group Three. I watched as many people I had known personally from the European Storm People were thrown hundreds of feet into ice and rocks or stomped on by the rock giants.

Once they had their feet under them, Groups Two and Four tried a couple of different tactics. Group Two went specifically for the legs of the giants. They used lifters to pull the legs off while the fire throwers burned at the giants' heads. Group Four had several strong men like Tony jump onto the giants. But instead of bashing at the giants' heads, they wrapped themselves around their necks and pulled, twisted or flipped to decapitate them. Unfortunately, their animation must have originated in their bodies, because the headless creatures kept moving.

As the giant bodies swung massive arms across the ground, the Storm People were tossed aside like dolls, either flying dozens of feet into the air and coming down with a sickening crunch in the snow or being thrown into another giant. Sometimes the lifters, like Jacob who could lift anything with their minds, could catch their friends, but that took their attention away from stopping the giants.

Blood quickly splattered the area as evidence of the horrific confrontation. My stomach threatened to churn as I watched. All the People of the Storm from around the world had donated their stocks of healing stones for the fight. Gretchen, Sheila and twenty other healers ran from person to person healing as quickly as they could, but many they couldn't reach in time.

Rather than watch in agony at the lives being lost around us, I turned to assist Ella, with Evelyn close at her side. Ella should've been searching for somewhere to hide her body when and if the time came to take control of Bam Bam, but, like me, couldn't tear her eyes away from the suffering around us. Experience dictated the need to force her to focus. I grabbed her by the shoulders and turned her to face me. Her eyelashes glistened. "We can't do this," she said, her bottom lip trembling, but I stared at her sternly.

"We can. We will," I said. She turned her head back to watch the fighting, completely distracted from the assignment at hand, so I scanned the landscape around us to find a spot for her body to wait. Evelyn also eventually shook herself from her stupor to help us search for a good place.

Behind us about twenty yards, a piece of lumpy ground protruded more than the expanse around it. During the warmer weather, it probably housed hardy plants or bushes but now lay snuggled in blankets of snow like everything else. A large slab of ice stuck out at a strange angle next to it protectively so I figured it might protect Ella as well.

Pointing it out to mother and daughter, we made our way toward it while trying to ignore the screams and yells behind us. Ella could only nod weakly before turning back to watch the fighting. She might have been watching through other peoples' minds or waiting to relay directions from Jancarlo, but I knew the fighting was in too much force for her to be of much use at this point. Plus, I had lived through enough wars in my time to know better than to watch too closely. Evelyn, focusing her attention on the proposed site, reached out her hand, and the snow and ice formed a small cave for Ella to lie down in.

I turned to see Ella still watching the fighting going on and pursed my lips in frustration. I took hold of her shoulders and turned to stare into her eyes again. Evelyn stepped toward us, but I held up my hand to stop her. I would not allow her to interrupt while I said what might be a good-bye.

As I put my hand back on Ella's shoulder, I wrapped my net around the two of us. Doubling over my net, I closed out all sound and sight from everything else around us. We were alone. Just two people in a rugged land of white.

"Ella," I said gently. I needed to make her understand her importance. I wanted to tell her how much I cared for her, but this wasn't the time. I needed to impress upon her the need to be careful, but at the same time, I didn't want her to be frightened. I needed her to be strong and powerful but cautious too. I had only one emotion left to promote. "Remember the time when the Shadow attacked the base?" She nodded, her lip quivering, but I plowed ahead. "Remember how you felt when you saw Kimi get hurt?" I knew how powerful she had realized she was at that moment. I needed *that* Ella back now. Immediately her lip stopped quaking, and she set her jaw, but her eyes still swam, being overwhelmed with the atrocities. "Onus is going to try to do a lot worse," I said. "Not just to Kimi, to everyone. You can help stop him."

She swallowed and blinked. I could visibly see her shaking off her fear. She nodded. "I never wanted you to see me get angry like that again," she said.

"I trust you," I said, giving her half a grin, "even when you're angry." I leaned down to her and kissed her, not knowing when I would be able to do it again. I gave us both a moment to savor it.

She forced a grin and reached into her back pocket. Pulling the flat cap out, she said, "Let's do it." All evidence of a quiver in her voice disappeared.

I gave her a wink. "That's my girl."

I released her from my net so Evelyn and I could watch her sit down on the ground behind the rock. She squeezed her mother's hand, and they had what must have been a short, silent conversation. Releasing Evelyn's hand, Ella put the cap on her head and disappeared.

Before I could tear myself away, Evelyn surprised me by calling me. "Liam," she said, then met my eyes, "I'm sorry."

I hesitated, waiting for her to continue.

"I've had a hard time trusting you," she said. "I should have listened to you, and I should have trusted your feelings for her." She took a deep breath. "I'll watch over her. I promise."

I watched Bam Bam and Jancarlo run forward, leading our group into the fight. Without turning back to Evelyn, I said, "So will I."

I ran back over to our group. My pep-talk had incited my determination as well. Meeting Jancarlo at the front, he asked, "Is Ella squared away?"

"Aye." I nodded.

While I had been helping Ella, Jancarlo watched for any strategic openings to get to Onus. Onus had two rockmen hanging back from the fighting to guard their ferocious leader, but he seemed unperturbed by the goings on. Jancarlo informed me we would have to make our own way to the demon. After a moment, Bam Bam, or Ella, I guess, approached to hover over us. Our own rock-giant had a chunk of his head missing in back from our first battle with him and no mouth to speak. Ella had once told me she didn't know if she would be able to speak even if he did have a mouth, so we never bothered to try to give him one.

Jancarlo looked up at the twelve-foot monster and said, somewhat skeptically, "Ella?"

The giant gave us a thumbs-up. This was only the second time I had ever seen Ella in Bam Bam's body, but I doubted I would ever feel comfortable with it. She spared me a glance but looked quickly back at Jancarlo and jerked her thumb in the direction of Onus.

"Yes, Ella," he told her and everyone else loudly, "It's time."

With a deafening scream of passion I hadn't known Jancarlo to possess, he led the charge into the fray. I had always been inspired by Jancarlo and his ability to rouse people when there was a need, but that was usually with words. He was naturally eloquent and extremely level-headed, so when he made a suggestion, folks wanted to follow his advice. I didn't know until that moment he could also incite others to combat with a single, guttural cry.

Jancarlo raised our group out of their seats and into the fight, but Ella quickly took the lead with the long strides of her oversized host. It was like watching Tony as a full-back barreling down a field. Apparently, the other rockmen didn't have any technique programmed into them. They simply tried to grab at everyone they saw and punch them or smash them into the ground or stomp on them. Ella could change tactics and fight on a different level. Every time one of the rockmen got in her way, she slammed her shoulder into them, tossing them out of the way. Where our people had been getting thrown ridiculous distances by the goliaths, the tables finally turned. It was the giants turn to feel the freedom of flying. Ella happily assisted.

As we ran into the fight, I noticed a blur of fiery red sweeping into my vision. The color clashed terribly with the gore soaking the ground. As if she had heard me, Theresa stopped, pausing in her efforts for a moment. She noticed our group coming out of our hiding place and focused directly on me. Her face formed a scowl I had only seen on a few occasions. Often right before she would give up on a situation as lost. I thought surely she wouldn't leave in the middle of a crisis such as this. But as I thought it, she softened her eyes and instantly disappeared. Setting my shoulders, I would not allow Theresa's abandonment to dictate my feelings about our efforts.

Our group followed in Ella's wake, trying to keep up until she jumped high in the air kicking her legs and flailing her arms to stabilize herself. All I could do was watch as she sailed some fifty feet in the air over the group of people in front of her, landing in a crouch between Onus's two bodyguards. I threw my hand out in front of me hoping to give her an advantage. Before she launched her attack on the enemy, she disappeared.

While Ella single-handedly and invisibly engaged the two defenders, we continued running towards her as fast as our legs could carry us. After a few more steps, Heather appeared out of nowhere in front of Jancarlo and me, making us stop short. She cocked her head to the side staring like she had caught an interesting bug in a jar. "Why are you running?" she asked. She had learned to move so quickly in the short time she had her powers, so much so that before I knew what was happening, she had taken hold of both of us and transported us right next to Onus.

As soon as he saw us, which didn't take long, he reared back his head and opened his maw. I saw a bubbling fireball develop in his throat just before Heather transported us behind him. I watched in horror as he melted a hole in the snow thirty yards in front of him. Ella had been a hair's breadth away from the fireball, but I assumed the fire didn't hurt her too badly because I could sense her under my net as she continued without interruption to fight the two giant rockmen.

I was about to cover our small group in my net, but in an instant, I decided to throw a separate net over Onus. I doubled it back again and again, closing off to the beast most sense of sight, sound and, with any luck, even smell. I alone could hear him raging from the sensory deprivation. He continued to rampage, tearing at his head with his razor-sharp claws and his whip-like tail, fighting the enemy of his own mind. Suddenly a familiar crackle stirred the air. Nathaniel had joined us.

The rest of our group caught up to us as thick clouds hung like molten lead over our heads. Resounding lightning bolts hissed down from the clouds striking the magnificent brute surprisingly accurately, seeing as the monster was invisible to him.

Unfortunately, the lightning was nothing more than a glancing blow, and the monster continued his blind rampage. I realized the longer I held him in my net, the more damage he would unknowingly do. Everyone, Storm People and rockmen alike, who tried to get close got brushed aside by a sweep of his tail or a swipe of his claw.

The rest of the battle fared just as badly. All of the groups had been fully deployed. Everywhere, the People of the Storm fell to the giants they fought. Group One had been able to take down six of them quickly, but it was taking more of them than they could spare to keep the giants from fighting their way back to standing. If a group was lucky enough to break one of the giants into pieces, those pieces would writhe around and continue to harm our people. We knew of no conceivable way to destroy the monsters, so we just persisted to clash.

The fighting had, at first, pushed the rockmen back against their ferocious leader. But with Onus swinging around so much, the fight again spread out over the length of a few football fields.

I watched the fighting, not knowing what else I could do. Keeping Onus at bay or Ella hidden were the best options right now. While I struggled with the idea of letting them go and trying to attack one of the giants myself, a familiar man solidified in front of me.

I knew his blonde, wavy hair anywhere, but the anguish on his face didn't match the way I remembered him. Wiki was usually so jovial. It had been too late when I realized he used the joking demeanor to mask his true feelings of pain. These were the emotions he displayed when he appeared in front of me. "Liam," he whispered to me. His hands hung slack at his side, so I assumed he wasn't much of a threat. He opened his mouth to speak and then closed it again thinking better of it. Pursing his lips, he swallowed his pride. He held out his hand to indicate Onus. "This isn't what I wanted."

"Then help us stop this monster!" I pleaded with him.

"No one can stop him," he said with disgust.

He was trying to apologize, and I imagined he must be terrified to find himself under the rule of this dreadful being. I didn't move my hands because they were busy, but I made sure to keep eye contact with him. "We were friends once, weren't we?"

He gave a small nod.

"I can understand why you were so angry last time you joined the Shadow. I get your feelings about Kimi's rejection," I confided to him. "I would feel the same way if it was me and Ella." I tried to catch his eyes again, "But you're a better man than this Wiki." I shook my head. "We don't wish you any harm."

He finally met my eye. "Nor I, you." After another moment's pause, he nodded back to me, "Good-bye, Liam. Run while you can." And he disappeared in mid-run.

I couldn't find any fault with Wiki for leaving. No one would know whose side he was on at this point, even if he did fight with us. He had always watched out for himself. He knew his best bet was to sit back and wait for the fighting to end. We had had some good times together in the past. I hoped he would find happiness someday if we all lived through to whatever came next.

Whatever might happen, I didn't have time to dwell on it. Immediately after Wiki disappeared, I felt hot breath on my cheek and heard a whisper in my ear, "I, however, don't hold your comrade's sentiments." I turned slightly to see Perry Anderson addressing me. "I wish all of you self-righteous, self-proclaimed immortals would just DIE!" he yelled at my face.

I flinched away, but he landed a solid kick in my gut. For lack of concentration, I had to release my net from the rest of our group but I made sure to keep my separate nets over Ella and Onus while I sparred with Perry. We exchanged blows with speed and agility, but mine seemed delayed as I concentrated on keeping my nets in place. I stretched the net that covered Ella over myself as well, in time to avoid a jet of fire from Perry. He was trained with fatal skill. I couldn't measure up to him physically. Ella and Kimi always claimed I was too easy on people I fought. I never liked to hurt anyone, and it wasn't something I could hide. Today was a little different. I fought to protect my people. I had a reason to end those who opposed me. I didn't relish, in any way, the idea of ending someone's life, but if Perry had his way, he would end mine. I had more determination than ever before, and it showed as my little trick gave me the upper hand over Anderson.

In a rage, he swung wildly trying to find me and eventually connected. Stumbling, but keeping myself oriented, I kicked at Perry's ankles. He fell and I stood over him to deliver a fatal blow. Out of nowhere, I felt a thud and my head was knocked forward. One of Onus's claws swung over me as pain blossomed in the back of my skull and I tumbled over Perry, who knelt in front of me. Landing on the flat of my back, invisible or not, he could feel me, and I was all but blacked out. The world around me spun furiously, my vision faltering. I lay staring blankly up at the sky in front of a man who had sworn to kill all my people. My net came off me, and whatever else I had been doing with it ended as well, but I couldn't remember what that had been.

Perry smiled an evil grin down at me. He put both his hands in front of himself over my face. I saw a bright red scar on his wrist indicating he had recently been shocked and gained new powers. I wondered briefly if I might black out as his upside-down face faded and clarified. I thought maybe if I did pass out I wouldn't feel what was going to happen, but I was wrong. My mind came into sharp focus as my body was engulfed in white hot flames. All I could do was scream in agony and attempt to roll around to get out of the fire, but 'stop-drop-and-roll' doesn't work in these situations. The flames chased me as much as I tried to evade them. Perry screamed with maniacal laughter.

As I thought I must succumb to the pain, the flames disappeared along with my executioner. I was burnt over every inch of my body and couldn't see Ella/Bam Bam standing over me for just an instant. The enchanted flames Perry conjured had ignored my clothing and gone straight through to my flesh. In the back of my mind, I could understand why he might not want to waste the time burning my clothes before he could torture my skin, but I wished the snow on which I lay had direct access to me. I wasn't aware of anything happening around me until a gigantic rock hand plopped Gretchen down on the ground next to me.

Ignoring my groaning, which Gretchen was good at, she put her hand on my forehead. The pain immediately ceased in that spot. The pain subsided as if she poured a soothing ointment over me from head to toe. Ella watched for a moment before Gretchen, not fully concentrating on her, said, "He'll be ok. Go help the others."

After another minute of the soothing feeling spreading over my body, I could focus on the needs at hand. Gretchen pulled her hand off my head and told me sternly, "More needs to be healed, but you're stable now. Be careful." With those last words she ran off to help someone else.

I staggered off the ground and took stock in the commotion around me. Onus, now free of my restriction, flew above the battle grounds loosing torrents of flame on unsuspecting victims. Many human lives were being lost while only a dozen of the rockmen had been taken to pieces enough for them to stop twitching. Tony stood over one of these, using the remains as missiles to take on the rest of its companions. Jacob helped him by making sure they hit their mark with as much force as possible.

But as hard as our people fought, Onus and his men were stronger, and Onus did not appear susceptible to most of our powers. Whenever Tony or Jacob or anyone else would try to launch something at Onus, it would invariably deflect away from him mid-flight. Whenever lightning was thrown at him, he seemed to almost enjoy it. Seeing as he was "made from fire," the fire starters and throwers were completely ineffective. So they had mostly resigned themselves to keeping Onus's flames off our people.

Kin and Kimi had, early on in the fight, realized their inability to affect Onus so had turned their attentions to the rockmen. They used blasts of flame to light the rock on fire, but it was going as quickly as burning a rock would go. In one or two situations, they successfully melted the rock and turned the rockmen's legs into lava, but it took so long that they exhausted themselves. Besides that, whomever the giant decided to attack would also get caught in the flames unless they could work their fires around the other person. It was a tricky business.

Despite the best efforts of every one of the eighteen hundred Storm People who had come to the barren arctic waste, our people's blood covered the ground. Mangled bodies lay scattered like hideous debris. Bile rose in my throat as I saw how many people we had lost. The healers were having a tough time keeping up with the injuries. Our numbers dwindled rapidly, but we continued to fight with ferocity well after the sun had gone down.

Getting back into the fight, I gave anyone the advantage when I could. Mostly, I kept my net over Ella so she could take on the monsters without being seen. It seemed to help for a while. The tides of the battle would ebb and flow. When I thought we were gaining ground, we would quickly lose it again. Then once I would think all hope was lost, we would take down more of the giants and hope would be restored.

Onus began resorting to snagging individuals and ripping them apart in front of us. He got away with it a few times before the transporters figured it out. A few of them tried to get the others out before they could be hurt, but the transporters were torn apart as well. Once, a transporter named Sam had gotten a woman out, (I hadn't known who she was) but as soon as they solidified on the ground, they realized they had both been partly torn in half through their torsos. Luckily, a healer had gotten there soon enough to repair the damage.

Onus finally swooped down out of the sky and landed with an earth-shattering crash directly in front of Jancarlo. "You are their leader! Aren't you?" I couldn't hear or see if Jancarlo tried to answer, but it didn't matter as Onus drowned out his voice with a booming roar. "You will all die!" he bellowed in Jancarlo's face. Without another word, Onus thrust his right winged claw at Jancarlo and drew him into the other one. With a moist crack and a gush of blood, he tore Jancarlo in half and flung the bottom half away. He released a jet of flame at the top half, engulfing the remains in his claw. When he closed his mouth, ash slipped through his claw.

Chapter EIGHTEEN

I stared in utter shock, unable to accept the fact that Jancarlo was gone. He had been my friend and confidante as well as my leader. He had helped give my life purpose when I felt I had nothing left in the world. He had introduced me to the American People of the Storm and helped me find my place among them. I couldn't believe such a powerful man and meaningful life could be snuffed out so effortlessly.

"NO!" I screamed at the top of my lungs. I lunged forward at Onus with all the strength left in my limbs, abandoning those I had been currently protecting.

I was not alone. I heard others doing the same thing. Screaming foul oaths, dozens of us converged on Onus at the same time. For a split second, I thought with our combined outrage we might have a chance against the fiend, but before we could come within fifty feet of him, who should appear before us but Eva Winford herself. In her shadow loomed Rosa Gomez, her sister, Roy Simms, master of illusion, Jack, deadly metal mover, and Aaron Parker, lifter, transporter and fire thrower in one. The prisoners that had previously been in the cells beneath the Storm People's base stood in front of us with Eva holding the supposedly secret transportation rock she had used when she disappeared with Perry Anderson before.

Eva glared at me with a wicked smile, her lip curling back over her teeth. With what might have been considered a beautiful face, she mangled it into a snarl before she loosed her flames at me. I dove to the side to avoid them at the same time wrapping myself and Ella back in my net. The fight seemed to start all over again.

I don't know how long it dragged on, but it seemed like the carnage would never end. I was locked in a fight with Rosa Gomez when suddenly the ground beneath us became unstable. As the earth shook, I tried to determine if she had anything to do with it, but she seemed just as unsure. We tottered around trying to keep our footing. I surveyed the area for the source of the quaking. I looked at Ella who had stopped her fight with one of the rock monsters as well. She widened her eyes and I couldn't figure out if it was good or bad. She pointed to the horizon with one of her massive rock fingers.

I scanned the area where she indicated just as a dozen large helicopters rose into view. The markings on them signified that they were from Canada and America, six of each. Everyone stopped fighting and cheered as they watched the birds fly purposefully into the fray. As they got closer, I noticed someone with fiery red hair that whipped unchecked around her head. A moment before I realized who it was, Theresa materialized right next to me.

"Vonce again," she threw her hands into the air, "I have come to save de day!" She reached over and squished my cheeks together. "Do you love me, or do you love me?" she asked in her thick Russian accent.

"How did you....?" I stuttered out. "Who did you...?"

"I told you your president vas a lovely man." She winked at me. "Not half as good as you are, my dear, but I think I shall vork vit' him some more all de same."

I watched as our rescuers launched a volley of missiles at the rock giants. The shots hit their marks. Onus was down to only twenty rock giants, but we were still easily outmatched. The helicopters fired again and took down five more instantly. Again, they fired, neutralizing five more.

I couldn't help myself. I knew Ella was just as grateful, so I grabbed Theresa's face and planted a big kiss on her lips. "I knew you loved me!" she yelled into the air triumphantly as she disappeared. I spotted her back in the lead helicopter a moment later, and she flew off with them to finish off the enemy.

The rest of the Storm People retreated from the giants as they were attacked from the air. Onus watched as the helicopters obliterated five more of his army, but he only bellowed his belligerence and vaulted into the sky. I thought surely he would circle around to rend the choppers from the sky, but he kept moving into the distance. I watched him, waiting for the moment his wrath would sweep the enemy away, but he didn't come back. Like all evil, he abandoned those that stood by him.

I surveyed the scene to see the helicopters fire again at the giants. I wonder what the pilots must think of the exhibition they had come upon, but if they met

Theresa, then nothing else could come as too much of a shock. Firing again, the giants were down to five. The choppers had obliterated the giant's comrades, and their remains didn't even have enough strength to move.

Eva had also seen Onus leave them. She screamed in anguish as the military choppers mowed down her creations. From fifty yards away, she met my gaze with her own raging, malicious eyes. The next moment, I watched as she hurled herself into the path of an incoming missile headed for one of her giants. I knew she was fireproof to some extent, but no one could survive such a blast. Pieces of rock and debris skittered across the field.

Most of the giants stood their ground, throwing fire or fists at the aircraft, which our people nimbly deflected. But once Eva's army had been blasted down to three, I started to wonder if Theresa had told the pilots not to harm Ella. I saw Ella, in Bam Bam's body, running away from the scene and toward her body. I wasn't sure just how long she would need to get back into her body so I chased after her to help her if need be.

Unfortunately, one of the choppers gave chase to Ella as well. I could barely see the pilot inside, and I knew even if I tried to signal to him, he wouldn't be able to hear me. I threw my net over Ella again, knowing if the pilot fired in her direction, she would be hit anyway. For a second, time stood still. I waited to see if the pilot would fire as I sensed Ella hidden underneath my net, although she wasn't moving anywhere. I continued running towards her when, thankfully, the chopper suddenly maneuvered away from the area.

I tried to breathe again and ran up to the rock giant. I removed my net and stared up at the twelve-foot behemoth. It still intimidated me. "Ella?" I questioned. No response. Suddenly the air broke with a blood-curdling scream coming from the spot where I knew Ella's body to be. The last time she had tried to come out of Bam Bam's body, she had screamed for a few minutes when she did it. "Bam Bam," I yelled up to him, "stay here." He gave me a sharp bob of his head in acknowledgement.

I ran around the rock that jutted out over Ella while her screaming subsided. She wasn't screaming as loud or as long as the first time, so I harbored a hope that it didn't hurt as much this time. Evelyn sat behind Ella with her arms wrapped around her daughter. The ice cave had been moved away to allow more room. I scrambled to her side as she opened her eyes, panting for breath. "That is….very….disorienting," she stuttered out between shaky breaths.

"Are you okay?" I asked, taking her hand.

"Yes," she nodded back at me. She sat up and took a few deep breaths to steady herself. "I figured it was safer in my own body about now."

"Good timing."

I was about to explain to her about the misguided pilot when Heather appeared next to us. She looked at me seriously. "Kin needs you." She turned to Ella and added, "Both of you."

"Ella, are you up for it?" I asked.

"Wait," Evelyn barked, grabbing Ella's hand and yanking her away from Heather. "She was almost blown up by those helicopters. Now Jancarlo wants more?"

"Jancarlo's dead," Heather mumbled.

"Exactly," Evelyn muttered. "If a man as strong and experienced as Jancarlo can't survive, how can he ask children to put themselves in danger?"

"Mom," Ella snapped. "This is my job. I need to help."

"You're only sixteen," Evelyn pressed. "They shouldn't be asking anything of you. Either of you," she gestured to Heather. "Definitely not asking you to put yourself in this much danger."

"Mom," Ella gentled her voice. "We don't exactly live the normal lives of teenagers, do we? I've seen too much. Not just in my life, but in the minds of others. I've experienced far more than you or Jancarlo or Liam or anyone. You need to trust that we are capable and know what we're doing. That's the only reason Jancarlo or Kin would rely on us at all. They trust us. Can you?"

"We're saving lives," Heather whispered.

"Besides," Ella said, placing her hand on Heather's shoulder as I did the same on the other side. "I love you, Mom, but you couldn't stop either of us anyway."

A moment later we stood outside the battlefield next to Kin, Jacob and Tony.

The choppers, having finished their work, headed back to their bases. No doubt their excursion would be written off as a training exercise of some sort. I knew one of the Canadian Storm People was a general and pulled strings like that all the time.

"Where's Kimi?" I asked Kin.

"Helping clean up." Kin indicated the field. Where he gestured, I could see Kimi walking around in the mushy, blood-soaked field burning debris. Adam, the water mover, was covering the charred ground with fresh snow. At another time it would've been fascinating to watch the mini blizzard following him around. "Heather, would you mind collecting Evelyn. I imagine Adam could use her help."

"Of course," she said and was gone.

"I'm proud of everyone," Kin said, as we watched the activity going on around us. Gretchen, Sheila and a host of other healers continued working to heal people. As they were healed, groups formed, and everyone was taking account of their remaining numbers or helping clean up the mess. The American People of the Storm slowly congregated around Kin.

"What did you do with Jancarlo?" I asked quietly.

I knew it would evoke strong feelings in everyone. Jancarlo had been the leader of our people for almost forty years. Everyone here knew him very well, and we were all loyal to his memory.

"We thought it disrespectful," he answered me quietly, "to drag around half of his body." As he said it, I could see the tears filling his eyes. "So, Kimi and I burnt the bottom half." He stuck his chin out and ground his teeth together fighting back emotion as he usually did. He gave a loud sniff then added, "We'll have a memorial later. For everyone."

By unspoken consent, we observed a moment of silence, dwelling on the fate of our fallen leader. Ella closed her eyes, and a silent tear slid down her cheek.

After a minute, Kin cleared his throat and said a little more firmly, "We still have work to do." He addressed everyone standing nearby. "Jancarlo knew as well as any of us the threat Onus poses. We can't stop until that threat is neutralized. For now, let's focus on cleaning up then re-group back at the base."

Cleaning up wasn't a fun ordeal. Heather brought supplies back from the base, and I kept track of those we still retained. Out of the eighteen hundred Storm People that had transported up here, we had lost seven hundred and thirty-nine. Unfortunately, most of the casualties were from the other groups around the world. The Americans had either fought the rock giants before or had trained with Bam Bam so we had more experience with the foe. Most of the Storm People lost had been those with lesser powers. They had simply been outmatched.

Out of our initial three hundred who tried to take on Onus, we had only lost twenty. That was mostly due to the efforts of Gretchen and Sheila, with Heather transporting them. They had done a spectacular job of keeping everyone healed, for the most part.

The most gruesome part of the task was trying to account for the human enemies. We found most of the remains of Eva and knew she wouldn't be back to take her revenge again. Kimi seemed to savor burning those remains.

We found Perry's body some two hundred feet from the fighting. Ella must have hit him pretty hard to send him that far. We approached cautiously, wondering if he was still alive, but when we got close enough, we saw the gore from his head on the cold ground underneath him.

Aaron Parker and Jack had also been killed. It seemed they had been overwhelmed by our people. They never even had a chance.

As for Rosa, she had fallen apart in hysterics when her sister had been blown apart by the choppers. She was sobbing on the ground on her knees. She made no attempt to get away nor to harm anyone, so Kin had Migan and a few others from security watching her. As we cleaned up around her, she sat in the frozen snow with her face in her hands. At least her shoulders had stopped convulsing.

While the fire throwers went about their work with water movers following them, Ella and I approached Kin. "What's going to happen to her?" I asked him, gesturing to Rosa.

"I'm not sure." Kin shook his head. "Suggestions?" he asked.

"We should heal her," Ella spoke up. "She just wants to forget everything that's happened. Her sister dragged her into all this because of her love for Devin Ross. Rosa wants to go back to a normal life without all the supernatural chaos."

"She'll always know about us," I put in. "She might try to forget, but hatred has a way of festering."

"She's not much of a threat." Kin pointed out. "All she can do is block powers. She's a tough fighter, but that's about it. And if she's healed of her powers, that threat goes away."

"But she knows all about us." I insisted. "She can't just be turned loose with that kind of knowledge."

"I might be able to change that," Ella almost whispered while she found a profound interest in the snow by her boot.

"What do you mean?" I asked soberly.

"I was working with Gretchen once, and she made the suggestion that I might try to see if I was capable of such a thing…removing memories from someone…permanently." She finally met Kin's bewildered eyes. "I haven't had someone to try it on yet." She watched Rosa sitting in the snow. "I think if I approached her about it right now, she'd be perfectly willing."

Kin came out of his reverie. He took a deep breath. "Go talk to her about it then," he said.

Without looking back, Ella approached Rosa.

Kin stepped closer to me and said in a low tone, "I take it you weren't aware of this either?" I shook my head. "I wonder how many of us are capable of so much more than we realize. I think we should devote some resources to helping our people realize their full potential."

I nodded agreement. "But in the meantime," I said, "we still have a dragon to deal with."

We got everyone cleaned up, healed up, warmed up and transported back, all before morning, collapsing in exhaustion just as the sky grew a lighter shade of blue. We were allowed to grab a few hours of sleep, but Kin requested myself, Ella, Tony, Kimi, Gretchen, Heather and Jacob to meet back in the conference room at 0900 sharp. The group leaders from around the world had offered their assistance to Kin and our group, should we need it, to detain Onus. Kin told them he would certainly keep their numbers handy.

At 0855 we dragged ourselves down the hallway. I realized Evelyn hadn't necessarily been invited, but I knew she would be coming all the same. None of us had bothered to shower. Evelyn hadn't even complained when I crashed on their couch rather than walk all the way back to my room. She even tossed me a blanket.

We shuffled into the conference room and saw everyone else had the same idea. Minus the parkas, we all wore yesterday's clothing. The adrenaline from the night before had left our bodies and minds drained, but the reality of the danger we still had to face sobered us quickly.

"I've been thinking about this," Kin started once we all sat down. He stood at the head of the table in Jancarlo's place and seemed perfectly comfortable there. "Wiki is the only person left that spent time with Onus and might have some insight. We need to find him."

"That's easy enough," Heather spoke up. "I just need a picture of him." Her eyes glanced up, as I assumed Ella put a picture of him in her head, then she nodded slightly. "I can find him."

"Good," Kin said. "Liam, go with her. You probably know him best." I nodded my consent. Kin added, "Go now. We have other business to attend to here, but that's the most pressing matter."

We stood up to leave, but before I left the room, Ella said in my mind, *I'll most likely be working with Rosa while you're gone. Good luck.*

You too. I answered back.

Chapter NINETEEN

Heather and I stepped into the lobby, the only place where security measures had been temporarily lifted. I put my hand on her shoulder, throwing my net over the pair of us at the same time. I felt the all-too-familiar sensation of breathlessness before we solidified in a bright bedroom with a window view of a white beach.

"Where are we?" Heather whispered so quietly I barely heard her.

I inspected the blue walls and slowly rotating ceiling fan. We were obviously at some sort of tropical resort. The sun blazed through the window, and the salty smell coming from the ocean outside was overwhelming. "Definitely somewhere Wiki would disappear to," I whispered back, "But where is he?"

In answer to my question, a toilet flushed behind a white door in front of us. The water ran as someone washed their hands, and I held my finger to my lips to keep Heather silent. I stepped to the side of the door, situating Heather behind my back.

The door swung open and Wiki stepped out. Wearing a Hawaiian shirt with large hibiscus flowers and swimming trunks, he was obviously looking forward to a long vacation.

"Hello, Wiki." I said without pulling my net off.

Wiki stopped dead in his tracks. "Liam?" he asked scanning the room.

I pulled the net off myself but left it on Heather. I opened my mouth to speak, but Wiki disappeared from in front of me. I sighed and shook my head. "I guess it'll be the hard way then."

"Not hard for me." Heather shrugged.

"Well, I guess I'll have to introduce you to him properly." I winked at her.

Taking the hint, she nodded to me with a grin on her face. I put my net over us again, not knowing what to expect of the next few places we might go. I took hold of Heather's shoulder again, and we disappeared only to reappear on the same white beach the windows had been overlooking. Wiki didn't have much imagination. We reappeared facing him as he sat down on the sand with worry on his face.

"Not very unique," I said to him as I pulled my net off myself again. His eyes bulged in shock.

"Try this," he said before he disappeared again.

"Again," I said to Heather, replacing my net and my hand.

This time we landed in a dirty street outside some sort of bar. From the heat and the sound of the voices inside the establishment, I assumed we were in Mexico.

Wiki cowered in the shadows only a few feet in front of us, peeking into the sparsely filled street warily.

This time I didn't speak, I simply let my net sink away from me while my eyes bored into him. He caught sight of me immediately and shook his head violently. "It's not possible."

I opened my mouth to speak, but he disappeared. I closed my mouth and sighed, signaling to Heather to go again.

Next, we materialized in a museum; it must have been the Louvre. When the building materialized around us, I found myself standing nose to nose with a large statue of a Greek goddess. Although beautiful, it was an uncomfortable proximity. I turned to Heather, questioning her placement with my ear brushing the statue. Before she could respond, we realized why I was kissing a statue when Wiki stepped out from behind it. Heather smiled at her accomplishment, and I had to accept her smugness.

Again, Wiki glanced cautiously around, but I didn't think it was because he was standing in the middle of the Louvre in a Hawaiian shirt and flip flops. I allowed my net to melt away from me again, and he disappeared without a word.

Reappearing in a very familiar mountain cabin, he didn't stop when I revealed myself. Again. We found him next to a pyramid in Egypt, then in a small village in China. Every time we appeared in front of him, I noticed we got closer to him in proximity.

I was impressed when Heather transported us and I found myself nose to nose with Wiki. "I think you're getting the hang of this," I said.

"Yeah," she said. "I think I've figured out the spatial positioning."

"That's great. Can you do me a favor?" I asked.

"What's that?"

I hugged the glass window in front of me while trying to keep my feet on the slim ledge under me. Wiki stared out the window in front of me, seeing right through me. I tried to carefully peer over the ledge of the building I attempted to remain glued to. I'll admit, I clutched her shoulder a little tighter. "Get us down from here."

After a few more jumps, we finally landed under a set of stairs in an underground tunnel in London. "Stop!" I said firmly to Wiki as I slowly pulled my net off again. Luckily, this time, he didn't disappear. Unfortunately, a homeless man in the corner might have thought he was losing his mind.

"How are you doing that?" Wiki asked, cautiously pointing a shaky finger at me.

I took the initiative to keep him talking. "Heather, here," I explained as I pulled my net off her as well, "can do this all day."

Still under my left hand, she greeted him as if they were old friends. I hoped her cheerfulness would help bring back the old Wiki. The one that was always ready with a joke or a smile. His lips twitched as he fought back a smile in response.

"How?" he asked again, this time addressing her.

"I can transport to people," Heather answered, "as well as places."

All Wiki's suspicions disappeared as quickly as he had previously. "No kidding?" he asked with all his buoyancy back. "How does that work?"

Before Heather could answer him, I stepped in. "She can tell you all about it later." People had started to file onto the platform in front of us, so I stepped closer to him. In a lower tone I said, "For now, can we please just talk to you?" I eyed the mortals and added, "Somewhere else?"

Wiki glanced around, "All right," he nodded. "But not back at the base. I know you have it locked down, and I don't want to get trapped there...again."

"Fine."

"Onus never said much to me." Wiki put down his drink in front of himself. "He looked at us like we would be his next snack if we stepped out of line. Do you confide in your food?"

We sat at a little café on the beach having gone back to Wiki's previous accommodations. I explained the situation to him and our need for any help he might have. We ordered some drinks, and Heather and I listened intently, but I felt like I kept asking the same questions.

"He must have said something." I struggled to get some kind of information out of him. After this conversation, he would probably try to disappear again. Not that it would be possible with Heather around, but I knew he wouldn't come back and help us.

He shook his head as he swirled his drink, "He only talked to Eva," he insisted, "And that was only because he needed her." Wiki shrugged his shoulders. "I honestly can't think of anything important that might help you. Really. I would tell you if I did."

Then it dawned on me. "Would you be willing to let Ella check?" Immediately I could see Wiki's defenses being thrown up around him. He was very private, very protective of the one that mattered most…himself.

"Wait a second, Liam…"

"You know she won't get too personal…" I interrupted.

"I don't want anyone…"

"She is very good at what she does…"

"But that's my mind we're talking about! There's personal stuff!"

"Ella has everyone's secrets in her head. She's never divulged anything that would incriminate someone else."

"Yeah, but I'm a traitor already, remember?" He glanced around at the wary vacationers then leaned forward. "Everyone is going to want details on everything I've been up to," he said in a lowered tone. "You really think she's going to pass up a chance like that?" He gave me a moment then said, "Would you?"

I couldn't answer. I knew I wouldn't pass it up. I took a drink to keep from answering.

Heather attempted to dispel the awkward silence that followed. "Did Eva report everything to you?" Heather asked. She sipped politely on a glass of water. "Did she ever report any suspicions of him at all?"

"Wait," Wiki said, sitting up straighter. "There is something that might help you." I leaned in so the three of us formed a small circle with our heads close together. "I heard Eva and Perry talking one night. They didn't trust me any more than you do, but they thought I was asleep. They said something about the gemstones in the cavern. Said they were keeping Onus prisoner. I think they were discussing the possibility of him being freed." I glanced sideways at Heather, but she was listening intently to Wiki. "I heard something about the four elements of the earth containing him. I didn't pay much attention after that because I figured it would never be my problem."

I leaned back in my seat as Heather and Wiki tried to interpret any possible meaning from what had been said. After listening quietly, I finally voiced the coming problem. "We'll have to go investigate the cavern."

Wiki nodded. "Take Kathryn with you. She'll be able to discern any powers in the cavern that might have been keeping Onus locked in there."

I nodded then stood to leave. "Thanks, Wiki. I'll tell Kin that at least you tried."

"Kin?" Wiki asked.

I nodded solemnly. "Onus killed Jancarlo before he left."

Wiki's mouth hung open in shock. Before he dropped his eyes to the table, I could swear I saw tears in them. "Are you going to have a service?" he asked in a weak voice.

"Eventually," I said. "I'll let you know when it will be."

Heather and I stepped away from the table, but before we could go far, he spoke up again. "I guess he passed his gem on to Kin, then, huh?"

I glanced back, but his face was still downturned. "What gem?" I asked a little harsher than I meant.

He turned his face up to me, and I could see the red around his eyes that he was trying to hide. "Didn't you know?" He must have been waiting for some kind of answer, but I just stared back at him. When he saw nothing forthcoming, he explained. "The only reason Eva kept returning to the base was because Onus wanted the gemstone Jancarlo has."

"Jancarlo doesn't have a gemstone."

"Yes, he does…or did." Wiki swirled his drink. "All of the Storm organizations have at least one. They're passed down from leader to leader through the generations. They've been around since Onus's time." He looked up at me seriously. "And he wants them. All of them."

"You never said anything about this!" I roared at Kin. We were in his office giving him my report, and I couldn't help feeling betrayed that he left out a key piece of the puzzle. Maybe it was just the fact that I had to hear it from someone else. Maybe it was the fact that that person had been Wiki, I wasn't sure, but I felt deceived.

"I wasn't *supposed* to tell you. That's the whole point." Kin answered me in a calm voice I had never known him to have. It only infuriated me more.

"So, what *are* they?" I seethed.

"The gems have powers in them," Kin explained. "Our gem contains the most powerful concentration of rock shifting known around the world and throughout history. Together, with the other gems, they act as a sort of key to Onus's prison. They can be used by regular mortals but were kept secretly with the Storm People. They were spread out among the different countries in order to not let Onus get his hands on them. I think he only wants them to ensure that he can never be held prisoner again. If he kills the only people with the power to do that, he prevents it as well. If he kills us and destroys the keys, he'll never be captured again."

"Does he have any of the other gems?" Heather asked.

Kin shook his head. "No, I think he met Devin Ross, (no idea how that happened) who introduced him to Eva, and he was using Eva to try to find the keys. He must have started with us. If he had gotten all the keys before we met him, we wouldn't have known about him until he was on our doorstep."

Heather sat quietly watching us, but I paced around the small room. With Jancarlo gone, I guess I felt someone should be pacing.

"But this is what he's been after the whole time," I insisted. "Not knowing everything puts us all at risk."

"It was a necessary risk," Kin answered. "Even Jancarlo told me that." He stood but dropped his voice. "And I expect both of you to keep this quiet as well."

I turned on him in shock. "How could you even suggest…" I started, but Heather interrupted me.

"Of course, we wouldn't tell anyone," she insisted, standing up between us. The girl was more mature than I gave her credit for. I'm sure she could see our temperatures rising, so she struggled to keep the situation under control.

With my frustration about not being told about the gemstone, we hadn't gotten much reporting done, so Heather tried to keep the report going. "Wiki also said we should check out the cavern again." She turned to me. "Right, Liam? He said something about the four elements of the earth keeping Onus prisoner."

I took a deep breath and nodded. "Yeah," I said trying to gain control of myself. I knew I shouldn't let a disappointment like this get in the way of working with Kin. Tensions had been high and nerves frazzled, so I tried to manage as best I could. "He suggested we have Kathryn check it out."

"Sounds like a good idea." Kin nodded. "Ella couldn't get any information out of Rosa. It seems Eva kept her in the dark as much as possible because of Ella." He walked around to the front of his desk watching the ground. "For now, let's go get Kathryn and head to the caverns."

"You're coming with us?" I asked. Jancarlo had been a hands-on leader, but I didn't really see Kin as that sort. Then again, I had never really seen Kin as my leader.

"Yeah," he nodded. "If there is information in that cavern of how to defeat Onus, I want to know about it firsthand."

We all turned to head out the door. Kin, however, touched Heather on the arm. "Heather," he said in a low voice, "could you give us a minute?"

Her eyes bounced between Kin and me for only a second before she agreed to go get Kathryn. She stepped out of the office, closing the door behind her.

"Liam," Kin started hesitantly, "I understand you being upset about the gemstone, but I really need you, of all people, to support me if this organization isn't going to crumble into chaos." He held my eyes like a vice. Even though I stood a head taller than him, he was still very intimidating. "I'm going to need the same support, help and advice you always gave so willingly to Jancarlo." I tried to shake off his gaze, but he held onto it. "Everyone here knows and trusts you, Liam. I can't do this without you."

For the first time in the thirty some-odd years I had known Kin, he seemed vulnerable. I was ashamed of myself for lashing out at him the way I did. "You're my friend, just as much as Jancarlo was," I told him sincerely. "I'll support you to my death. I'm sorry for my conduct."

Kin's shoulders dropped, releasing an invisible weight. "Don't worry about it," he said giving me half a grin and shaking his head. "These aren't exactly easy times. We're all under a lot of stress right now." He grabbed my arm and squeezed it, saying, "Let's go get rid of that monster so we can grow old in peace, huh?"

We met Heather and Kathryn in the lobby on their way to collect us. Heather had briefly explained the situation to Kathryn, and they were ready to leave. It was a good thing Heather had been to the cavern before because Ella was busy dealing with Rosa.

When we got to the cavern, it was very different from the first time I had seen it. It was still very dark, but a small trickle of light came from the now gaping hole in the ceiling. The speck of light hovered a good distance off, but for a room otherwise void of all lumen, it made a difference in our vision. We landed in the same spot Heather had rescued us from. The stone that had rained on us before now lay strewn all over the cavern floor as well as the entrance and a good distance down the hallway leading to it. What had once been a smooth-surfaced, gem-encrusted, enormous cavern room now had rubble littering the floor. The walls that had seemed so secure now showed huge gashes the size of cars. It looked as if a giant jackhammer had gotten out of control.

We picked our way over the treacherous boulders and saw football-sized gemstones that had once adorned the walls among the rubble. I bent to pick one up, but Kathryn stopped my hand. "Don't touch the gems." She said it to everyone, "I can feel the powers in them from here." She concentrated on them so fiercely that I decided it would be best to listen.

"What will they do to us?" Kin asked her.

She walked over to the wall and passed her hand an inch away from the gems in the wall. "They have strong powers in them. The worst they can do is pass on the powers to you temporarily, but there's no telling what kind of adverse effect it might have on you while it lasts."

"Like Jacob when he first got his powers?" Heather asked.

"Exactly," Kathryn said. Heather stepped away from the gems as well.

"How exactly do your powers work, Kathryn?" I asked her as she gazed at the stones, occasionally passing her hand over them.

"It's hard to explain," she said with the far-off airy voice of one distracted. "I can manipulate powers, copying them, changing them, taking them on myself," she explained. "Perry Anderson and I had much the same powers. I could do what he did if I wanted." She shrugged, "But I don't want to. In this case, I can sense what powers reside in these stones." Her voice dropped dangerously low, "And how powerful they are." She took a deep breath. "If we could somehow harvest these stones, not even Onus could stand against us."

"And these are what kept him trapped in here," Kin finished.

Kathryn nodded then stood up to look at Kin. "Wiki was right. These stones hold the four elemental powers."

"Water, air, earth and fire?" I asked.

"Yes, amplified by lightning." She turned back to the wall. "I'm sensing water manipulation, which is of course a very base power. Fire manipulation, also obvious. And air."

"Air? In what form?" Kin asked.

"Transportation."

"Like my powers?" Heather asked.

"Yes," Kathryn said. "In fact, exactly like your powers."

"What about earth?" Kin asked.

Kathryn pursed her lips and slightly shook her head. "I'm only sensing a small amount of that power." She gazed at the hole in the ceiling. "I'm guessing the rock manipulation was used to create this cavern and hold the gemstones in place, but there are no gems that contain it.

Otherwise, Onus might have been able to use his claw to scratch it out and use it himself. That power particularly is contained within the walls itself."

"That would explain," Kin spoke slowly, "why Onus needed Jancarlo's powers to move the gems restraining him."

"And," Kathryn pointed out, "I have a feeling that's what we'll need to conquer him again."

Chapter TWENTY

I tapped on the door leading to the living area that Ella and her mother shared.

"She's not here," Evelyn said, once she opened the door and saw me. "She's busy doing stuff for Kin."

"I know," I said, before she could close the door, "I'm actually here to get your help."

Evelyn's eyebrows creased. "That's new."

Standing in the doorway, I quickly explained the situation and the need for elemental manipulators.

"We need someone powerful," I finished. "Probably more than a few people to help."

"Of course, I'll help," Evelyn said. "Let me grab some stuff." I turned to leave, but before she closed the door, she called to me again. "Liam," she said, "thank you."

"For what?" I asked. "I'm coming to you for help."

"For watching over Ella," she said, her eyes cast down. "For watching over her while I couldn't. I…" her voice trailed off, but I knew what she was thinking.

I turned back to face her as she stood awkwardly in the doorway. "Evelyn," I said, "I would do anything to protect Ella. You know that."

She nodded. "I do now."

We had to take time to gather people, but we finally got everyone necessary, and more, in the lobby of the base that evening. Along with Evelyn, we asked Adam to help as an extra pair of hands.

We had Heather and Boris there to represent transporters, thankfully Theresa was on assignment. Apparently, she and the president had gotten along so well that she was spending some time relating to him how our people live and filling him in on the specifics of our latest encounter in the arctic.

Kathryn and Kin had decided that having lifters, people that could move objects, might be helpful as well, so Jacob and Henry Tate joined the group. Theresa, having explained the situation to the president, procured a temporary leave of absence for Henry. Theresa claimed she could protect the president while he was away. Henry, of course, didn't like the situation. But things like this usually happened when Theresa was around. Instead of arguing, he decided his efforts would be well spent helping us.

As for rock movers, we had called in four very powerful people. Without Jancarlo around, our resident, most powerful, rock movers would be Dallin Larkin and Zeershis (everyone called him Zee). Dallin was from Denmark but had been in America for almost forty-five years. Zeershis had come to us from India only a decade ago and was still working on fitting in with the American Storm People. He was a hard worker and a fun guy to be around but very quiet. Being rock movers, both men had helped build the clinic on the surface. And they had added many transport stations and underground tunnels the mortals would never know about.

The other two rock movers were from Africa. They were extremely powerful but sometimes hard to understand. Thankfully, we had Sophia, our translator, there to relay their instructions and their questions. Their names were something like Paktel and Kurisi…I think.

For fire starters, all we needed was Kin and Kimi, but Kin agreed to allow Migan and Brendan from the security team to come along as well. Kin was afraid his attentions would be divided thus not allowing him to focus his energy properly.

Tony, Kathryn and Gretchen would be coming along as back-up. Tony would have been furious if he had been left out of this little venture, and Gretchen insisted that precautions needed to be taken. Ella told me in confidence that Gretchen felt so guilty about the lives lost in the battle that she was not willing to risk possibly being too late to help.

Kathryn would be there to direct the flow of everyone's powers and how best they should use them. According to her, with these specific powers used the right way, we should be able to defeat Onus, but she would be there in case of miscalculations or anything else. She would be there for analysis.

Ella would round off the group. She couldn't allow much communication in our minds because Onus would hear us since he too could read minds and was much more powerful than her, but she would work on breaking through his mental defenses. I didn't envy the position she would be in. She confided in me that he could very well use the same overload of information that she used to knock people out against her. She had no idea what was going to happen, but she hid her fear well.

Nathaniel came to listen to the briefing and say good-bye. He would hold down the fort while we were away. He said he felt bad that he couldn't help out much, but he would be on point to coordinate from the base.

I would go along to keep everyone invisible. Kin decided, and I agreed, that if we contained Onus in a confined space in my bubble like I had in the arctic, it could do much more damage than good. We would at least have a slight advantage if Onus didn't know our numbers or our positions. So that was my job.

After we finalized our strategy, Kin finished explaining as much as he could about the foe. "We know Onus can breathe fire and lift objects. We also believe he's capable of taking powers. That's why we doubled up all the powers." Kin addressed the group in the lobby. "The plan is for Heather and me to lure him to the cavern, but if we must, we'll force him. Ella will be shielding our minds from Onus, so we won't be able to communicate that way. Should anything happen to Ella, and Onus engages you, make sure you try to clear your mind of our plans or you could give us away.

"You all have your assignments, but we're going to have to think on our toes here." Kin looked around gravely. "Onus has sworn to destroy the People of the

Storm, so our lives are in danger as well as anyone who might get in his way. We cannot fail today."

"Who is he?" Tony spoke into the silence that followed. "Why does he hate us? Why do we have to capture him?"

Everyone turned back to Kin, but Kin waved a hand to Ella.

"I caught a portion of his memories when he escaped the cave," she said. "He must have been so distracted by the thought of getting out that he let me into his mind a little. It seems dragons had been hunted and killed for centuries. But the Romans were especially brutal, killing dragons by the hundreds until there were only a handful of them left. Onus was the last one left, and they decided to humiliate him further by capturing and imprisoning him rather than killing him. That's why he spoke his threat in Latin. It was the language of his mortal enemies. I guess many Roman leaders were Storm People. They didn't even have to hide their powers, which might be where the stories of gods and demigods come from. Either way, Onus's anger against humans and especially the People of the Storm has driven him to a raging madness over the past millennia. He won't stop until we're all dead. Then he'll go on killing all humans just for fun."

When she stopped speaking, everyone was as silent as the rock surrounding us.

Kin cleared his throat to break up the tension. "Like I said, we can't fail today."

He turned to Nathaniel who leaned against the desk. "Nathaniel will be connected to me." He indicated the leather strap on his wrist that held the communication ruby. "So, I'll be able to call for reinforcements at any time. All the Storm People around the world are on high alert. We're trying to capture Onus, but, as much as I loathe the idea of destroying this creature, if it comes to that, so be it. Good luck everyone."

He scooped up a large velvet bag with a pull tie on top. Only a few of us knew it contained the gem Onus had been after. It was a large emerald the size of a pineapple. Dallin, our other rock mover, had extracted it from the small vault encased in rock in the wall of Jancarlo's office. Kin had known where it was but couldn't get it because of the powers surrounding it. Kin planned on trying to tempt Onus back to the cavern with it. If that didn't work, Heather would have to transport him back.

Everyone gathered around Heather. As soon as we were linked together, Kin gave her the go-ahead to transport us to the cavern. In an instant, we all stood amidst the broken boulders and gemstones strewn on the cave floor with one goal in mind. Imprison the creature Onus.... again.

We sat quietly in the dark, speaking only occasionally and only in whispers. I felt like some kind of criminal or runaway hiding away in the gloom. I was profoundly reminded of the time Ella and I and a man named Eddie had taken refuge in the crypts of the Shadow.

We soberly contemplated our different assignments in a mounting tension. Adam and Evelyn had collected as much water as they could find with more waiting in reserve. Their stock waited in a large pool hidden behind the rocks. It was kept securely in place by the rock shifters.

The lifters and rock shifters didn't dare disturb any of the boulders or gems on the ground for fear Onus might realize things were out of place when he showed up, thereby giving away our deception. They also made great hiding places for us, but Onus would be too large to utilize them.

Ella and I sat on the floor, leaning our backs against a wall in the tunnel, our hands clasped together tightly. Evelyn watched quietly from nearby. We spoke in our minds about the possible outcomes of this skirmish as well as what we knew of Onus and how to exploit that knowledge best.

He'll never come willingly, she said. *He's able to outlive us. It would be easier to wait for us to die off then try to trick the next generation of Storm People.*

Or eat us, I countered.

She gave me a sideways glance. *I'm just saying they're going to have to force him. And if he comes against his will, it will be difficult from the start.*

After a moment's silence, I finally confessed, *I wish I could do more to help.*

All of us help in our own ways, you know that.

There's no "I" in "team," right? I asked sarcastically.

Something like that.

Still there must be something I can do.

All I can suggest is to examine your powers. Play around with them. Maybe you'll figure something out, she said. I knew she was trying to be helpful, but at the same time I knew we didn't have that luxury.

"What will he do?" Evelyn whispered in the darkness. When Ella and I glanced at her in confusion, she elaborated, "What will Onus do? How will he fight us?"

Ella shrugged. "He has lots of powers at his disposal, so I can't be entirely sure. I don't think he'll bother taking Heather's powers. He can transport himself with his wings just fine. If she can get him here, I think his desire to have the gem will keep him here long enough for her to get clear."

"The rest of us will just have to fight him from a distance?" Evelyn asked.

Ella nodded.

"I won't be able to wrap him up again," I said to both of them. "Kin and I decided it would be even more dangerous to try that in an enclosed space like this."

"What about his stone moving ability?" Evelyn asked. "Won't he just be able to open up the stone again and leave?"

"No," Ella said. "We have rock movers that will be fighting him, plus there are other, less powerful, gems in the cave to prevent it. Besides, the gem Jancarlo touched was one that allowed Onus to take people's powers. He didn't have the ability before he swallowed the gem. The gem dissolved into him, giving him that ability to take powers, but the actual power to move rock didn't keep. Kind of like how Kathryn's powers only allow her to hold or use other people's powers for a short amount of time. The only way he could be a rock mover permanently is to swallow the gem that Kin brought. So, he has even more incentive to follow it here."

"So how did he get all of his powers?" Evelyn asked. "Did he get some of the other gems?"

Ella shook her head. "No, he was struck by lightning, just like us."

"Is it very responsible of Kin to tease Onus with that gem?" Evelyn said. "He should have left it at the base and not even brought it here. He could just pretend to have it."

"He thought about it," Ella said. "But he decided that Onus would have to at least see it. He'll take it out of the bag for a moment, so Onus knows he has it, then he'll send the real gem back to the base as quickly as possible. He's going to do everything he can to keep it as far from Onus as possible."

"But we have to act like we have the incentive to keep him away from it," I added.

"What about his lifting powers?" Evelyn said. "Can't he move the rock with those powers?"

"Any lifter will tell you," Ella said, "you can't lift a whole mountain."

"Not that Onus won't try," I said.

"Mom," Ella said, "I think your powers are going to be extremely important. Onus is supposedly 'made of fire', so water is the best to combat fire, right? Where's your water?"

"Behind that wall," Evelyn said, pointing to one side of the cavern. "We have about a swimming pool's worth and we can pull more from the cave system as well. It would only take a small crack in the rock to bring it out, but I'm more worried about Onus evaporating it with his fire."

"I guess we'll have to wait and see," Ella said.

I didn't voice it, but I had my doubts. Was water really the best way to fight him? Didn't people say "fight fire with fire"? If only we had more time to prepare for this fight we might have been able to figure it out.

As if in answer to my thought, Kin appeared in front of us with a blur of blonde hair. Kin's face was streaked with ash and dirt. "He's coming! Get ready!" he yelled to the group, then stooping, he pulled open the velvet bag and pulled out the large smoky gem. He turned and tossed the gem to Boris. "Get rid of that," he said. "No matter what happens, we can't let him have it." As Boris disappeared, Kin took a random rock from the floor, put it in the bag and tossed the bag to the floor nearby. "Liam," he said, pointing to the bag, "cover it as if we have something to hide."

I barely had enough time to throw my net over our group. I was still pulling it tight onto the separate individuals and setting a connection between them so they could see each other when the viperous monster appeared in the middle of the cavern.

Heather rode on his tail when he appeared, but she disappeared quickly, materializing next to me and Kin although she couldn't see us. She stood still for a moment staring at Onus so I swiftly included her under my net to protect her as much as I could from the beast. She flinched in surprise when we appeared next to her, but I held my finger to my lips.

"How dare you presume to force me here, child!" Onus roared to the entire room. His voice reverberated off the walls menacingly. "Who do you think you are?!" He shook the rock with his accusation. He searched for Heather but only found an empty cavern. We all waited to see if, for whatever reason, Kin might be able to rationalize with him. While we waited, Onus prowled the cavern, tossing rocks and random bursts of fire. What he didn't pay any attention to was the fact that our rock shifters were already sealing up the crevice in the ceiling. Far away, the faint light was dimming.

But Onus didn't notice the light dimming because he loosed a jet of fire around the walls and towards the human-sized entrance. The fire starters easily kept the flames from touching anyone in our party but allowed them to engulf individuals so as not to give away our numbers. It was a fascinating sensation to watch the brilliant flames steal about me but only feel a fraction of their heat.

"Please, Onus!" Kin yelled as the inferno raged around him. "It doesn't need to be like this! Just listen to us!"

When he clamped his maw shut, everyone held their breath as Onus's eyes swept the cavern silently. He must have been searching for minds because he said smoothly, "There are more of you than I expected."

I immediately tried to pry my mind away from our task at hand as his gaze turned toward me. I looked away to my left to see Ella. Her face was always an easy distraction for me. Unfortunately, this time I started wondering how she was doing with her assigned task as I saw the deep concentration on her face. Knowing I shouldn't be thinking about it, I searched for something else to contemplate.

My gaze fell on my hands which hung at my side, with fingers slightly splayed out as they usually were when I engaged my powers. I thought about my hands and how dissimilar they were from Onus's talons. His might be more powerful for destruction, but I had an opposable thumb, which was better for minute tasks. Could either be better than the other? His could tear through flesh easily, but mine could carefully skin the carcass of an animal to be used for other things. They both had their uses to fit our individual needs.

I silently relaxed as his eyes moved away from where I stood.

Good job changing your mind, Liam. Weird but effective. When I heard Ella's voice, it took me by surprise because I had assumed she wouldn't be communicating with that method at all, but I nodded succinctly in response.

"Speak with us, Onus," Kin continued his pleas. "You are a logical creature. I know we can figure out a way to have peace between us."

Suddenly Onus, who had been turning a slow circle in the cavern, snapped his head sharply to the left to stare down at Dallin and Zee furiously. In only a brief moment, he must have penetrated Ella's defenses because in the next split second his head shot straight up to inspect the almost sealed ceiling above him. Without warning, he launched himself into the still slightly gaping hole.

"NO!" he snarled as he pressed his wings hard to the ground over and over. Before any of us could blink, he was in the hole, tearing at chunks of the rock and gems. Deafening rumbles shook the walls of the cavern. I couldn't tell if the tumult was from Onus's voice or from the rock being smashed. Over and over his defiant bellows were heard in harmony to the thundering of rock being thrown down upon us.

The rock continued to close around Onus as he desperately tried to free himself from his remade prison. Roaring, thrashing, and stone-rending amidst brilliant bursts of flame, he continued to fight the inevitable, until finally, the grit threatened to encompass him, and he was forced to concede his campaign. He landed in the cavern so hard he cracked the stone surface beneath him.

His head hung for a moment, and I prayed he would relinquish this fight. But my hope dissolved when he whispered, "I will kill you all."

Kin shook his head, dejected. "I'm sorry it has to be this way. Now!" he yelled, but the last word was drowned by the crashing boom of rock scraping against rock.

Onus's head snapped up along with both his front claws facing straight forward, his razor-sharp talons spread wide. The rock covering the floor in front of him lifted. Hundreds of stones, large and small, came hurtling through the air as if a giant broom swept them all in our direction. I flinched away from the onslaught with a raised arm…like that would help, but the stones fell helplessly to the floor in front of us. Onus knew he couldn't move the rock as easily as the rock movers, and I don't think he knew we also had lifters in our numbers who were just as potent as he was, but he continued to fight. He swept his wings straight out to each side. With them flew all the rock on either side of him, rolling, bouncing, scraping all around the edges of the cavern. He had sufficiently swept clear the entire cavern, leaving the rubble in a large pile behind him.

"Aaaaagggghhhhh!!!" A tortured cry rose from the pile of rubble. The rock shifters must have missed one. Boris lay next to the pile, his leg trapped beneath a boulder as large as a car.

"Don't let him touch you!" Ella yelled. "He'll get your powers." But Boris couldn't move. One heartbeat later, as if he had seen him clear as day, Onus reached his claw out to Boris.

Fast as Heather could, she transported Boris out from under the rock, but Onus had enough time to swipe his claw across Boris's chest. The pair reappeared behind us, further along the hallway where Onus couldn't reach them, but the damage had been done. Gretchen immediately reached her hands out to his sundered chest and mutilated leg.

"No," Kin breathed then he locked eyes with Heather. "Go."

If Heather hadn't been so fast, Onus might have transported away, but she left Boris's side to go back to riding on Onus's tail. "Don't let go of him until the powers start to fade!" Kin yelled at her. "Everyone, go!" He screamed at the top of his lungs.

Kin's voice reverberated around the cavern. Everyone knew what they were to do. Mass chaos ensued. As everyone attacked Onus with their powers at once, a blurry image of Heather appeared next to Kin as well as the fuzzy image attached to Onus's tail. He watched her with a crease in his brow and stretched out his hands to her as if he wanted to catch her from falling. Lowering his chin in concentration, I could practically see the gears turning in his mind. "We need another transporter," he whispered almost to himself. I knew he would be communicating this to Nathaniel at the base, but I didn't know if we would be able to get one soon enough. None of the others had been here before. Kin's eyes lifted back to watch Heather again as he added, "she can't breathe."

Chapter TWENTY-ONE

Heather's face began to crumple. She flickered as she and Onus fought for control of the transport he was attempting to enforce. As I watched the two struggle, I remembered the breathless sensation every time I transported with her or Wiki or anyone else. Now Heather was stuck in that same state, unable to breathe until the transporting ceased. She was pushing herself so much further than we ever would have asked of her under normal circumstances. I felt even more helpless as she began to curl her shoulders in on themselves. This poor girl had trusted us, and we were helpless to assist her.

Suddenly, from behind us came a very familiar voice. "Man, you guys are hard to find!"

Kin and I spun to see Wiki running down the hallway towards us. He took in the sight of our people struggling with the massive creature whom he had once assisted. Then his eyes strayed to Heather as her fuzzy form fell to her knees.

"Wiki!" Kin started, but Wiki cut him off.

Without taking his eyes off Heather, Wiki said, "Don't worry, Kin. I got this." He transported next to Heather and put his hand on her shoulder. His image faded as Heather's solidified, and she collapsed on the floor. She gasped air into her lungs and coughed a few times, but she seemed okay. Wiki's visage replaced Heather's riding on Onus's tail as he relieved her of the transporting burden.

After that, Wiki and Heather worked together to keep Onus from transporting out of the cavern. Every ten seconds or so, the other one would take over stopping Onus from transporting away. Onus disappeared and reappeared all over the cavern trying to shake off his attacker, but he remained in the cavern with us.

Rock shifters weren't concerned with throwing rocks at the creature, but they were afraid those rocks might hit someone else. Their main focus was to rebuild the cavern with all the gems in place and completely fill in the hole in the ceiling all the way to the surface. But in order to make sure Onus wouldn't be able to harness their powers for himself, all four of them sunk backwards into the rock. The stone slowly surrounded them like coffins, only stopping with a small opening around their faces so they could see and breathe but the monster's claws couldn't reach them.

Someone cracked open the rock so the water movers could access their stores. This one act made the most impact on Onus, and he displayed fierce anxiety by focusing his attention on trying to use his lifting powers to keep the waters away from him. Evelyn and Adam stepped from the shadows with their hands in front of them, twisting the water in the air around the dragon.

"No!" Onus yelled, transporting away from the water as far as he could go. "You will not trap me again!"

Everyone attacked Onus with all their strength, but the beast didn't seem to weaken. Kin and Kimi and the others turned the fire he produced back on him, but it didn't bother him in the least. The lifters, Jacob and Henry tried to use their powers to hold him down, but he would transport out of their grasp, forcing them to start over.

Heather finally transported next to Kin. "His power to transport is weakening," she yelled. "He can't get out of the cave anymore! If I touch him again, he'll take my powers, and we'll never see him again!"

"Stay put!" He yelled back to her and Wiki as everyone wrestled, inwardly and outwardly, with the monster. Kin's face twisted in frustration. "This isn't working!" He turned to Kathryn. "What are we doing wrong?"

"Let me think." She closed her eyes and cocked her head to the side slightly.

We didn't have time for this. A thought Tony echoed. "I'll hold him down!" he yelled, running towards Onus.

"No, Tony! Wait!" Kathryn yelled at him, reaching her arm out towards him, but it was too late. In a few bounds, Tony had grabbed one of his back legs. The second the creature noticed him, his strength drained and transferred to Onus. He shook his back leg like a horse kicking a small creature and took a deep breath. I could see the power flowing through him as he attacked our people anew. Tony was thrown against a far wall and fell to the floor unconscious.

"Idiot!" Kathryn sobbed in frustration. Then she turned quickly to Kin. "I have to drain his powers, as much as I can." She had a fierce look of determination. If I had been Kin, I would have shied away from her ferocity. Luckily, Kin kept his head.

"You said it might kill you," he said, anguish etched across his face.

"I know." She nodded. Without another glance, she started towards Onus.

"Kathryn," Ella yelled to her. Instead of saying anything aloud, their eyes met for a moment, and they communicated silently. Kathryn nodded again then ran towards the monster as he continued his rampage on our people, throwing stone and fire while deftly avoiding water.

"What did you tell her?" Kin asked Ella quietly.

In response, we both heard in our minds, *I told her not to take all his powers. Just concentrate on lifting and strength.*

Is it safe to communicate like this? Kin asked her the same thing I was wondering.

As long as he's not concentrating on us, she answered. *Just like us, he has to focus on using his powers and which one he's using at one time and concentrating on how he's using it. Heather and Wiki could stop him from transporting because that's the power he was focusing on using. He's pretty good at using more than one power at a time though, so we can't do it often.*

Kin nodded and turned his attention back to Onus. *Keep working, Ella.*

We watched as Kathryn ran around the cavern to Onus's flank. I knew she couldn't be seen, but I wasn't sure how he was pinpointing our party either. Luckily, he didn't notice her as he bashed on the wall protecting the rock shifters. Softly, as if petting a small, scared animal, she reached her hand out to touch his back end, which was the only part of him holding still.

The moment she touched him, he ceased his assault on the rock. His pupils dilated, and he froze for a heartbeat. I harbored a hope that she was weakening him, until he turned on her.

Kathryn's mouth hung open. Her hand slowly crept to her chest. She doubled over as if in pain.

"Kathryn, stop!" Ella yelled beside me. "That's enough!"

Before she had all the words out, Onus lifted his back leg and kicked Kathryn across the room to join Tony on the floor.

Next to Kin, Heather twitched in Kathryn's direction, but he put his hand on her arm. "Don't touch her," he told her before she could move, "it could mess up everything she did."

Onus's attacks became less pronounced. Kathryn must have taken his lifting powers like she had been instructed because he didn't throw any more rocks. He belched fire at everything, but it had no effect.

Kimi came running up to Kin. "This isn't working," she barked at her brother. She would be the only one allowed to use that tone with him. Meanwhile, Jacob and Henry pressed the creature to the floor almost completely restraining him from movement, so his jets of fire couldn't be aimed at anyone in particular. However, the more we seemed to gain control over him, the harder he fought. He was an animal backed into a corner, all the more dangerous for being more frightened. His fire snaked around him and seemed to fill the entire cavern. He could make it burn longer than any human would have been able to hold their breath. The flames blared a brilliant white for the heat they presented.

Kin's eyes narrowed as he surveyed the situation. Finally, he turned to Ella. "How does he know where we are?"

"He can see our heat." She shook her head and avoided his stare. "I'm able to keep our thoughts from him right now." Her eyes met mine apologetically. "But no matter what either of us do, he'll know where we are."

My only job was to keep us all invisible. Once again, my efforts were expendable.

"Have you been able to get in his mind yet?" Kin asked her.

"No," came her defeated response. "His mind is a fortress. It would take me years to learn to copy what he's doing, let alone bypass it."

"We've tried talking to him," I pointed out the obvious to Kin. "We have no choice but to imprison him again and hope we can talk sense into him later."

"His powers will return shortly," Kin said while he examined the floor. "Ella, make sure Kathryn is okay. Search her mind for any ideas she might have of how this is supposed to work."

As he said it, Tony began to stir from being knocked unconscious, and he reached over to Kathryn. His strength returned to him the second he touched her. Her eyes flew open as she gasped for breath. Ella and I watched them with indifference. Heather began to question Kin, but he said, "It's okay. We need everyone at full strength to regroup."

With a nod, she materialized next to Tony and Kathryn to transport them back over by Kin. When Kathryn woke and gave up her powers, Onus's efforts were multiplied. With his lifting powers back, he immediately started hurtling things through the air.

Seventeen-on-one is pretty good odds unless the one happens to be a very powerful dragon. He caught Henry off-guard, which I didn't think was even possible. Henry took a boulder to the head. Heather transported him away from Onus before he could get squished. The rock movers stayed safely entombed in their stone coffins, although with repeated attacks, Kurisi had to move himself up along the wall, so he overlooked the fight. Onus stayed well away from Adam and Evelyn as if they were extremely dangerous, but he clawed and kicked at all the fire starters. Brendan took a swift kick that sent him flying, but he was brought safely down by a hook of rock stretching like water dripping from the ceiling. Kimi had a large boulder thrown at her, but Tony batted it away only to miss the next one that hit Migan. She ended up in the tunnel with Gretchen watching over her as well.

I struggled watching everyone around me fight with the beast, knowing I was useless. When Migan got hit, I actually had to look away. I stared down at my hands again. I was a light shifter. I had been living for one hundred and eighteen years. I had one hundred and one years of experience with my powers. I had hidden entire buildings before! I had once hidden a small mountain in order to prank Wiki! I was the most powerful light shifter known in the world! Was I missing something? I could make things disappear, right?! But Onus could still see us. Could I make the cavern disappear? Kin and I discussed this. It was too dangerous for him to lose all senses. But what if he could see *too* much…?

I stared at my hands, not really seeing them but inspecting my powers in my mind's eye. Onus headed our way, bellowing something about taking down the leader. That seemed to be a consistent strategy with him. I examined the net as I extended it. Onus raged about Ella being a murderer. I tried to widen the intersections in my net by spreading two of my fingers further apart. They moved. As the monster swept Brendan aside, a small light appeared in my palm. I turned my hand over to inspect it. As a light shifter, I could not only manipulate the light so only certain things appear…I could create light! How had I never tried this?!

I widened the cross sections of my net. The light in my palm grew. Onus reached a claw for Ella. I widened the section of my net. Just four strands of my net, but stretched wide enough to encompass Onus himself. Then I flex the net to make a bubble between the four threads. The light directed itself toward Onus, magnified to a blinding degree. Ella turned to flee from Onus, but there was no need. The creature pulled his talon back and used his wing to cover his eyes.

He bellowed his defiance but continued to fight. Jacob, with much effort and from a distance, pulled him away from us so we were just barely out of his reach. The rock movers threw nets of rock over the creature to try to physically hold him down. He arched his back and tore at the rock. His claws were broken and bleeding, but he continued to fight. His wings had gashes that made speckles of light glitter on the floor, but he continued to fight. He attempted to burn anyone that came near him.

Evelyn yelled to Kin, "He keeps evaporating the water! We can cycle it back again, but it doesn't seem to be doing anything!"

"What are we doing wrong, Kathryn?" Kin hollered to her over the din.

"I don't know." She shook her head and put her hands on her forehead. "There's earth all around him to contain him." She checked off everything verbally. "Air, being transported, which he can't do either. Water to quench the…."

She stared up with horror in her wide eyes. "Fire!" she yelled.

"We're using fire!" Kimi hollered back.

"No!" Kathryn yelled, but she was cut off by Onus roaring at the top of his lungs. He stretched out the roar for a long time in order to cover Kathryn's voice.

Kathryn clamped her mouth shut and with pursed lips pointed at Ella then to her head.

A moment later we all heard her answer. *You have to draw the fire out of him instead of using it on him!*

Kin and Kimi shared a glance, but with determined eyes, lifted their hands to Onus again. I kept him blinded by light while they fidgeted with a talent they had very seldom used. I watched as streams of dancing flames flowed from the monstrous beast in front of us into Kin and Kimi's outstretched hands. Slowly the reverse flow from the beast to themselves manifested itself in Onus's appearance.

"NO!" he thundered again, but this time his defiant scream was noticeably weaker. My eardrums didn't feel on the verge of bursting at least. His writhing lessened only slightly. He seemed like a worm trying to wriggle off a hook that already had him impaled. He still broke the bonds the rock movers threw over him, but after a few more minutes of struggling, he stopped. The rock bonds lay over him like a grotesque net. I kept thinking at any moment he would free himself from his bonds, but eventually, he lay still. Dallin, Zee and the other rock movers cautiously emerged from their stone confines. We all stood before the mighty beast.

His grumbles lessened like a passing storm. Kin and Kimi continued pulling the fire out of him. His vibrant, rich green hide drained to a lusterless dull wash. The menacing brute took on the appearance of an overlarge science experiment gone wrong in front of our eyes.

Evelyn and Adam smothered Onus in the stores of water without having the supply dry up before it even touched him. Instead of trying to drown him by keeping the water around his head, they tried to contain him by keeping the water around his heart and belly, thus quenching the fire of which he claimed to be made.

Jacob, Henry and Tony stood close by, but I could see from their stances they no longer had to use their powers to struggle with Onus. They watched with crumpled faces as the monster was cowed.

We all watched…and waited. My heart broke to see this unique creature brought so low before us. I wished this could have been handled differently. I wished we could have found peace with him. We could learn so much from him!

In answer to my pain, Kin stepped forward and held a hand up to Kimi. The stream of fire had dwindled so small it was barely enough to light a room, so they both ceased pulling. Onus lay groaning, but instead of his sounds being murderous, they were suffering. Kin held a hand up to the water movers as well. The water danced away from the creature to hang in the air above him.

Finally, he squinted in my direction. "Put that thing away," he said. I realized I still had a blinding light projecting from my hand in front of me. I had almost forgotten it because the light hadn't affected my vision as much as everyone else's. I immediately closed the crosshairs of my net back together. The light dimmed. I recoiled my net altogether, and the light ceased.

"Onus," Kin said loud enough for everyone to hear. "Ella tells me your name means 'Last.' You're the last of your kind, are you not?" He waited a moment, but Onus just groaned, turning his head away from Kin. "We don't want it to be this way," Kin said with pleading in his voice. "We want you to survive as much as you do. We want to learn from you and work *with* you."

Onus tried to push from the floor again, but his rock bonds held him tight. He sagged against the ground, and his eyes met Kin's then drifted to the velvet bag behind Kin's feet that had reappeared when my net fell away. Without a word spoken, we all knew what he wanted. Kin retrieved the bag, and opening it, allowed the chunk of useless rock to fall with an echoing thunk. Onus closed his eyes, sank to the floor and stopped moving.

"Onus," he continued, "you can read our minds, you know we don't mean you any harm. Please, forgive ancient wrongs and work with us in peace. Try to trust that we're not like your previous captors."

Onus sat silently for another minute, then slowly he turned back to face us, his rock-hard scales scraping on the floor. With labored breath, he quietly said, "Ella."

Kin and I both turned to Ella. She's a hard one to catch off guard, but she looked as confused as I felt. She had been crouched against the wall in a mental struggle with Onus to gain access to his mind. But she stood and addressed him. "I'm here."

"Come closer," he whispered.

Immediately, Kin and I were on our guard. Evelyn took a few steps forward. I reached out to Ella, and she turned partially back to me. I shook my head slightly, but when we looked at Kin he just pursed his lips. He wanted us to show that we trusted Onus, I knew, but did we have to put Ella at risk in order to do that?

She nodded slightly, knowing what Kin wanted her to do. As she stepped forward again, I was frozen, but Evelyn took another step and called out to her daughter. Ella held up a hand to stop her mother then slowly walked toward the massive beast. As she passed me, she squeezed my wrist briefly to remind me, I'm sure, that she would be careful.

"I'm here, Onus," she answered him softly.

"I'm dying," Onus whispered back to her.

"No." Kin shook his head in disbelief.

"Once you have broken a dragon, they can no longer live," Onus replied, turning to look Kin in the eye. "The only thing that kept me alive this long was the determination to escape. Now I know I will continue to be captured so I have lost the will to survive."

"No," Kin said louder this time, taking a step forward. "Let us help you."

"You cannot," Onus insisted. "I will not let you take me alive again. This is my only option. I have known that all along."

"There must be something we can do," He answered back weakly.

"There is nothing you can do." Onus turned his eyes to stare at Ella again. "But there is something *she* can do."

Without warning, Ella took a sharp breath in, her eyes widening. She stood with her back as straight as I'd ever seen it. Her jaw went slack, and her breathing got shallow.

I couldn't exactly hear what Onus said to her, but it sounded something like, "Take them. Take them all."

"What's he doing to her?" I asked Kin.

"I don't know." His eyes were locked on Ella as well.

"Ella?" I called to her and heard it echoed from Evelyn.

Ella's trembling hands reached to her head. Her back arched further, and she was quaking all over.

"Ella?" I called to her again and moved towards her.

Evelyn and I both approached from opposite sides, but Ella held her hands out to us. With a weak voice she stuttered, "S-stay b-back." I stopped next to Kin. She shuddered again, her back arched and her chest pulsing in an attempt to breathe. Finally, she reached her right hand out and said, "Kathryn…help me."

In a flash, Kathryn ran up to Ella and clasped her hand. Immediately Kathryn's eyes widened as well. Her lip quivered like she was going to cry, then her face switched to pain. Pulling her free hand up to her head, she tried to disengage her other hand from Ella, but Ella kept hold of her in an iron grip.

Ella now breathed easier, but Kathryn began shaking her head. "Too…much…" she forced out from clenched teeth. Ella nodded and her face twisted in pain again. All the while, Onus stood like a statue with his eyes locked on the two women.

Now both women reacted as if they had been programmed to repeat the same movements. They both fell forward onto their knees and cried. Then they arched their backs to scream at the ceiling. Panting and heaving, they sat up and clutched their heads.

"Onus," Kin yelled at him. "Don't hurt them!"

With one final blood-chilling scream, the two women fell backwards, unconscious. The cavern was silent for a moment as we watched the two women lying on the floor. I stared in horror and prayed I wasn't imagining the minute rise and fall of Ella's chest. My eyes met Evelyn's, and I saw the horror I felt mirrored in her eyes.

The cavern was filled with life-like statues for a few heartbeats. Finally, Onus turned his serpentine head to gaze at Kin and a few of the rest of us. With a final, weak gasp he whispered, "Farewell," to no one in particular. His head slumped to the ground with a dull thud. As we beheld the beast with bated breath, the precious, ancient light in his eyes faded into darkness. Onus was dead.

Chapter TWENTY-TWO

A few days later, I sat in Kin's office on the edge of his desk as we watched a streamed news program from back in Ohio.

The news announcer spoke as Heather's high school picture showed up next to her. "The young woman was a patient at St. Anthony's Institute and has been listed as missing from the hospital for almost two months." The view on the screen switched to show a clip of Heather walking out of the hospital in her original scrubs with her mother and father on both sides of her, protecting her from the surrounding cameras. "While the custodian that found the young woman locked in a closet is being hailed as a local hero, the authorities are now launching a full investigation of the hospital and other personnel."

The video switched again to show Jacob standing at a pulpit crowded with microphones. He had shaved his head completely clean, sported a severe beard along his jawline and fake glasses. "People struck by lightning are often misunderstood and misdiagnosed," he professed with confidence. Under him appeared the title of Dr. Mark

Jancarlos and listed him as "Therapist for the Lightning Strike Victims Clinic." "It is appalling to see the level of care has declined to such abuse. Thus, the family has determined that Miss Lancaster will be receiving services in an environment with those of us who have experienced similar trauma in order to assist her on the road to recovery."

"Jacob certainly plays the part well." I said as Kin switched off the screen.

"Yeah," he nodded. "Good thing the family doesn't know he's dating their daughter, though, huh?" He added with a grin.

"Probably for the best," I said with a smile as well. "It's good that she's back with her family for a while." After another moment, I gestured to the television. "Will they be able to make it back in time?" I asked.

Kin nodded, "Yeah. That footage was from yesterday."

Silence fell between us again. I slowly stood and tugged at the black suit jacket I wore. I liked wearing suits, they made me feel more professional, but today I hated it. I glanced at the clock on the wall.

"It's about time, I guess," Kin muttered. I nodded as he stood to don his own black suit jacket. "You ready?" He asked me.

"I guess. I have to go get Ella first." I headed to the door.

"See you in there," He said as I slipped out.

I trudged down the hallway to Kathryn's office and swung the door open slowly. Kathryn and Ella sat hunched over some papers. They didn't move except for an occasional scratch on paper nor did they say anything out loud, but I knew they were hard at work. "Ella." I said, Both women sat up and spun at the sound of my voice.

The first thing I could see was the red encompassing their eyes. The next thing I noticed was the tissues overflowing the waste basket next to them. "It's time," I muttered. Both women abandoned the papers that lay in front of them. Kathryn put a long black sweater on over her black dress and promised to see us in a few minutes.

Ella put a small navy-blue sweater over her bare shoulders to accent her short black dress. The dark colors brought out her soft ivory skin nicely while also emphasizing her soft brown hair. She was so beautiful I might have complimented her on it but couldn't bring myself to say anything cheerful today. The only thing to mar her was an odd smudge of ink on the side of her hand left from rubbing across the pages.

"Seems you two have started without the rest of us," I mentioned to her as we walked hand in hand down the long hall.

"Today was especially…difficult," she whispered back. As her chin trembled, I wished I hadn't said anything.

After Onus died in the cavern, I had rushed to Ella's side. Both she and Kathryn had been fine, but she informed us that Onus had forced many millions of years' worth of memories into her mind. His species had the ability to pass information through generations. His ability to read minds also allowed him access to countless other such thoughts. All of which he had seen necessary to pass on to Ella. As much information as she could process at a time, it had still been too much for her. She and Kathryn together barely withstood the overload. Now they worked together tirelessly to record everything. The reason for his attack had not been violence, as I had assumed, but a desire for his kind never to be forgotten. Their work would be recorded in a series of reverse sequels. Onus's life first, then his parents, then their parents and so on.

"Kathryn and I," she continued, "were discussing Onus's admiration of his own leader." She shrugged. "He admired her as much as we admired Jancarlo. Our own emotions became muddled with the memory of his," she finished with a sigh.

"Will you be okay?" I asked. I took out my handkerchief and offered it to her.

"I'll be fine," she insisted as she blotted at her eyes. "I need to be here for this." I nodded to her as we turned the corner into a separate entrance for the massive practice arena.

We made our way past many of the American People of the Storm. No one was in the mood for conversation. In the front row gathered many dignitaries from around the world who had worked closely with Jancarlo in the past. With them sat Kin. He was officially the head of the American Chapter of The People of the Storm so that was where he belonged, but I knew his heart would have been with his sister.

Luckily Kimi sat with Tony. I had never seen Kimi cry or break down even a little bit. Even her imprisonment by Eva seemed to have hardened her more. But as she sat, stone-faced, in one of the hundreds of chairs that filled the arena, her eyes seemed to glisten as she nodded to us.

Tony's arm stayed firmly around her. An unheard-of display in any other setting, but today was very different.

I saw Heather and Jacob sitting next to each other holding hands. Sophia was a few seats away. Even Henry Tate had left the president's side to be here. I spotted Nathaniel and Evelyn in the second row, so Ella and I moved to join them. We sat at the end since I would have to get up and deliver one of the eulogies.

When it seemed everyone was present, Kin stood up at the front to officiate. Kin had truly become a well-spoken leader. I marveled at the changes Jancarlo's tutelage had wrought in him. A large boulder had been placed at the front of the assembly with a microphone embedded in it and speakers off to the sides. Not a fancy set-up, but enough for everyone to hear.

The rock movers had been busy. They used rock for the podium, rock for the chairs and had even taken the time to perfectly sculpt large wreaths of flowers of rock. They weren't a dull, lifeless type rock though. They had used different types of rock with varied hues to mimic the colors of the flowers. Although not the same color as the real thing, the swirls of green, red, orange, yellow, brown and blue made them just as beautiful.

To the right of the speaker's podium, an outcrop of rock protruded sculpted very carefully by the rock movers to resemble Jancarlo. It had been done with such skill and detail that it felt like the man himself had been turned to stone and laid on a bed of the same.

I noticed a familiar shock of blonde hair on the far left of the audience. When I inspected further, my suspicions were confirmed. Wiki sat in the crowd, trying not to be seen. After the fight with Onus had ended, Wiki had hung around long enough to make sure everyone was all right. He hadn't wanted to return to the base, but Kin made it clear he would be welcome again. Heather had promised she wouldn't hunt him down… unless it was important. Then he left again.

Give him time, Ella had told me. That was all we had left to give.

Only a few people would be speaking before we all had to say our last farewells. Each would speak about a different aspect of Jancarlo's life. Kin spoke of the business aspect, which was probably the biggest part of his life. Sophia spoke about him as an ambassador to nations and other Storm People around the world. She had been by his side for almost all those occasions. I was going to speak about the personal side of his life, his loyalty and friendship to myself and others.

As Kin spoke, I couldn't help but compare the ends of Jancarlo and Onus. Onus had given up his life because he couldn't be a prisoner any longer. Jancarlo had had his life, literally, ripped away from him. But the two beings would be entombed the same way.

After Onus had been confirmed dead by Gretchen, we had used the gemstones in the cavern to surround his body and encapsulate him against anyone ever finding his remains again. The rock movers brought the cavern crumbling down, creating a depression in the surface above. But they assured us the alteration would be stable and go unnoticed.

It was mostly Kathryn's doing, but she was able to use the powers in the gems to deter every living being away from the final resting place of the creature. She kept a small stone to help her or anyone else locate the tomb in the future if it was necessary for any reason. Once her deterrent was in place, I suddenly remembered many pressing items to tend to, and the urge to run back to the base almost overwhelmed me.

I was yanked out of my reveries when Sophia finished speaking. It was my turn. Ella gave my hand a squeeze, and I left her side to stand at the pulpit in front of the audience.

"As I thought of Jancarlo's personal life, I thought of what he meant to me." I choked back tears. I wouldn't allow myself to break down. "I came up with one word to sum up most of his relationships as a whole. That word was 'Trust.' Jancarlo was the most trustworthy person I've ever met. We have all trusted him with our secrets and our lives." I prattled on for a few more minutes about what that trust meant to me. I ventured that Jancarlo's trust made us live better lives. "As we think back on his life, we should always honor his memory. The only way I can see accomplishing this is by the trust we place in each other. We should live worthy of the trust of our fellowmen, our fellow Storm People and ourselves. Only then will we live up to Jancarlo's memory."

As I took my seat again, Kin motioned for Dallin and Zee to step forward. While Kin read the names of the many other Storm People who had died in the battle with Onus, the rock movers stood at either end of Jancarlo's likeness and placed a hand on the rock wall. The effigy moved on its bed of stone into a vertical position. Then the bed melted back into the wall behind it as Jancarlo's face watched the assembly. Jancarlo's last wish was to remain watching over The People of the Storm forever, and so he would. The likeness continued to move backward until it seemed as if it would sink into the rock altogether, but that was not their aim. Once the memorial was flush with the wall it remained still. Next to it the names of the fallen were sketched into the stone. Later, Kathryn and others would place protective powers in the stone so it could not be marred or broken.

We would all say good-bye in our own due time and be able to look into Jancarlo's eye again and again. An epitaph would be created over the memorial, but Dallin and Zee etched a temporary one as a final farewell.

Jancarlo Mecina
Born 22 January 1919
Empowered 13 August 1952
Died 23 September 2023
Honored Leader, Beloved Friend, Powerful Rock Mover

THE END

Looking for more books from HRB Collotzi?
Try…

The Secret of Avonoa Book One in the Avonoa Series

Note to Readers!

I hope you are enjoying the adventures as I enjoy writing
them! Although I love to write and create these stories,
being an independent author is hard. I don't have teams
of people ghost-writing, editing, formatting and
marketing for me. I do it all on my own, so my only
support comes from readers like you! Thank you for
supporting me and my craft.

Another way you can support a lowly indie author like
myself is to leave me a review. Feel free to use the link to
let others know how much you enjoyed the story and you
can pick up the next book at the same time! Enjoy the
adventure!!

You can also sign up for my newsletter to be the first to
hear about sales, signing events and new books! Sign up
at avonoa.com, hrbcollotzi.com, or
peopleofthestorm.com.

Or follow me on social media…
Facebook @hrbcollotzi
Instagram @hrbcolloti